Imagine a cross between  Millhone, a female sleuth a thirtysomething Lauren pretty good portrait of K. Jane, a former lounge singer who has been the chief (and only) investigator for Seattle's Foundation for Righting Wrongs, can collect on her uncle's vast inheritance only when she solves worthwhile "hopeless cases." She's a lady who values her independence, yearns for a healthy bank balance, and appreciates a good wine, a Cole Porter tune, a great clothing sale . . . and a fine-looking man. Now Beck is back with her fourth mystery in the acclaimed Jane da Silva series . . .

COLD SMOKED

"Beck tells a story with a compelling narrative drive."
—*Chicago Tribune*

"Jane da Silva's character is made of just the right proportions of cynicism, good humor, avarice, determination, and resourcefulness."
—*Denver Post*

"This is Beck's best work to date. . . . COLD SMOKED is a hot treat."
—*Seattle Times*

"This fourth Jane da Silva novel by K. K. Beck treats readers to a smorgasbord of intrigue dished up for a humorous and savvy heroine."
—*Mostly Murder*

more . . .

"Beck has created a breezy, modern detective . . . a delightful series."
—*Publishers Weekly*

"Beck writes in a wry and appealing style, and Jane is a well-realized protagonist."
—*Cleveland Plain Dealer*

"A fresh and cockeyed look at the way an amateur sleuth can be invented."
—*Murder Ad Lib*

"Beck's da Silva is daring, determined, clever, and spirited."
—*Booklist*

"Jane da Silva is the kind of woman you wouldn't mind having a long cup of coffee with on a rainy day."
—*Wisconsin State Journal*

"Beck has a style that is slightly comic but wholly interesting."
—*Greeley Tribune (KS)*

"Beck is a mystery writer with a splendid gift for spinning out a story that catches up the reader, with a mesmerizing fascination for plot and character that stands her in the company of the Agatha Christies and Conan Doyles of the mystery tradition."
—*Midwest Book Review*

"Jane is one of the few detectives who manages to be endearing yet tough at the same time."
—*London Free Press*

"Beck is a charming storyteller with a lively sense of humor."
—*San Jose Mercury News*

COLD
SMOKED

COLD
SMOKED

K.K. BECK

THE MYSTERIOUS PRESS

Published by Warner Books

A Time Warner Company

For Alex, who loves fish

MYSTERIOUS PRESS EDITION

Cover design by Julia Kushnirsky
Cover illustration by Daniel Pelavin

The Mysterious Press name and logo are registered trademarks of Warner Books, Inc.

 Mysterious Press books are published by
Warner Books, Inc.
1271 Avenue of the Americas
New York, NY 10020

Visit our web site at
http://pathfinder.com/twep

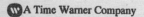A Time Warner Company

Printed in the United States of America

Originally published in hardcover by The Mysterious Press.
First Printed in Paperback: July, 1996

10 9 8 7 6 5 4 3 2 1

CHAPTER ONE

It was in the middle of her first number, "Blue Moon," that Jane da Silva realized the Fountain Room smelled heavily of fried fish. It must be coming from the clothes and skin of all these conventioneers attending the international seafood show, she thought. She hadn't noticed it earlier when she'd been working the lobby lounge. Now, however, she was in a private banquet room, doing a party for a group that had something to do with salmon. She shifted a little on her tall stool, closed her eyes, tilted her head back and began the chorus.

The fishiness was mingling with the smells of cigarette smoke and the chlorine fumes from the room's circular fountain. This pathetic structure, an apparent attempt to create an upscale atmosphere, seemed to be made of an old Jacuzzi with a mosaic of the chunky white rocks used in gas station landscaping cemented to the outside. A weak stream of water came out of a copper pipe in the middle of the thing. Jane had cranked up the mike in an attempt to drown out the persistent *whoosh* that sounded exactly like a running toilet.

The Fountain Room also had crushed velvet draperies with satin cord tiebacks and plastic wood tables with cigarette burns. It was in the basement of the Meade Hotel in downtown Seattle, a bland, recently renovated hotel from the fifties that catered mostly to the business traveler on a skimpy expense account.

Jane had been working at the Meade for two weeks now and had been under no illusions from the beginning. She'd known this was a tacky gig the minute she'd clapped eyes on the piano. It was white.

Still, she supposed she was lucky to get the job. The surly food and beverage manager, a young, dark, hulking man with heavy eyebrows, hadn't asked to see a promo book or hear a demo tape. He'd taken her word for it that she knew five hundred songs, which was a slight exaggeration. (Actually, she knew the opening lines to five hundred songs and relied on her fake book and her accompanist Gary's heavy chords to do the rest.)

He hadn't asked to see Gary's ID, either, which was a blessing because Jane suspected he was under twenty-one and therefore too young to work legally where booze was served. Jane, pushing forty, wondered if she and Gary looked like a mother-son act.

Gary had been here for a few months on his own, and because of dwindling business in the lobby lounge, he'd been told to come up with a female vocalist if he wanted to stay on. "Get a babe with some class," the manager had said. Now Gary had to split the take, but the tip glass—a brandy snifter the size of a baby's head, baited every night with fives and tens—took the edge off the low pay.

Yesterday the manager had muttered something about a beat box, a synthesizer that provided fake percussion sounds, to jazz up the act. Gary and Jane had managed to fend him off. The thought was anathema to them both, definitely sleazy, with its soulless, jangling, thumping cha-cha beats. Not to mention unsightly. The equipment sprouted ugly wires and plugs and looked like something from Radio Shack. But what else could you expect when the piano was white?

Anyway, she'd been happy to take on this party. It was an extra five hundred dollars, and she and Gary had brazenly brought in the tip glass, which was a nervy thing to do at a private gig.

Jane smiled in the direction of a nest of conventioneers with plastic name badges. A few of them were swaying and singing along to "Blue Moon." She'd watch them. All this karaoke had made mike grabbers out of people, and she wasn't about to let that happen.

One of them came across the room to make a request. She leaned down with a half smile. He was a tall thin man with fine silvery hair, slightly bloodshot blue eyes and a light brown suit that looked definitely European. In a slight Scandinavian accent, he asked for "Just One of Those Things." What a break. She actually knew all the words. Cole Porter was her strong suit.

She caught his name badge, which said he was Trygve somebody from the Norwegian Fisheries Ministry, and nodded. He patted her proprietarily on her shoulder. She felt the clammy warmth of his hand through the fabric of her beige silk dress. Still smiling, she turned slightly and executed an accidentally-on-purpose maneuver that involved flicking the microphone so that the cord snapped at his Adam's apple and he stepped back.

When she had sung his request, and done a pretty good job of it, too, she thought, the Norwegian came up and stuffed a measly two dollars into the glass. She gave him a two-dollar nod of thanks: about a quarter of an inch. She sighed and signaled to Gary that they should take their break a little early.

Jane felt herself teetering on the brink of a major depression. Maybe a shot of cognac would take the edge off and get her through her next set.

She smiled nicely to the scattered applause that floated over Gary's final chords, turned off the mike, set it carefully on her stool, and went over to the bar, where she sat down and ordered her usual tapwater with a wedge of lime, then decided what the hell and changed it to a small Courvoisier.

Two men with conventioneers' name badges were sitting there. One was about forty, dark and elegant. Jane read his name badge. He was from Santiago, Chile. She took in the dark good looks, the expensive tailoring and the wedding ring. The other was younger, with sandy hair and an open, amiable sort of face and pale skin. The two men watched the Norwegian make his way back to his table. He seemed to be having a little trouble negotiating the fountain and was following its curve with his head down like a pony in a child's zoo ride.

"Poor old Trygve. He's looking a bit pathetic. He always drinks too much at these gatherings," said the Chilean with a slight accent and a disapproving click of the tongue.

The younger man answered in a strange accent she assumed was Scottish, but was thicker than any she'd ever heard. "Spirits are desperately expensive in Norway, so they sometimes tend to crog it on a bit when they leave home." He paused and went on indulgently, "He was pairfectly sober for his speech today. He doesn't generally do these fish shows. I heard he was a last minute replacement for the assistant fisheries minister. He hasn't lairned yet that you wait for a late night until the last day of the show, once you've packed up your stand and all."

Jane liked having foreigners around. A recently reformed expatriate, she felt homesick for the rest of the world.

Just then two young women came into the Fountain Room. They were wearing short, tight velvet jackets, thigh-high Royal Stuart kilts, black mesh stockings and spiked heels. They did a showy turn around the fountain, and then the blond half of the team waved at the Norwegian, who seemed delighted and gestured them over to his table.

The Chilean rolled his eyes. "I can't believe the Scots, using those prostitutes to sell their salmon."

"It's their American distributor, actually," said the other man.

"Oh!" replied the Chilean, as if that explained the lapse in taste. "I didn't mean to malign your countrymen," he added with a little smile.

"They aren't my countrymen."

The younger man sounded testy. Jane's eyes flitted down to his name badge and read the computer-generated letters.

His name was Magnus Anderson. Hardly a Scottish name. The second line read "Shetland's Finest Smoked Salmon," and the last line read "Lerwick, Scotland." The word "Scotland" was crossed out in pen and replaced with block capitals that read "Shetland."

Magnus Anderson glowered. "We were stolen by the Scots. We were part of a dowry for the ugliest queen in the world."

"Yes, yes," his companion said impatiently. "You explained me this. They had to give away the most beautiful islands in the world to marry her off."

"And the Orkneys, too," said Magnus, peering gloomily into his beer. "By rights, we should be part of Norway."

"Then you could have Trygve's job, and maybe we'd accomplish something at the salmon exporters meeting. Oh, excuse me, but there is a customer I must see." The dark man drifted away toward an elderly Japanese gentleman and executed a very un-Latin bow.

Anderson now turned to Jane and said, "It's grand to have you singing for us. Perhaps you'll cheer us up. We just had our yearly meeting, and there are a lot of problems in salmon farming. Things got a bit heated." He sighed. "I'll be glad to get back home."

Jane glanced at his name tag as if reading it for the first time and repeated the name of his company. "Shetland Smoked Salmon. Really! Smoked salmon is one of my favorite things."

"The very best in the world comes from Shetland," he said. "World" came out "weereld." "You've heard of Shetland, haven't you?"

"Of course," she said. "The Shetland Isles at the northern tip of Scotland. I've always wanted to go there." Jane had French friends who'd raved about the place in the romantic way the French did about mist-enshrouded northern spots.

He beamed happily at her enthusiasm. "We prefer to call it Shetland." He indicated an enamel lapel badge showing a blue flag with a white cross. "This is our flag."

"The best smoked salmon in the world?" said Jane. She was prepared to listen to any sales pitch if she could hear more of that fabulous accent. There was something so wonderfully cozy about the vowels.

"We start out with the best fish," he intoned, like someone telling a child a much loved bedtime story. "In the voes of Shetland, the water temperature is perfect, and the wave action is strong, so the fish swim against the current and develop proper muscle tone. And then, of course, we prepare it properly. Cold smoked. Very slow."

"And I imagine you've been doing it for centuries," said Jane, prompting helpfully.

"Well, not exactly," he said. "In actual fact, we've only had salmon for the last fifteen years or so. We've no rivers. But now it's all farmed, you see. In pains in the sea." It took Jane a minute to figure out what he was getting at. He meant "pens," not "pains."

"Smoked salmon," she murmured, and closed her eyes, imagining it sliced thinly on buttered toast with some onion and caper and a lemon wedge as a garnish, with a cool glass of wine.

"Come by the seafood show and I'll give you some," said Anderson. "After the show ends, and I take down the stand"—an operation that became "tack doon" when he said it—"I'll give you what's left. We canna ship it all back." He handed her his card. "But there's just one condition."

"What's that?" said Jane.

"Sing my favorite song," he said.

"And what might that be?" She was alarmed because, as was her habit, she seemed to be absorbing the cadence and accent of whomever it was she was speaking to and selling it back to them. He didn't seem to notice. Despite his almost American friendliness, there was something feathery and otherworldly about him. His skin looked translucent, and his voice was soft. She could imagine his favorite song being some keening old ballad from a few centuries back.

" 'Walkin' after Midnight,' " he said. "You know, the

Patsy Cline thing?" He clearly sensed that she didn't expect him to be a Patsy Cline fan. "Country music's very big in Shetland," he said. He tapped at his card. "If you ever come, look me up. We're always happy to see visitors."

She drank the last delicious sip of the cognac and slid off the stool. "I'll be glad to sing that," she said, thanking God for her fake book.

Before she started again, she went to the ladies' room, tastefully done up in pink Formica with some bouquets of dried roses in baskets. She examined the skin under her eyes for mascara smudges.

The two young women in Highland attire, one blond and one brunette, stood in front of the mirror.

"Jesus, Marcia," said the one with brown hair in a squeaky voice that sounded as if she were on helium, "my feet are fucking killing me."

Jane could well believe it. The spikes were at least four inches high, enough to jam her toes painfully down into the point of the shoe and throw out her back. It was one of life's major ironies, thought Jane, that something that made your legs look so good made your feet feel so bad.

"I know," said Marcia. She had taffy-colored hair and too much makeup around her small, wary blue eyes. "And these mesh stockings sort of cut into the soles of your feet, don't they?"

Jane, who had dismissed these girls as mindless twits because of their tacky outfits, felt sorry for them. They seemed suddenly young and vulnerable. After all, who was she to sneer? She was strutting her stuff, too, in her own middle-aged, subtle way. Hadn't she chosen the beige silk dress she was wearing for the way it curved over her hip, made her waist look small and revealed just a tasteful slice of leg?

"Plus, my hair smells like fish," said the brunette lass thoughtfully. She took the end of a strand of her hair between her fingers, brought it to her nose and sniffed. "Yuck," she said, then examined the hair sample visually in the time-honored split-end-inspection gesture. "So do you think those guys who said they'd meet us here will show?"

"Probably," Marcia said in a flat voice. She was rubbing a line of blusher along her cheekbone. "We can wait for them with that guy from Norway. He's really friendly."

The brunette dropped her hair and watched Marcia rub color into her face in the mirror. "You put on makeup weird," she said with the air of having reached a great insight. Jane, who was now brushing her hair, cast a curious glance at Marcia's reflection.

"People usually make a special face when they put on makeup," explained the brunette. "Like opening their eyes big and kind of smiling a little, maybe. Checking out how it would look when you were talking to people."

Marcia was just rubbing that old blusher on there like someone slamming paint on a fence. Jane gave her another look while she took out her own lipstick, realizing the squeaky brunette was right. There was such a thing as a putting-on-makeup expression, and Marcia didn't have one.

Jane touched up her own face, keeping half an eye on the two women. While the brunette looked about twenty-two, it was hard to tell how old Marcia, the blonde, was. There was a solemnness about her that made her sleazy outfit look even more grotesque.

Marcia went over to the sink and scrubbed her hands like an obsessive compulsive. "I smell like dead fish," she said. She sounded angry.

Back in the Fountain Room, Jane noticed that the mood of the gathering had changed. The rowdier element in the corner seemed to have cleared out. The place was now full of knots of gloomy, dark-suited men, not mixing and looking far from festive.

Still, why should she care if the party was dying just as it had begun? Her job in the lobby lounge was to sell drinks by keeping the customers in their chairs. Here, all she had to do was sing. She'd get paid whether or not this grim little party ever took off.

But what should she sing to these dismal-looking men? "Gloomy Sunday," the infamous Hungarian suicide song, might be just the ticket. She certainly wasn't going to do anything bouncy. The only dignified way to deal with a dead crowd was to reflect their mood and pretend everything was just fine. She decided "Autumn Leaves" might be a good choice. As soon as she played her request for that nice man from Shetland.

After her next set, she stepped off the dais and Magnus Anderson came up and thanked her. "Lovely," he said. "Do you know anything else by Patsy Cline?"

Before she could answer, he glanced over Jane's shoulder, clicked his tongue and snapped, "Here's that annoyin' lass, come to torment me."

The woman who came up to them was about thirty, with pale skin, light brown hair and large greenish eyes like peeled grapes. She wore silver drop earrings in the shape of fish, and a big fish pin fastened the matronly-looking scarf that she had draped over a stiff, boxy brown suit. Way too much shoulder pad, thought Jane. It made her look artificially squared off, as if she were a fish out of water, soft and squishy, wearing a not entirely successful human disguise.

"Hi, Magnus," she said in a grating but perky voice. "Remember me? Carla Elroy from *Seafood Now* magazine?"

"Oh, yes," he said without enthusiasm.

Carla looked over at Jane with just a flicker of curiosity and turned back to Anderson, who was scowling. "So how did the salmon meeting go?" she demanded. "They wouldn't let me in."

He shrugged noncommittally.

"Listen," she said, "there's rumors."

"Oh?" Anderson narrowed his eyes a little.

"That's right. Something funny's going on in farmed salmon. All over the world. Strange rumors about pigmentation problems. Did you guys talk about that?" She gave him a little smirk of triumph.

Jane watched Anderson's own pigmentation change from

pale to florid. He blinked hard a few times and looked furious, but in his soft, feathery voice, he just said, "I don't
know a thing about it." Then he nodded to Jane and walked
away.

Carla turned to Jane. "Are you a member of the Women's
Seafood Network?" she said eagerly, apparently unaware
that she had driven Magnus Anderson away in a choler. Jane
expected this woman to give her the secret handshake of this
organization. A dead-fish handshake, no doubt.

"I'm here to sing. I'm afraid I'm not in the fish business."
Actually, she was glad she wasn't in the fish business, but it
seemed tactless to say so.

Carla's green eyes grew even bulgier and her expression
more earnest. "It's a fascinating industry. Really global and
dynamic. But there aren't a lot of women in it. That's why
we have the Women's Seafood Network. So we can help
each other deal with these old boys." She wrinkled up her
nose. "A lot of these guys are totally macho."

Jane reflected that while overbearing jerks were undoubt-
edly the downside, there were plenty of single women who
would be only too glad to find themselves in an industry full
of men. She checked Carla's ring finger—naked—and
stopped herself from congratulating Carla on the great odds
she should be enjoying. Maybe she wasn't interested in men.

"So do you eat a lot of fish?" she said to Carla. "It's supposed to be very good for you."

"Full of Omega-3. It fights cholesterol," Carla said
solemnly. "The only problem is, I want to know all about it
first. Where it was caught, how it was processed, how it's
been handled. It all starts with proper on-board bleeding
techniques." She was getting quite animated now.

Jane felt slightly queasy and was relieved to see that
Gary was waving to her. She was afraid Carla would move
on to evisceration any moment now. "I'm so glad you enjoy
your work," she said. "Now I'm going to have to do mine."

From the dais at the end of the room, Gary played in his
own moody, introspective way, and Jane sang and watched

the party fizzle. Throughout the next hour she observed Carla buzz at the knots of suited men, trotting over to them in her sensible pumps, turning her white face up to them eagerly, occasionally whipping out a notebook and standing there, pencil poised. Everyone seemed to make short work of deflecting her.

Jane doubted that with her gauche interview technique she'd ever advance beyond *Seafood Now* magazine. It was so simple, really. All she needed to have done was look sympathetic instead of delighted when confronting Anderson with the suggestion there was some problem with salmon. Jane would have got the whole story out of him in five minutes by making it clear she was on his side.

Carla finally left the room. She looked satisfied despite having been universally rejected. Perhaps she thought she was being fended off because she was a woman trying to penetrate the old boy network. She was wrong. Jane could tell from Carla's assertive, overeager mingling technique, not unlike a dive-bombing insect at a barbecue, that the rejection was personal rather than gender based.

Jane sang "Somebody Loves Me" and began to think about her love life, mulling over in her mind how she could dump Jack Lawson, a singing rancher she'd met in the eastern part of the state last summer and with whom she had been carrying on a long-distance romance for some time. He was expecting to meet her after work tonight. Maybe she'd sleep with him just once more—for old times' sake and because she knew realistically she wouldn't be able to resist his physical charms anyway. Then she'd dump him. Nicely, of course.

These basically recreational affairs, no matter how they were dressed up, worked only to a point. Jane was determined to end it while it was still fun. She'd never expected the thing to go on as long as it had.

Her thoughts were interrupted by the entrance of another woman. Maybe the Women's Seafood Network took turns sending in its members in shifts to make sure the old boys weren't conspiring against them, and this amiable-looking tubby blonde was here to replace Carla.

The new arrival wore a bright blue crepe dress draped artfully over firm and ample flesh. She had the good legs that often went with a big torso, especially on women who drank a lot, and she strode confidently around the room on a pair of very expensive Italian shoes with high heels that showed off those legs.

Unlike the tired tartan tarts Jane had observed earlier, and who now seemed to be gone, this woman was used to dressing for success, and the muscles in her calves had adapted.

She seemed more welcome than poor Carla. Jane watched her purposefully knocking back what looked like a gin and tonic and beaming and bubbling around the room, shaking hands and exchanging air kisses like a politician. At one point she even thwacked the elegant Chilean on his elegant back in a hearty, one-of-the-boys manner. He blinked his Bambi-like eyes and smiled nervously.

She exchanged some words with the men around him, and when Jane stopped singing in one of her dramatic pauses, she heard the woman's deep laugh and voice. She was English. "We'll jolly soon set things right," she said in the booming, assured tones of the captain of a girls' hockey team.

She left soon after, and Jane started to think about Jack again, then decided it was all too boring, just as boring as this gig.

Maybe she should move to Prague. Jane had been to Prague in the bad old days and had felt a Mitteleuropisch Ernst Lubitsch charm under the oppressive surface. She'd heard they liked American jazz singers, and it was cheap and lively right now, full of expatriates. The Left Bank for the nineties and all that. Of course, all those buzzy people were probably a lot younger than she was—young and eager and looking for a buzz instead of creating one.

The hours crept by. The partygoers drifted in and out. At one point, Magnus Anderson left with a group of men and gave her a friendly wave. Jane kept on singing, although her repertoire was getting thin and her voice was tired. She reminded herself that the extra five hundred would come in handy. She was in the middle of "Smoke Gets in Your Eyes" and wondering if Budapest had a shot at being the next Prague, when Carla Elroy of *Seafood Now* magazine reappeared in the banquet room.

This time she was harder to ignore. She was wearing pajamas with tropical fish all over them, and she was screaming. She rushed to the front of the room and said, "My God, my God!"

The cuff on the sleeve of her pajama top was dark red and wet, and there was another paler red stain on her outer thigh, probably where the cuff had touched it. It looked very much like fresh blood.

CHAPTER TWO

Jane stopped singing. Gary stopped playing. What little conversation there had been ceased. The men in dark suits all stepped back in the nervous, embarrassed way men do when faced with a woman displaying strong emotion.

Jane stared at the wet pajama sleeve. It was blood all right. There was nothing else it could be. Jane let her mike fall. It made a thud and a crackle as it hit the floor. She stepped toward Carla and found herself putting an arm on her shoulder. "Are you all right?" she heard herself say.

Carla let out a sob and reached for Jane, looking up at her with those bulging eyes now shiny with tears. Her sleeve made a red streak across Jane's beige dress. "In my room," she said. "It's horrible. We have to help her. What shall we do?"

Jane pushed up the pajama sleeve and looked at the woman's soft white arm, turning it over just to make sure Carla hadn't hurt herself. Or been hurt. The skin was intact, smooth and white with a fine down of pale hairs, but looking heartbreakingly fragile somehow, so pale, with the tracing of blue veins at the elbow. The blood hadn't come from Carla, who submitted passively to the examination, then burst into tears and buried her face in her hands.

"Carla, tell me your room number." Jane made her voice firm. A very specific request often calmed down hysterical people. She kept her hand on Carla's shoulder and felt it shuddering with sobs through the thin cotton. Carla looked up from her hands and whispered, "Two ten."

Jane turned to Gary, now standing up. "Send security to two ten." He nodded and rushed away, and Jane turned back to Carla. "What happened? Is someone in trouble?"

Carla was still trembling. "I'm scared. I don't want to go in there."

"You don't have to," said Jane. "But maybe you could show me the way." Somebody had to get up to the room to see if someone was in trouble. It might take Gary a while to scare up security, and Jane didn't think Carla should be left here in her pajamas with no one to take care of her but these gloomy suits. Carla, who had tried to act tough before, now seemed helpless.

"I'm going up there now," Jane said in a kindergarten teacher voice. "Will you show me the way?"

"I'm not going in that room," Carla said, snuffling.

"Okay. You can wait in the hall. You don't want to stay here, do you?"

Carla looked around at all the curious faces. They all looked interested and puzzled, but none of them looked particularly sympathetic. "I'll come with you," she said.

In the elevator, Jane knew the poor thing was pulling herself together when she put a hand to her cheek and said, "Oh, my God, all those guys saw me in my pajamas."

"Thank God they're such chic pajamas," Jane said in a kindly way. Actually she felt they didn't really do a lot for Carla. Their tropical gaiety was a little overwhelming and made her look, by contrast, even more like a codfish.

The elevator doors opened, and they walked down the narrow corridor, lit at intervals with metal wall sconces that left blotches of yellow light on the textured wall paper. Behind one of the blank white doors, they heard music and laughing. It sounded as if a dorm party were in progress.

In front of room 210, Carla stopped. The door was slightly ajar. "In there," said Carla. "In the bathroom."

Jane knew she should wait for security. But what if someone were hurt? She could call 911 from the room and get help right away. She left the door wide open and went inside.

It was a large suite, filled with puffy-looking sofas and glass coffee tables. A laptop computer sat on one of the tables. The floor-to-ceiling turquoise curtains were drawn. On one side of the room was a bar, littered with dirty glasses and an overflowing ashtray. Through a doorway she saw a pair of double beds with turquoise-and-rose spreads. There were a few other closed doors.

Jane knew which door led to the bathroom because she heard a loud fan coming from behind it. She held her breath, pulled open the door and jumped back about a foot.

She half expected someone to rush out at her, but instead there was just the sound of the fan and another sound: the sound of dripping liquid. She stepped inside the doorway. The drip came from the sink faucet. She could see a drop of water clinging to the tap, fattening, then falling, and producing another rhythmic blip.

The bathtub's white plastic shower curtain was drawn all the way across. At the bottom, though, one end of the curtain was bunched up, and Jane saw a smear of blood. At her feet, she noticed that the terry bath mat, with its raised letters reading "Meade," was speckled with a fine spray of blood. She took a deep breath and lifted the other end of the shower curtain away from the tub.

There was no doubt in Jane's mind that the young woman in the tub was dead. The limbs were arranged so unnaturally, the elbows jutting akimbo, the knees wedged against the sides, in a position that would have been uncomfortable if this woman could feel anything. It looked as if she had been pushed into the tub and hastily abandoned, something messy to be cleaned up later.

And the face. Jane could bear only to glance at it. The jaw was in some kind of spasm, and the eyes showed white all the way around. They were small, milky blue eyes with pale lashes.

She looked to be in her late twenties. She had dark blond hair pulled back in a ponytail. Slightly darker roots were showing around the hairline. She wore faded jeans, a plain gray sweatshirt and a pair of slightly dirty Reeboks. One of them was hooked over the edge of the tub. The front of her sweatshirt was soaked with blood. It looked very dark, not red at all. There were flecks of blood on the white tiles behind her and still more on the small bottle of hotel shampoo and the tiny piece of pink soap that sat primly in the ceramic soap dish.

Jane backed out of the bathroom, feeling dizzy and slightly nauseated. Behind her, from the room, she heard a footstep and a man clearing his throat.

She turned, feeling physical fear for a second before she realized that the man who stood there staring at her was a young guy from the hotel security staff. She'd met him the week before when he'd bounced a few drunks out of the Fountain Room.

She heard herself say, "There's a dead woman in the tub," in a voice that shocked her because it sounded so calm.

The security man hustled into the bathroom as she was leaving, and they managed to collide in the doorway. He shoved past her and ripped back the curtain, the rings making a ratchety sound as they slid along the pole. He stood there for a second, his hand on the shower curtain, then drew in his breath, let the curtain fall back, turned to Jane and said, "Fuck."

"Yeah," said Jane.

He'd know what to do. If he didn't, he should. She wasn't going to try to calm him down. Back in the hall, Carla stood there all by herself, while a few of the men Jane had seen at the reception, apparently drawn here by curiosity, stood a few paces away, staring into the room.

Jane touched Carla's shoulder. "The security guy is there now. It's going to be all right."

Carla nodded. "I was pretty scared," she said. "I'm better now."

"Good. Who is she?"

"I don't know," said Carla. "I know she's not part of the Women's Seafood Network."

Jane tried to imagine the contorted face alive, relaxed, safe. It was hard to do. It was as if the woman in the tub had always been a corpse.

The security man came out of the room. He looked pale and slightly angry, as if he resented someone messing with the space for which he was responsible. "The cops are coming," he said. "They've asked you two to wait. I can put you in two fourteen across the hall." He glared at the collection of name-badged rubberneckers. "There's nothing to see," he said with a trace of contempt. "Please don't block the hall."

They began to drift away, and he led Jane and Carla to another room and let them in with a passkey. "I don't know if the maid has had time to make up the room," he said apologetically, in some hotel management reflex way that was ludicrous considering the circumstances. But trivial thoughts often appeared in the midst of horrors. Jane had found herself focusing on the soap and shampoo spattered with blood next to the dead girl. She remembered it was Caswell-Massey shampoo and was surprised that the Meade would have something so nice.

Inside room 214, the bed was unmade and there were crumpled pieces of paper in a circle around the wastebasket where someone had tried to sink them. Next to the television was a collection of empty liquor miniatures and toothbrush glasses flanking a plastic ice bucket full of water.

"Will you girls be okay?" the security man said, wrinkling his forehead as he surveyed the trashed room. "I gotta go get a hold of my boss." Carla didn't even bristle at the appellation "girls," she just sat down in a big chair.

"Go do what you have to do," Jane said firmly. As soon as he left she pulled up the sheets on the bed and smoothed the bedspread over it. The room now looked less repulsive. She investigated the tiny empties and ascertained that a bourbon drinker had stayed here. And he or she had left the key in the minibar. She knelt and pawed through the collection. "How does a drink sound?" she said to Carla. "It might be a good idea. The ice has all melted, though."

"Is there any vodka?" Carla said plaintively.

Jane made her a vodka Collins and poured herself a double cognac. They prepared to wait for the police. Carla took a deep breath and a sip of her drink. She seemed still shaky but much more calm. "Will this go on someone else's bill?" she said, staring at the glass.

"Who cares?" said Jane. She sat on the end of the bed. "This is an emergency."

Carla gave her a loopy smile. "Thanks for taking care of me. I really was pretty blown away."

"Of course you were," said Jane.

"I hit the tail end of the North Pacific Factory Trawler cocktail party after the salmon reception," said Carla. "Those guys party on later than most people. Then I went upstairs. I spell-checked my report on the show and added a few lines about the last events I'd covered, and then I put on my pajamas. I was just going into the bathroom to brush my teeth, and I found her. She was there the whole time I was spell-checking. It's horrible."

Carla had backed out of the bathroom and decided to pick up the phone and call for help, but then she had wondered if anyone was still lurking in the suite. That's when she'd left the room and gone down one flight of stairs to the salmon exporters reception.

"I wasn't thinking clearly. I just went to the first place where I could find people I knew. I guess I panicked." Carla sounded apologetic. "You're so calm."

"I expected I'd find a body. You were surprised by one," said Jane. "It's not the same thing at all."

How long would this take, anyway? Jane remembered Jack Lawson was coming by. Suddenly the choice between dumping him and having wild, abandoned sex with him (or somehow combining both) seemed less important than it had earlier. He would have let himself in with his key by now. She supposed she should call him.

From right outside the door she heard an irritated male voice say, "Let's get those witnesses separated. I don't want them reinforcing each other's wonky stories." Then there was a businesslike rap on the door, and a thirtyish man in a blazer and polyester slacks came in.

"I'm Detective Olson," he said, looking serious but friendly and not at all as if he thought they were a bunch of hysterics concocting wonky stories. "I understand you ladies found the body in room two ten."

"She did, actually," said Jane, pointing to Carla. "And she came downstairs for help, and I went up with her to check it out."

"Okay," he said, pointing to Carla. "I'll talk to you first. Will you come with me, please?" Carla rose obediently. To Jane he said, "If you don't mind waiting, I'll talk to you next, okay?"

They left the room, and Jane called home. Jack answered. "Where the hell are you?" he said in a nice but puzzled way.

"I'm still down at the Meade, and I'm going to be even later. There's been a murder at the hotel. The police are going to question me, and I have to stick around."

"Jesus," he said. "And I thought you played those nice, quiet rooms. Shall I come down there?"

"No, no," she said. "Just make yourself comfortable. I'll get home when I can."

"Well, what happened? A bar fight or something?" Jack was a country-western singer who'd played more than his share of wild honky-tonks.

Jane felt suddenly tired, too tired to tell him all about it. "I was singing and someone came in screaming that they found a body. I went upstairs with her and checked it out. There was a young woman dead in the tub. There was a lot of blood."

"Maybe she killed herself," said Jack.

"I didn't see any weapons lying around," said Jane. "Anyway, the police are here now. It's all under control."

"Are you holding up okay?" he said. "It must have been a shock. I'm glad I'll be here when you come back. You shouldn't be alone after something like this."

"You are very sweet," she said, touched.

"So are you." His voice softened. "You pretend you're not, but you are."

After she said good-bye and hung up, she wondered if that were true. Jack apparently wanted to believe it, but his remark had seemed both patronizing and presumptuous. After all, he was younger and much more naive than she was.

Jane would have liked to be sweet, and maybe she had been once, when she was very young and her husband, Bernardo, had taken care of her. It had been easy to be sweet then. Now it was probably too late. Now she could be kind in a brusque, superficially maternal way, taking care of Carla, for instance, without actually liking her very much.

A little while later a uniformed officer came in and escorted her down the hall to another anonymous hotel room. This one had been made up. Detective Olson asked her a few questions at a table at the end of the room while a battery of other people came in and out, barked into the phone, stood around chatting and managed to create an air of organized chaos.

Olson ignored all this activity and asked simple, clear, direct questions, waiting patiently for a simple answer. It was easy to fall into his polite, impersonal rhythm of questioning. He established that Jane worked at the hotel, wanted to know about Carla's demeanor, asked her if she had ever been in the suite before.

"Carla's room?" she said.

"Apparently it was a hospitality suite run by her magazine," he said. Jane had wondered how Carla rated such a luxurious room. "Were you there earlier for a party or anything?"

"No. I just went in once. When Carla told me there was

someone in trouble." She felt compelled to apologize for having possibly contaminated a crime scene. "I thought I'd better go up there in case someone needed help before security got there."

"Sometimes it's better just to call the police," he said gently. "But I understand you were trying to help. Still, there could have been someone in there."

Jane nodded, and he asked her what she had handled in room 210. She tried to reconstruct her movements, and he made a few jottings in a notebook, then took her name and address and thanked her for her cooperation.

Jane found herself disappointed. She wanted to ask him a lot of questions. Was there a weapon around anywhere? How had the woman died? How long had she lain there? She would have to wait and read about in the paper, she supposed. But she did blurt out, "Do you know who she is?"

"Not yet," he said, rising to indicate the interview was over.

As he walked her to the door, the uniformed officer came into the room with Trygve, the Norwegian fish bureaucrat she'd seen much earlier in the Fountain Room, the one who'd requested "Just One of Those Things." His two-dollar tip seemed like something that had happened a week before.

Jane was startled to see him in a homey plaid bathrobe. He looked vexed. He had one hand jammed angrily in his robe pocket, and the other hand held a passport. He looked reasonably sober, but flushed. "I hope this won't take long," he said. "I have a very early flight tomorrow, and an important meeting with the Norwegian cabinet." The policeman didn't look particularly impressed.

Jane turned once and looked back at him. He seemed fairly self-possessed considering the circumstances, but she caught one odd detail that indicated he was disconcerted or maybe still slightly swacked. He was wearing only one slipper, a childish-looking thing of some bristly fur. His big white naked foot made him look pathetic and vulnerable somehow. She wondered if they'd woken him up, but that wet hair seemed to indicate he'd just come out of the shower.

At home, Jane discovered Jack sound asleep in her bed. He lay on his stomach, his head turned toward the wall and half buried in his pillow. His gorgeous, tapering back emerged from the sheet, and one hand stretched out across her pillow. His clothes lay neatly folded on a chair, and his very expensive felt Stetson was sitting on the foot of the bed.

Didn't he know it was unlucky to leave a hat on the bed? Jane hated herself for being superstitious, but she plucked it away and put it on top of his clothes, then undressed herself and slid under his warm, heavy arm. She put one hand on his back and tucked her knees into his side. Maybe he would wake up and maybe he wouldn't. Jane wasn't sure what she wanted and soon fell asleep herself, thinking that maybe they would make love as soon as they woke up.

CHAPTER THREE

Instead they had a fight.

It started when Jack uttered his first words of the day. "Why didn't you wake me up last night? I wanted to make you feel better. I wanted to take care of you. I thought you needed me, but you don't." He had propped himself up on one elbow and was glaring at her.

"Well, it's a good thing I don't," she said sleepily, "because you're never here. You just shuttle in once in a while from L.A., and then you go back down to the studio and party with your buddies or do a gig at some state fair."

"Is that what you think? I thought you understood. This recording thing is very important to me. I invited you to come down there."

"I'm sorry, Jack, I don't want to sit around on a folding chair in a cold studio like some groupie. I'm too old for that."

She hadn't meant to be so blunt. He'd caught her unawares by starting in while she was still half asleep.

"You know what your problem is," he said solemnly.

She sighed and put the pillow over her face. "Go ahead," she said. "Tell me. What is my problem?"

"Inability to commit," he said.

She tore the pillow off her face. "Oh, for God's sake, Jack. That's supposed to be my line. There's one of those why-he-won't-commit articles in every women's magazine in the beauty parlor."

She realized she was on dangerous ground now. Telling a guy he was behaving like a woman, was, in her experience, never a good idea.

She barreled on, trying to change the subject a little. "Maybe I should remind you that what you liked so much about me was that I wasn't possessive. That we could just have a great time. That I didn't want to snare you or change you. It seems unfair to attack me for what you considered to be one of my better points."

He fell back down on his back, bouncing the bed. "That was pretty good strategy," he said.

"It wasn't strategy," she said. "I'm way beyond that kind of thing. You may not believe it, but it's true. Come on, Jack, let's not fight. You're leaving for the airport in just a couple of hours. Don't go away mad." She stroked his hair. "Besides, I had a perfectly horrible time last night. I'm too tired to fight."

"You poor thing," he said, kissing her forehead. "I'm sorry I got bent out of shape." She relaxed a little, but then, instead of comforting her in some carnal way that she felt would unkink both of them, he managed to start in on himself again. "But you have to understand, it's hard on my ego that you don't seem to need me to be there for you. It's not that I want a codependent relationship or anything. . . ."

When Jane had first met Jack Lawson, he'd seemed straightforward and uncomplicated, a nice all-American hunk with a great baritone voice who could ride a horse, was a terrific dancer, and was unashamed of his endearingly greedy level of physical passion. Where had he come up with these mushy clichés—"inability to commit," "be there for you," "codependent"?

She ran a hand along his shoulder. "Jack, I know this recording thing is very exciting, but do you think you're spending too much time in L.A.?" He was clearly a victim of cultural contamination.

"You mean you think I should make more time and space for our relationship?"

"Oh, never mind," she said in a tactical retreat. (She might not operate strategically, but she still used tactics.) She could see it now. He'd stop writing his appealingly sordid drinking and cheating songs and start composing New Age odes to dolphins before too long. By which time Jane planned to be out of the picture. He was sweet, though, looking at her now rather blearily with boyish, tousled hair.

"Darling," she said, "I'm very tense. I wish you would do something to relax me. Something not too verbal."

Fortunately Jack's personality hadn't changed at its deeper core. He swung immediately into action. Pushing her shoulders down onto the pillow, he climbed on top of her, twisted her hair in his hands and started in delicately on her earlobe with the tip of his tongue while sliding one smooth knee up the inside of her thigh in his usual decisive manner.

A few hours later she stood on her porch in her bathrobe, waving good-bye to him as a taxi took him to the airport. Maybe I'll dump him later, she thought. But for now, I won't worry about it. He was scheduled to be gone for three weeks. By then maybe everything would take care of itself in some mysterious way. Maybe he would dump her. He had to be surrounded by gorgeous women in L.A. On the whole, Jane would have preferred to dump him before he dumped her, but Jack was so sweet that she wanted to make sure she didn't hurt him. She sighed and reminded herself to drop by the seafood show on her way to work and pick up some of that smoked salmon from that nice Shetland man.

When she got inside the convention center, Jane was confronted with rows and rows of booths, each fronted by a flounce of shiny blue fabric. In the booths were salespeople offering samples of cooked fish, men in suits, women in bright dresses, all smiling and friendly, all wearing plastic badges.

There were glass cases full of mounds of ice with shiny-

looking dead fish lying on their sides and neat overlapping
rows of fillets and steaks, garnished with lemons and limes.

In the Hawaiian area (things seemed to be arranged on
roughly geographical lines), Miss Hawaii in traditional
muumuu with sash and rhinestone tiara posed for pictures
with conventioneers, and there were big tropical fish
trimmed with waxy pink and white and scarlet flowers. Jane
stopped to admire a huge round orange fish with white polka
dots.

Some of the booths featured videos showing clean blue
waters, fishing vessels pounding through foamy waves, smiling women in white smocks and caps cleaning and slicing
fish in spotless factories.

As she walked the aisles in search of Magnus Anderson's
stand, jostled by lots of conventioneers carrying plastic bags
bulging with brochures, Jane was offered toothpicks impal-
ing shrimp, breaded fish in the shape of stars and half moons
and squares of white fish in various sauces—Cajun, teriyaki,
dill. Also available were glossy brochures, price lists, logo-
laden oven mitts and pot holders, pens, luggage tags, key
chains and fridge magnets.

The New Zealanders, whom Jane had never thought of as
particularly fishy, were out in full force with a section of
their own, blowups of photos of pristine fjords and artful dis-
plays of emerald-green mussels and bright white fillets of orange roughy.

The Chileans seemed to be serving some final little meals
of salmon and Chilean wines to a few select customers. Their
stand was staffed by elegant gentlemen in beautiful suits.

There were lots of Canadians in a section plastered with
red maple leaves. A man from Newfoundland was demonstrating a machine that removed cod tongues—and various
Quebecois accents floated through the air. A sign said that
lobster races would be held at the New Brunswick stand
hourly.

The Norwegians had a nest of booths all to themselves.
Everybody there seemed incredibly tall. A blue-eyed chef,

draped with medals and even taller with his toque, was
demonstrating a cod dish, and a gray-haired man with fierce
eyebrows was feeding some salmon into a huge
stainless-steel slicing machine.

She made her way past a Scottish piper and a brace of men
in kilts and trews, a gaggle of pale-complected New Englan-
ders in sweaters and L. L. Bean gear, and various aerobicized
young women in black Spandex, handing out large shrimp in
a stand full of garish fake marble columns. They looked a lot
slicker than the two babes in Highland fling outfits she'd
seen last night.

A certain amount of packing up was going on, with people
bent over cardboard boxes and running around with wrapping
tape, scraping off grills and taking down signs.

Finally she found stand seventeen, where Magnus Anderson was leaning over his refrigerated case, pointing to a map
for the benefit of an American customer who looked clearly
puzzled. "It's right here, at the sixtieth parallel," Magnus was
explaining patiently. Jane imagined every pitch began with
that basic geography lesson.

She stood a little to one side as he went on about the fact
that nowhere in God's creation was there a better place to
farm salmon than in Shetland.

Behind him she watched a pretty dark-haired girl and a
florid middle-aged man stacking up piles of brochures and
stowing them in a big box. They spoke to each other in a language that sounded vaguely like English, but which Jane
slowly realized was completely incomprehensible to her.

She must have looked startled, because when Magnus's
prospect, stuffing more brochures into his plastic bag, left,
Magnus turned to her and said, "They're spickin Shetland."

"You have your own dialect?"

"We prefer to call it a language." He smiled. "It's got
words from Old Norn, and Old Scots and some of our own as
well. After a week on the road, we get weary o' knappin."

"Knappin?"

"Speaking English so other folk understand." He smiled. "So you've come for your salmon?"

"Is there any left?"

He rummaged around inside his glass case and came up with a neatly wrapped package. "I've got it all ready for you," he said.

"Thank you very much. I hope you approved of my Patsy Cline," said Jane. "She's not easy to do."

"Your Patsy Cline was brilliant," he said, adding a delicious row of extra *r*s to the word. She imagined he meant brilliant in the British sense—what an American would characterize as an understated "just great" rather than in the American sense of the word: dazzling and near genius.

She gestured in the fishy-smelling air and said, "This show is pretty amazing. I didn't know there was so much to fish."

"This is a pretty small show. The Boston Seafood Show, that's the big one. And I do shows in Paris and Tokyo and Spain as well. We have to travel to let people know about us."

A new tacky lass, wearing fishnet hose and a tiny kilt and spiked heels, walked by. This one was a redhead. She was carrying a tray of smoked salmon.

"Your competitors?" said Jane. Magnus seemed to be staring at her.

His face took on a serious look. "Did you hear what happened to the other one?" he said. "Murdered. Shot. They found her in a bathtub in the hotel."

"The other one?" said Jane, staring at the redhead.

"The blond lass. She was in the bar where you were singing."

Jane realized at once that the woman she'd seen in the tub was the woman she'd seen putting on makeup the night before. Without her makeup, and without that ridiculous outfit, she looked entirely different. But those small blue eyes were the same. Jane remembered her scrubbing her hands and her strange expression. She even remembered her name. Her brunette friend had called her Marcia.

A couple of Japanese men came up to Magnus. "Got to be nice to them," he said to her in a whisper. "They're the biggest fish buyers in the world. And very pernickity."

"Thanks again for the salmon," she said.

"Have you got my card?" he said as he sidled away. "Come see us in Shetland. We'll hire the community hall for you and you can give us a concert."

She left the convention center thinking about Marcia. Being able to imagine her alive made the whole thing much more horrible. She'd seemed so sullen and strange. Maybe they'd know more at the Meade. Maybe they had a suspect now that they knew who the victim was.

When she arrived, she popped back into the kitchen and asked the chef if she could keep the salmon in his fridge while she worked. The food and beverage manager loomed up behind her.

"Never mind about that," he said, stepping between her and the fridge. "Hang on to it. I need to see you and Gary outside."

The way everyone in the kitchen turned away in embarrassment made it all painfully clear. Carrying her package, she followed him out into the bar, where Gary was seated at the piano in a dinner jacket—white to match the piano.

"Listen, guys," the surly manager said, "while you did your own gig last night I auditioned another act. With a boom box. They do a nice Hawaiian thing. We're gonna tie it in with a mai-tai special, get a whole tropical Trader Vic kind of thing going. Here's your last check."

"I guess there's nothing to say," said Jane. "Except why didn't you phone us and save us the trip downtown to this depressing place?"

He handed them each an envelope.

"You could have mailed those," she said.

He shrugged. "You guys were classy, but, hey, we gotta

look at the bottom line." He shuffled away, then turned and said, "Have a farewell drink at the bar, on me."

"Thanks a lot," said Jane. "But I'm not a mai-tai drinker." She turned and gave Gary a brave smile. "Well, think there's somewhere else for us?"

Gary cleared his throat and looked guilty. "Um, I sort of saw this coming, Jane. I've got another job."

"Do they need a singer?"

"I'm going to play piano at Nordstrom's."

"You mean you're going to be the guy by the elevator near ladies' shoes playing 'Lara's Theme'?"

"That's right."

Jane gave this some thought. "Well, at least the piano's black. And maybe you can get an employee's discount."

"I'm glad you're not pissed off," Gary said gratefully. "I should have told you I was looking, I guess. So you could have been looking, too."

"Never mind," Jane said recklessly. "I think I might be off to Prague. Or Budapest. Or maybe the Shetland Isles."

"Gosh, I'm sorry," said Gary.

"Yeah, okay," Jane said. "I'll be by to put the arm on you to pass along the discount next time I'm shopping at Nordstrom's. Which may not be for quite a while." She didn't know why she was giving the poor kid a hard time. She was actually rather relieved to be out of the Fountain Room. "I'm going to take my salmon and go home."

Once at home, she was more than relieved, she was delighted. She got out of her green crepe number with a little tasteful beading at the shoulder and into a pair of soft old jeans and a sweatshirt. Then she made herself a supper of smoked salmon on toast and ate it with some nice Chardonnay and listened to the Maria Callas *Tosca*. That would blast piano bar standards out of her mind. And country music, too. She was in the mood for something sublime. And tomorrow she'd give the house a thorough cleaning. Then she'd decide what to do next with her life. Or wait and see what happened. Mr. Micawber's optimistic phrase "Something will turn up" bounced around in her head.

Two days after that, Marcia's parents came to see Jane. The father had phoned first. "I'm sorry to bother you," he said. "My name is Phil Hunter. I understand you were the one who found my little girl. I got your name from the hotel. My wife and I are going crazy wondering what happened to her. The police are doing what they can, but it would help a lot if we could meet you. We have to know what happened, and no one seems to want to tell us." It was a plain, straightforward voice, but with a strained, desperate note, as if it were trying very hard to stay controlled.

"I can't tell you much at all," said Jane. "I wish I could." There was a pause, and she said, "I'm very sorry—about your daughter."

"If we could ask you a few questions," he said. In the background she heard a woman's voice, unintelligible but clearly urgent and coaching him, the way wives sometimes did. Marcia's mother.

She was unable to turn them down. She doubted she had anything to tell them, but it sounded as if they wanted to be doing something to stave off helplessness. "Would you like to come to the house?" said Jane.

The Hunters came over about half an hour later, two big people in their late forties. He was tall and broad and balding, with ruddy, weathered skin, and he wore a checked shirt and jeans. She was wide and solid with light brown hair streaked with gray and a slack, soft, hurt face, blotched with red from crying. He introduced her as Barbara. She had small blue eyes like Marcia—round and glassy like doll's eyes, a loose dark green sweater that covered her wide hips, and black knit pants.

They sat very close to each other on the sofa. Although he had spoken on the phone, now she took the lead. She held her husband's hand in her lap and rested her other hand on a huge purse propped up beside her. She told Jane that they were cattle ranchers from Ellensburg, east of the mountains, and that they had just come back from burying their daughter.

"We took her home," she said. "She hadn't been home for a long time."

Jane nodded, then told them very simply what had happened. How Carla had rushed into the banquet room, how Jane had gone back up with her, how Jane had seen the body in the bath.

Phil Hunter held up a hand. "We've talked to the coroner about all that," he said.

Jane was relieved that they didn't want to hear any gory physical details. Instead she told them she had seen their daughter earlier, wearing her costume. "I'm sorry I don't know more," she concluded helplessly. "What do the police say?"

"Not much," said the father. "They don't seem to know much at all. We talked to Stacy, the little gal that was with her that night, and she says Diane was with this Norwegian fellow, but the police let him go. He had the room next to where she was found."

"We don't think they should have let him go," said the mother.

"I saw that Norwegian, too," said Jane. "I'm afraid he was pretty drunk. Earlier in the evening, anyway." Jane wondered why they had called her Diane. She distinctly remembered the girl's name was Marcia.

The parents exchanged glances. Apparently Marcia's cohort hadn't told them that Trygve was drunk. It was the kind of thing a young girl wouldn't tell someone's parents—teen solidarity carried through into young adulthood.

"But your daughter wasn't drunk," Jane assured them. "I saw her in the ladies' room earlier that evening."

"How did she seem?" said the mother, leaning forward greedily.

How *had* she seemed? Very strange, really. Not silly or giddy, like some girl waiting to be picked up. If Jane had known she'd be killed in a few hours, she would have paid more attention.

"She seemed rather serious," said Jane. "Not frightened in any way. Just serious. Putting on makeup."

"She was always very serious," her mother said. "Even when she was a little girl."

"She came here to go to the University of Washington," said her father. "She graduated with a degree in English. I don't know why she had that job running around handing out samples."

He seemed to be apologizing. Jane didn't think it was unusual in the least for an English major to be working as a demo temp. "Young kids do all kinds of jobs these days," said Jane. She started to add, "Before they find their niche in life," but realized Marcia or Diane or whatever her name was had done everything she was ever going to do.

"There's a lot we don't know," said her father. "Her being over here in Seattle and all." He looked away.

"We found out where she was living . . . ," began her mother. "Kind of near here."

Ellensburg was only a couple of hours away. Why hadn't they known where she was living until now? Jane wondered. They'd said she hadn't been home for a long time. "It's hard when they move away," she said.

Mrs. Hunter sighed. "At first, at the U, we'd visit her and she'd visit us a lot. Then something happened. She moved out of the sorority and didn't seem to want to have anything to do with us."

"Sometimes when people start out in life on their own, they go through a phase like that," said Jane, horrified that murder had transformed an adolescent estrangement into a separation until death.

The Hunters might have been the kind of rigid parents who drove their children away, but they seemed like well-meaning people who didn't deserve to spend the rest of their lives wondering what they could have done differently and what their daughter had become. Now she understood why they were pursuing an investigation of sorts on their own.

"You need to know more about your daughter's death, but also more about her life here in Seattle, don't you?" said Jane.

"That's it exactly," Barbara Hunter said. "It's so hard not knowing." She began to weep without any struggle to contain it, without any spasms or shudder, just tears filling her little doll eyes and flowing out onto her cheeks.

"We found out she had a boyfriend. His name was Curtis. Curtis Jeffers. She was living with him. But he won't speak to us. We don't understand it."

"Maybe she thought you wouldn't have liked it that they lived together," said Jane.

" 'Course we wouldn't have," said her father. "But she was over twenty-one. We couldn't have stopped her." He sounded quite rational about it and genuinely puzzled at the estrangement.

"Our other daughter lived with her husband before they got married," said Barbara. "It couldn't have been that."

"Maybe her boyfriend was too upset to talk about her," Jane said.

"We don't know," said Phil. He looked over at his wife. "He wouldn't let us in the house. It was pretty bad. And I sure wish we could have talked to that Norwegian before he left town. We'll keep trying, but it's hell. It's hard on Barb, but she won't let me do it alone."

"Maybe you need a good professional investigator to find out some of these things for you," said Jane. "For your own peace of mind."

Phil sighed and said, "To be completely honest, I'd thought about it. Especially after we had such a bad time with Diane's boyfriend. I even talked to a friend of mine in the sheriff's department back home about how much it would cost." He sighed. "What people don't understand about ranching is that you can be land rich and cash poor. Or even deep in hock to the bank."

Jane took a deep breath and went into her pitch.

Uncle Harold would have been proud of her. Her first instinct had been to help these people. Of course, that initial spurt of pure altruism, keen as it was, hadn't lasted very long.

A second later she had felt an added thrill as she realized the problems of these two people might form the basis for a satisfactory case. A case she could take before the board. A case she could turn into big bucks. Bucks that could allow her to tell the food and beverage manager at the Meade Hotel, for instance, what he could do with his job. Bucks that could allow her to lead the life she felt she really deserved after years of living out of suitcases and managing a sort of genteel, stylish poverty that had its on-the-edge thrill but was beginning to take its toll on her spirit.

Under the terms of her uncle Harold's eccentric will, Jane was in a position to benefit from a large trust fund if she carried on his work—providing investigative services to people who otherwise wouldn't be able to get help. Uncle Harold, rich in his own right, had been motivated by the idea of helping his fellow man and wanted Jane to carry on after his death. A board of his cronies, nervous, querulous old men who hated publicity and feared oversight, decided whether her cases were worthy or not and doled out the huge income from the trust.

Now, looking at those large, sad parents holding hands on her sofa, Jane tried not to think that they might find it strange or even suspicious that a lounge singer should rush in and help them find out about their daughter's life and death.

They didn't seem defensive when Jane suggested that she find out for them what she could about their daughter's life in Seattle and about the circumstances of her death. Maybe it was because they came from a small town and didn't have a shell of urban distrust. Perhaps their reason was undermined by grief. There did seem to be a streak of fatalism in Barbara Hunter that made it an easy sell. "It seems like it was meant to be," she said. "Because we do need some help." She looked up at her husband. "We don't know our way around Seattle. We've already come up against a wall with that boy. And the police. They won't tell us about the Norwegian."

Phil Hunter looked down at his wife with an expression that seemed to say "I will agree to anything that you think could help because I don't know how else to console you."

He turned to Jane and said with a defensive bristle: "You really mean it when you say you do this sort of thing for free?"

"Absolutely," said Jane. "I represent a family foundation that provides investigative services to people who need it. In your case, I feel strongly that this is the sort of work you are in no condition to do by yourselves right now. Emotionally. And practically. You live far away. You have a ranch you probably can't neglect."

"Is this some kind of charity thing?" said Phil.

"No," Jane said. "This is what I do. I do it well, and it's what I want to do. It's the work my uncle chose for me." She stopped for a moment and tried to imagine their lives and think of some way to reassure them. "In a smaller town, when there is a tragedy like yours, people can help one another in a more direct way," she said. "This is the way it can happen in a city where people are more cut off from each other."

They nodded, and she decided to assume the sale was made and get down to business before they fretted themselves out of letting her help. "I'd like a picture of your daughter," she said in a calm, low voice. "Also the name of her boyfriend and her old address. And some way to get in touch with the other young woman you spoke with. I'll see what I can find out.

"And maybe you can tell me," she continued, "why you call her Diane and I heard the other girl that night call her Marcia. Was that her middle name?"

Barb Hunter looked genuinely confused. "She didn't have a middle name. We don't understand it at all. The police tell us she was calling herself Marcia St. Francis. There's so much we don't get at all."

Before they left, Jane had written down all the pertinent addresses and phone numbers, including the phone and address of Marcia's sister, Lisa, who lived in Kent, a suburb to the south.

Jane took a look at her list, thought about it for a moment, and added, "Carla? Fish magazine," to the list. After all, Marcia (Jane persisted in thinking of her as Marcia, at least until she discovered the reason for her name change) had been found in Carla's bathtub.

CHAPTER FOUR

Carla Elroy was in the phone book, and although Jane assumed she was at work at ten-thirty in the morning, she tried her home number anyway. Maybe Carla had a machine.

She answered on the first ring.

"Hi, Carla. This is Jane da Silva. The singer from the Meade Hotel."

"Hi," Carla said in a sad little voice.

"I was wondering how you were getting along," began Jane.

"I'm not getting on very well at all," Carla said. "My whole life has been turned upside down."

"Oh, I know, it was awful," said Jane, alarmed.

"It isn't just that," said Carla. "Even though I'm still upset, naturally. It's that after that happened, I was let go."

"You mean fired?" Jane said.

"I guess you'd call it that. I've devoted my life to seafood, and Norm just went ahead and fired me. Because of that dead woman."

It took a while to get the story out of her. Carla had been fired because an advertiser, a smoked salmon company, objected to her piece on the Seattle Seafood Show, specifically the sidebar entitled "Tartan Tarts? Is This Really the Way to Sell Seafood?" The piece had apparently included a long statement from the Women's Seafood Network about tasteless exploitation of women at trade shows.

Carla had written it before making her ghastly discovery in her hotel room. The magazine's editor, Norman Carver, hadn't bothered to read it. Norman never bothered reading any editorial material, because he was really only interested in selling ad pages.

He had, however, faxed the copy to an advertiser, the smoked salmon company that had hired Marcia, so they could read what had been written about them before it went to press.

The company had complained that the whole thing was in poor taste, considering what had happened to its hapless demo girl. They had canceled a four-color insert. Norman had fired Carla immediately, citing the cancellation and other complaints from advertisers who felt Carla wasn't as interested in providing editorial support for their businesses as she should be. Norm had to be a first-class idiot, faxing the story without reading it.

"Now I won't get that trip to the Norwegian cod grounds I lined up at the seafood show," said Carla. "I was really looking forward to it." Her heartfelt sigh was clearly audible over the phone.

Jane offered some sympathy and worked the conversation around to Marcia. Carla, it turned out, had been working on writing up the murder for the magazine until about an hour before she was fired. "I knew it wasn't strictly seafood oriented, but I thought people in the industry would want to know what happened," she explained.

Jane wanted to hear all about Carla's investigation. "Listen," she said, "I got fired, too. How about if I use my last check to take us out to lunch to cheer us up. To be honest, I'm kind of curious about Marcia. Maybe you could fill me in. It would take my mind off my own troubles."

"Wow, that would be great," Carla said, her voice taking on a new animation.

Jane suggested her own favorite restaurant, Ray's Boathouse, in Carla's neighborhood. She thought Carla would approve, as seafood was their specialty.

"Good idea," said Carla, sounding even happier. "I think they have some great Copper River salmon, and some of the Canadian halibut that's just been landed."

Jane cut her off before she had a chance to give more details of the menu or went into how the catch of the day had been bled and gutted; she arranged to meet Carla at one, then called and made a reservation.

Jane was eager to talk to Carla in person. She was a firm believer in in-person interviews. It was much easier to get things out of people face-to-face.

Feeling pushy, but sticking by her tried-and-true method, Jane decided she should also try to touch base with Marcia's boyfriend in person, on her way to the restaurant.

She showed up twenty minutes later on the porch of a surprisingly elegant old house on Capitol Hill, not far from her own house on Federal Avenue. She hoped he'd be home.

It was a big square house, painted white and embellished with lots of fancy moldings, classical columns along the deep front porch, leaded diamond-shaped windowpanes and a couple of Moorish keyhole windows thrown in for good measure. There were lots of houses like this in Seattle, dating from the early decades of the century and nicknamed "classic boxes." There was a big, messy garden around it and a curving driveway leading to a porte-cochère.

What was Marcia St. Francis, cheesy model, doing living in a place like this? It seemed a more suitable home for a blue-haired lady who belonged to the Sunset Club, or some youngish yuppie couple who would have the landscaping all redone and a paint job in three colors picking out all the little details. Rich people, in any case. Maybe Curtis Jeffers was some well-heeled doctor or dentist who had ditched his wife and been shacked up with a younger blonde. But no, the Hunters had called him "that boy."

She rang the bell. The door had a big oval of beveled glass in its center, and she tried to peer through a heavy, yellowish lace curtain into the hall. All she could make out was a human shape coming toward the door.

The man who answered looked about twenty-five. He had oily-looking dark curls that hung to just below his earlobes, a thin, intense-looking face and olive skin. He wore a woven cotton tunic in purple and red that Jane guessed came from Central America, over what looked like pajama bottoms. On his feet were black cloth slippers.

From behind him came the powerful smell of cat. More than one, judging by the intensity, Jane imagined.

"Are you Curtis Jeffers?" She tried to look sympathetic yet firm and businesslike.

"Yes, I am." He blinked slowly. There was a strange passivity to his voice.

"I'm glad I caught you at home," she began.

"I don't work," he said in that strange, flat voice. "I'm always here."

"My name is Jane da Silva," she said. "Marcia's family . . ."

At that he scowled. "Her parents?" he demanded.

"Yes. They—"

"They have blood on their hands," he said. "Tell them I said so."

Maybe he'd gone crazy with grief, she reflected, hesitating. Then: "I wonder if I could ask you a few questions," she ventured. "The Hunters—"

"Ha!" he said in some strange little cry of triumph.

"They're very upset, as I'm sure you are," Jane said.

Curtis Jeffers's face changed suddenly. The anger drained away, and Jane thought he was now on the verge of tears. The sudden shift was slightly scary, but she thought she had an opening now.

"They're wondering about a lot of things," she said. "They'd lost touch. They want to know what she was up to."

"Marcia was a saint," he said. "A wonderful, brave person. Ethical and decent. They wouldn't understand that."

"They're wondering about her death, too," she said.

He stepped back a pace, then whined: "No, I'm not talking about it."

Now he acted as if she were accusing him. "There was a Norwegian," she began, thinking to deflect attention from him.

"What about him?" said Curtis.

"Her family wonders—"

"He has blood on his hands, too. They can all go to hell," he said.

This wasn't going anywhere. Jane sighed and took a card from her purse. "I know this is a terrible time for you," she said. "Maybe later you might want to talk. Other people cared about Marcia, too."

He took the card, stared at it, then thrust it back at her. "Go away," he said quietly, and then he slammed the door. Hard. The glass shuddered and the lace shook.

Jane stood on the porch for a second, feeling like a failed door-to-door salesman. Thank God she hadn't put her foot in the door. That heavy slam could have done some real damage. And it had come without any accompanying physical signs of anger. Curtis Jeffers seemed to be wired rather differently from other human beings. He gave her the creeps.

It wasn't until she was back at the curb that her feeling of painful rejection subsided. After all, it had been pretty aggressive to just show up without an appointment and expect someone who might well have been grieving to confide in her.

At the restaurant, Carla was waiting eagerly for Jane, carrying a large tote bag with a stenciled crab on the side and wearing a T-shirt with a salmon and the words "Protect the Resource" on it. Ray's was a nice, airy restaurant right on the water. Jane loved it because the food was simple and beautifully prepared, and the atmosphere was low key and unpretentious. If the place hadn't been in Seattle, it might have been tarted up and snobbish.

They got a nice table by the window, where they could

watch an occasional fishing boat or green-and-white tugboat go by and admire the misty hills over the water.

After a lengthy discussion with the waiter over the provenance of all the specials, Carla settled for some Alaska rex sole. To avoid further fishy discussion, Jane ordered the same thing.

"Tell me what you found out," said Jane, digging into her first course—a salad of wild tasting greens with a wonderful walnut vinaigrette dressing.

Carla said her informants from the Fountain Room (she'd made about thirty calls to conventioneers who'd been hanging around the Meade that night) told her that Marcia and Trygve Knutsen, a Norwegian Fisheries Ministry official, were seen pawing each other in the bar. He was very drunk. They left the hotel together at one point in the evening. He later returned alone. His room was next door to the hospitality suite.

Carla already knew that there was a connecting door between his room and the suite. It had been open earlier that evening when the magazine had hosted a cocktail party.

Jane was beginning to see why the Hunters wondered why the police had let Trygve Knutsen fly out of Seattle a few hours after talking to the police.

"Did you find anything out about Marcia herself?" said Jane. "What kind of person was she?"

"I talked to her boyfriend," Carla said. "Twice. The first time I just called and said I'd found her and I was sorry and he said he thought this Norwegian guy killed her and—"

"He said that?" said Jane, startled.

"Yes," said Carla. "He said he knew they were together and that the guy was drunk, and that he was a sociopathic killer."

Carla had gotten more out of Curtis than Jane had. "How would he know?" Jane said. "Did she call him and say she was groping around with this guy and he seemed homicidal and she'd be home a little late? What kind of a boyfriend is he, anyway?"

"He's very weird," said Carla. "The second time I called, I told him I was writing the story for the magazine, and he said he had nothing to say to the press and that I had blood on my hands or something. Maybe because he knew she was found in our hospitality suite. He was kind of scary, but I guess he's in terrible shape."

Curtis Jeffers seemed to see blood on everyone's hands.

"I also called Trygve Knutsen in Norway," continued Carla. "I've interviewed him plenty of times, and he is usually pretty friendly, but he said he had nothing to say and hung up on me."

"What I still don't understand," said Jane, "is why you were staying at the hotel? You live here in Seattle."

"I know," said Carla, "but I wanted to be sort of in the middle of the action. Norm has a suite there he uses for entertaining clients, and sometimes I interview people there. He gets some freebie from the hotel for plugging it in our Seattle Seafood Show issue." Jane noted that poor Carla had used "our" when referring to the magazine. She still hadn't fully realized she wasn't working for them anymore.

"Anyway, he said I could spend the night there. I pick up a lot just hanging around the hotel. And that way I can socialize more and hit all the parties." Carla sounded as if the seafood show were the highlight of her social year. Hmm . . . like the dreary salmon exporters reception, thought Jane. Carla had hardly wowed them there, as she recalled.

"You said room two ten was sort of a corporate suite. Who else had a key to it?"

"I don't know. Norman gave me the key. He had a bunch of them and sort of handed them around. It was one of those cards with holes punched in them. It was when I started to ask him about it that he told me not to write about the murder, just to forget about the whole thing. Then those smoked salmon people called about an hour later and he fired me."

Jane produced another soothing murmur and then said: "Did you talk to the police?"

"That Detective Olson wouldn't tell me anything. The

public affairs department just told me what I'd read in the *Seattle Times*. She was shot and no weapon was found.

"But I did get the name of the other girl dressed in that stupid outfit from the demo agency." The Hunters had managed to do that, too, Jane recalled. "I was all set to interview her, but I had to cancel when Norm killed the story." Carla broke off to inspect the sole, which had just arrived. She smiled down at it happily, took a bite, looked thoughtful, nodded her approval and went on. "Norm said it was a downer and we were a trade publication and we were supposed to elevate the industry and not accentuate the negative."

"I'm hardly surprised," said Jane, who had already formed the impression that if Norm could sell an inside back cover to Jack the Ripper, he'd suppress the White-chapel killings. Besides, the fact that Marcia had been found in his hospitality suite hardly reflected well on the publication.

"It's really a shame," said Carla. "I think there are some really interesting stories out there, but I've never really been able to tackle them. Norm's had me so busy with all this advertorial stuff."

"You know, Carla," said Jane, "I got kind of close to Marcia's parents. They came to see me. I promised them I'd check into this whole thing for them. Do you think Norm would answer some of my questions?"

"If he thought there was something in it for him," she said. "He's a total creep." Her voice caught a little, and she said, "If you do, find out if he's found my replacement. They'll probably get that trip to the cod grounds."

Jane had an idea. If it worked, she could get in to talk to Norm, get herself to Norway to check out Trygve Knutsen without pushing the limits of her Visa card and give Carla some freelance work.

"Carla," she said, "if you briefed me, do you think I could get your old job? I'd let you ghost-write everything, and I'd hand over what he paid me to you. It might help while you're looking. Frankly, I could use that trip to Norway myself. To check things out for Marcia's parents."

"Make yourself a freelance, and he might go for it," said Carla. "He always likes to save money."

"Do you think we could fool Norman?" said Jane.

"No problem," Carla said, sounding enthusiastic. "He's majorly stupid." She sniffed contemptuously. "He doesn't even know that much about fish."

"Maybe you could prep me. Tell me what to say. Help me fake a résumé or something," said Jane.

"I took all my reference books and the Rolodex when I cleaned out the place, so we have everything we need to get you going." Carla sounded happy all of a sudden. "I can start you on a cram course this afternoon. You'll love this industry."

"Great," said Jane, who supposed it could be worse. Carla could have been a writer for an industrial zipper and fastener magazine or *Linoleum World* or something. "But let me get the appointment with Norm first." There was no way she was going to fill her head with fish facts unless she really had to.

CHAPTER FIVE

During the next few days Jane tried to get in touch with Norm, who never returned her calls, and Stacy, the other tartan tart from the seafood show. Stacy's machine was always on, leaving a squeaky little recording asking for callers to leave a message. Jane didn't, thinking it was too easy for Stacy not to call back. She'd keep trying until she got her in person.

Jane also called Trygve Knutsen in Norway. Carla had given her his office number. She said she was a friend of Marcia St. Francis's family, calling from Seattle, and he replied, sounding as if he meant it: "I have spoken to the police. I have nothing to say to anyone else. Good-bye." As he had done with Carla, he hung up.

When Jane called Lisa Rogers, Marcia's sister in Kent, she got her husband. He said his wife was east of the mountains with her parents, who were in pretty bad shape, but that she would be back in a week or so, "or whenever she thinks her mom will be okay. This has been hell for all of us." Jane halfheartedly thought of asking him a few questions, but he sounded weary and worn out, so she decided to wait until Lisa came back to town.

The person Jane most wanted to interview, however, was Trygve Knutsen, and the way she planned to get to him was through the magazine. Finally, after leaving a message saying she wanted to buy the back cover, Norm returned her call.

"We can draw up a contract right away," he said.

"There must be some mistake," said Jane. "Actually I was calling about something else."

"My God," said Norm. "I wonder who does want the back cover."

After he recovered from the possibility of a botched sale, Jane managed to get an appointment with him, then bit the bullet and called Carla for her cram course.

A few days later, as ready as she'd ever be, Jane found herself in the offices of *Seafood Now*. Norm Carver was much as Carla had described him: a weedy, self-important man with a dense thatch of hair that Jane thought might well be a toupee. "So how did you know we were looking for a writer?"

Jane went into her story. She hadn't rehearsed it too well. She'd discovered that her lies sounded better if she improvised the details. "Well, I was at the Seattle Seafood Show, covering it for a European seafood magazine, and I ran into Carla. She told me you'd come to a parting of the ways." She shrugged, as if to indicate she wasn't really a friend of Carla's and couldn't care less it she'd been fired. "I was interested in leaving Europe and coming back to Seattle, and I thought if you needed a stringer or a freelancer here, we might work something out."

She looked around his untidy office. It had a nice view of the docks and the fleet of fishing boats across the street at Fisherman's Terminal. There were some framed charts of fish species on the wall and a bulletin board with overlapping scrawled notes and computer printouts. On the desk and the table next to it were nests of files and memos spilling from in and out boxes. The whole thing had the look of a collection of fungal masses growing toward each other to become one whole sometime in the near future. A flurry of yellow Post-it notes, like wind-tossed leaves, embellished the whole composition.

Carver nodded with a serious expression, brow furrowed, mouth turned down as if to say "I have a powerful intellect and the ability to grasp complexities." But the dull glaze in his heavy-lidded, cowlike brown eyes gave him away.

"I'm not really interested in full-time," she said. "I have an income of my own."

Now she had his attention. There was an eager flicker in those dull eyes. He picked up a pencil and gazed at it thoughtfully. He nodded again. "Well," he said, "maybe we can work something out. On a per word basis. I guess you know the trade press doesn't really pay that well. And frankly, things are tight in the seafood business. It's no secret our ad pages are down. The book is half the size it was three years ago."

Jane nodded. Carla had said he would poor-mouth. "I understand completely," she said. "I just happen to love this industry, and I'd like to keep my hand in. And of course, a byline in *Seafood Now* would mean a lot to me."

He leaned back on his chair and made a pompous little cathedral with his fingertips. "We are the best seafood magazine around. No question. I'm sure you're familiar with our competitors, *Seafood Leader* and *Seafood Business*. Have you seen our sales materials?"

Carla had also told her that Norman had no interest in the editorial content that he was compelled to include between the ads. Jane looked attentive as he went into a canned pitch about the merits of the magazine. "We're reaching key buyers in all industry segments," he said, flapping through a sales kit with some bar graphs. "We've got decision makers all down the line—your big institutional buyers, retail fish buyers, wholesalers, distributors, executive chefs—and we've got key people at point of purchase—right down to your seafood manager at your local grocery store."

He leaned over in a manner Jane imagined he'd learned at some school for salesmen and looked her right in the eye. The effect was more bovine than dynamic. "They all rely on *Seafood Now* in their decision making. We keep them in the loop. We give them product information, marketing ideas, we let them know about pricing and supply, new value-added products, the whole ball of wax. Processing, too. If there's a new way to handle parasites or a new H and G concept, we clue them in."

Jane nodded. A new way to handle parasites sounded like a useful social skill, but he was presumably talking about marine rather than human worms. What "H and G" stood for, however, was a total mystery.

"Would you like to see my clips?" she said, handing over the sheaf of material she and Carla had dummied up together at Sudden Printing, pasting Jane's byline over the pseudonym Carla had used when freelancing for other magazines. Jane had skimmed the titles of the articles, which she had found oddly evocative: "Out of Africa: Is There Nile Perch in Your Future?"; "Abalone without You: A West Coast Resource Threatened with Extinction"; and the slightly heretical "In Cod We Trust." She had actually read "Trash Fish: Underutilized Species Can Be Gourmet Treats" and discovered that the Canadians especially had high hopes for various worms, barnacles, and fish that looked like an aquatic Quasimodo or the Elephant Man.

"I'll take a look at those later," Norman said without conviction. He placed the stack of photocopies between two large messy piles of papers so they formed a little bridge and made one large messy pile. "If I get you started right away, do you think you could give me a thousand words on Alaska halibut? I can sell a page right next to it." He plucked a Post-it note from his computer screen and examined it with a puzzled expression, then moved it to his phone, where he reapplied it with a decisive gesture.

"No problem," said Jane. Here was her chance to close. She gave Norman Carver a serious look, leaned forward just as he had done a moment ago and said: "If we can meet the client's editorial needs, everybody wins, right?"

"I really appreciate your attitude," he said. "Naturally, we'll interview the company concerned for the story.

They're very big in halibut, and they have strong feelings about how the resource up there in Alaska should be managed."

"Fine," said Jane. "Which reminds me, I was speaking with the Norwegian contingent at the seafood show. They were excited about having Carla come over and do that cod story. Would you like me to handle that?"

"I've been concerned about that trip," he said. "They'd worked up a whole itinerary, and of course, with the Norwegians paying, it seems a shame not to extend the magazine's editorial reach."

"Word is the Norwegians are going to be tripling their U.S. promotion budget," Jane said with a knowing air. "I think it might be a good idea to get over there right away." She paused, and then just to make sure he got it—it was hard to tell how much he got and how much he pretended to get—she said, "They might buy some ads from you."

"I had thought of taking that trip myself," he said.

"Of course, you couldn't possibly write," Jane said as if it were somehow on a par with making the coffee or sweeping out the place. "With business the way it is, I imagine you're really working hard on the big sales push. Your special talents are needed elsewhere."

"My wife and I enjoyed a lovely free trip to New Zealand," he said. "It is one of the nice perks attached to this business. We went in July, though, which is winter there. That's when the hoki are harvested, so I didn't have much choice. But they aren't into central heating down there. It was cold. And my wife found the food disappointing."

"Well, Norway in winter might be interesting," said Jane. "I think it's okay as long as you're inside. I don't know what it would be like on the deck of a boat out there above the Arctic circle. And I understand seagull eggs are a great delicacy there. Maybe they'll be in season."

Norman took this in and looked thoughtful for a moment. Then he said, "Perhaps you should go ahead and take that trip."

CHAPTER SIX

From the magazine's offices Jane drove to the Fremont Bridge and waited in line outside the Bleitz Funeral Home because the bridge was up. A tugboat pulling a barge with a stack of containers and somebody's tall yacht sailed through the channel, and the two halves of the bridge went back down again.

She wasn't really in the mood for another session of fish school, but she decided to get it over with. Besides, Carla was eager for the debriefing.

Jane drove along Leary Way past a microbrewery, lots of industrial businesses, and several boatyards to Carla's residential neighborhood, where she lived in a basement apartment underneath a big white house.

Basement apartments, some of them illegal, were a Seattle staple, and Jane had found the idea depressing. They sounded damp and cold, with the ghosts of old garden tools and broken croquet sets haunting the place, and the sound of the landlord's feet clomping around overhead all day. However, Carla's apartment, she had been pleased to learn on her last visit, was quite pleasant.

Jane walked on stepping-stones through the grass in the side yard and down the concrete steps that led to a blue door with a brass lobster knocker and rapped firmly.

Carla opened the door and peered out with her glassy

green eyes into the light. "How did it go with Norm?" she said. "Come on in."

Although the place seemed murky, there was an inviting sofa with lots of printed cushions and a big coffee table and a couple of chairs. Green light filtered through hanging ferns from high rectangular windows, giving Jane the feeling she was under water. As she sat down, she noticed all the cushions were in tropical fish prints. Perhaps any moment now bubbles would float out of Carla's mouth.

"He bought it," said Jane. "I got the Norwegian trip. But our first assignment is a thousand words on Alaska halibut."

She had expected Carla to act pleased, since she was getting some freelance ghost work while she looked for a new job. But instead she looked hurt. "Did he say anything about me?" she said.

"No, not really," said Jane, realizing she was dealing with grief. "He's probably ashamed of himself. He knows you're irreplaceable." Carla brightened just a little.

"After all," Jane continued in a reassuring tone, "the clips were all yours, so really he's replacing you with you. I can't imagine there are many people who could step in there and get the job."

Carla gave a bleak little smile. "Let me pull my files on Norwegian cod. And on Alaska halibut. You might want to borrow my multilingual fish dictionary, too, but be careful with it." She got up and went over to a collection of cardboard boxes clustered around her desk. Jane could just see her lugging those boxes tearfully to the car after the ax had fallen.

"I've devoted years to this industry," she said bitterly, kneeling in front of the boxes and stirring around in them. "I feel like useless by-catch."

Jane, who had had a great many jobs, always felt it was a mistake to identify too much with your work. "Any new job leads?" she said in a cheerful voice.

"Well," said Carla, "I went to the Women's Seafood Network monthly dinner last night. I networked a lot. I fact, I was Networker of the Night."

"You were?" said Jane. "What's that?" Whatever it was, it sounded grim and like nothing related to easy social intercourse.

"I was the seventh person to shake the hand of the secret networker," Carla said proudly. "It was a woman who sells marine insurance. I won a species identification handbook. Anyway, I put out the word I was looking."

"That's good," said Jane, imagining a dreary gathering of Carla clones, vestal virgins of fish, all draped with fish jewelry. "You must know tons of people. I bet you'll find something soon."

"Oh, sure," said Carla, sounding unsure about it. "After all, I'm one of the leading fish journalists in the country. People in the industry take me seriously."

Jane remembered Carla rushing around the salmon reception, bothering everyone. No one seemed to take her seriously there. But then Jane found it hard to take fish itself seriously. She supposed she'd better learn to if she was going to pose as an eminent fish journalist.

"Listen, Carla," she said, "what does 'H and G' mean? Norm was talking about that."

"Headed and gutted," said Carla, frowning at Jane's appalling ignorance.

Jane tried to commit it to memory. "I hope I'll be able to carry this off," she said.

Carla, defensive, said: "It took me years to learn the business."

Jane tried to look humble for Carla's benefit, but actually she was feeling smug. She was sure she'd be able to fake it. She realized that Carla had an awesome store of fish knowledge, but her own social skills were superior. When all else failed, Jane usually managed to talk her way in or out of anything.

Back home, she made herself an espresso in her new machine. She had justified buying it, despite her shaky finances, after learning about the heavy markup on all the coffee sold on Seattle street corners. The biggest mover, a tall latte, espresso with lots of hot milk, fetched around two bucks and apparently cost the *barista* around a quarter to make.

She took great satisfaction in tamping down the coffee in its little stainless-steel cup and pulling the handle over to one side, then watching the double stream of coffee come out into a little white demitasse cup, giving the kitchen the smell of Italy.

Just as she finished and flipped the grounds into the garbage disposal, the phone rang. Coffee in hand, she went into the hall to answer it. It was Norman Carver, who announced that an itinerary and some tickets from SAS had arrived in his office.

"I can give them to you later, when we see the Putnam brothers, those halibut guys," he said. "We're meeting them for a drink at Chinook's this evening. Did I tell you? I figure I can sell them half a page."

He hadn't told her, but Jane just said, "That's fine." She had hoped she wouldn't have to continue her fishy charade any more than was necessary. She'd try to get her hands on the airplane tickets first, in case she disgraced herself by her ignorance of halibut and he decided to take the trip himself.

She also had no idea what Chinook's was, other than remembering vaguely from her Pacific Northwest youth that it was a kind of salmon. She'd call Carla.

Carla gave her a brace of questions to ask and provided her with a few additional halibut facts. It was hard for Jane not to let her mind wander. There seemed to be some issue about how the resource was managed, short openings and high prices meaning that a few times a year a million boats went out and grabbed as much as they could for twenty-four hours, so that all the fresh halibut came to market at once, and the rest of the year it was frozen, only they were changing all that now.

"So who is it you're meeting?" Carla said with the forlorn

air of someone who wasn't being invited to a high school dance.

"Their name is Putnam," said Jane. "You know them?"

Even over the phone, Jane could hear Carla's tongue click in derision. "I'm afraid they are very poor representatives of the industry," she said primly. "That's all I'm prepared to say for now."

As Carla drew in a breath to tell her more than she wanted to know, Jane rushed in and said: "How about if I just tape the interview and you can write it up?"

"That'll work," said Carla. "Just let them talk. They have a lot of theories, and they can get nasty when people don't agree with everything they say."

Jane managed to cut her off again and ask what Chinook's was. Chinook's, it appeared, was a restaurant inside the Fishermen's Terminal complex on Salmon Bay.

After she hung up, Jane went into the little office across the hall. There was a tape recorder in the closet there, left over from Uncle Harold's day, and Jane thought she'd better make sure it had batteries.

In the office, she felt that something was different, but she wasn't quite sure what. Then she realized the air was strange somehow. There was a very odd smell here. It was familiar and reminded her vaguely of childhood, but she couldn't place it.

A glance at the desk gave Jane the impression that the papers there—just some letters and bills—had been moved. She told herself she was imagining it all and took a look around the room, then felt a stab of fear.

The top drawer of the file cabinet in the corner was hanging out. She hadn't left it that way. She had opened that drawer only once, some months ago when she was making a general inspection after first moving in. The drawer had been empty.

Jane went slowly through the house for more signs of invasion, telling herself she must have pulled out that drawer herself. The television, VCR and CD player were all where they belonged. She calmed down and went up into the bedroom and looked to see if her jewelry was all there. It was.

Jane sat on the side of the bed and tried to remember pulling out that drawer. She thought for just a second about calling the police. But what would she tell them? Somehow she didn't think that when she told them someone had opened an empty drawer and moved the phone bill a few inches, they'd rush right over and dust for fingerprints.

She walked back downstairs, wondering how anyone could get in. She had thought the place was pretty secure. Maybe she'd get an alarm system installed. She hated the idea that life in Seattle, a town that had always seemed so peaceful, required that kind of siege mentality, but she knew that lots of people here on Capitol Hill had alarm systems.

The problem was, she couldn't really afford it right now—she'd been trying to hold on to as much of the money she'd received for her last case as she could—but she could at least find out how much money it would cost.

She didn't like going back into the office. The space felt tainted. She decided she'd go ahead and get that alarm system no matter how much it cost. She hated feeling this vulnerable to intruders. Had she scared them away when she'd come in the front door? Would they have ripped her off if she had come in later?

She went to the closet and opened the door and heard a horrible half-human yell. A figure came rushing out of the closet toward her. She felt hands in some kind of cloth gloves pushing at her face and smelled that smell much more strongly. Now she knew it was camphor, the smell of mothballs.

Letting out a halfhearted scream, she landed on her back and felt the thing that had rushed out of the closet scrabbling over her. Jane felt as though it were an animal. No, it was human, she told herself, logic struggling through the fear, her heart beating hard and fast, but what kind of a human being was hard to say.

She tried to prop herself up on her elbows and looked up.

The thing was looming over her in a half crouch. It was wearing a ratty old fur coat, flapping with strips of torn skin. The effect was grotesque and hellish.

More frightening, however, was the fact that the creature was wearing a navy blue ski mask, so its head looked like a little knob coming out of the pile of matted fur.

Jane tried to scramble up. She felt at a terrible disadvantage being on the floor. "Just go," she said, trying and failing to sound calm. "Just go, right now."

She wanted the thing to answer her so she would hear a human voice come out of it. That initial cry, when she'd disturbed it in its lair, a mixture of fear and anger, had been frightening. She wanted to look at its face, see the human eyes there. She had a vague impression of them blinking, but fear kept her from looking at it directly.

A foot came out from under the fur and pushed her back down by her shoulder. The foot was wearing a scruffy-looking canvas tennis shoe in a style that could have belonged to either sex. That tennis shoe and the accompanying blue denim leg of a pair of jeans finally made Jane sure that she was dealing with a person.

The figure jumped back, as though it were frightened. She decided not to startle it. She propped herself up on her elbows and pushed back along the floor, away from it. "Go!" she said, watching it back out of the room, hearing crazy feet running down the hall, finally hearing the front door slam.

Shaking and angry, she made her way to the phone. She called 911 and told the dispatcher she had just come back and interrupted a burglar. "He was wearing a ratty old fur coat and a ski mask," she said, "and he just ran out my front door onto Federal Avenue." She had said "he," but she wasn't sure what sex the intruder had been. That foot pushing down on her shoulder had seemed strong, but she remembered reading somewhere that there was considerably less difference in strength between men's and women's legs than their arms.

From her position on the ground, Jane had no idea of the

size of this person. As soon as she put down the phone, she dashed onto the porch to see if she could see which direction her intruder had taken.

There was no sign of anyone on the quiet street.

CHAPTER SEVEN

When they arrived, the policemen seemed pretty blasé about it all. "It reminded me of some kind of vermin," Jane told them after giving a description of the fur-bearing creature.

"Vermin is right," said one of the cops. "Kids, mostly, burglarizing houses while people are at work. They go for jewelry and CDs. If you ever think someone's been in the house, don't go in yourself. Call us."

By the time they finished checking the windows and showed her how easy it was to get inside through her living room window, obscured by a big camellia bush, it was time to go talk halibut.

Fishermen's Terminal was tucked quietly between two Seattle neighborhoods, Magnolia and Ballard. Jane remembered a more or less ramshackle collection of buildings around the bay where the fishing fleet was moored.

The whole thing had apparently been rebuilt, and because she was early for her meeting, she walked around to take a look. The renovation was really quite nice, all galvanized metal with dark turquoise trim, pretty but still presenting a sufficiently industrial appearance so it seemed like a working facility and not some tourist trap.

The facility housed a collection of businesses catering to fishermen who'd been at sea for a while—a shower and a barber shop, and a bank; various stores that sold gear and clothing; some corporate offices of seafood companies; and a fish market and a couple of restaurants.

Jane walked along the dock, with its fibrous-looking heavy planks and the smell of creosote, and looked at the vessels with names from the north like *Alaska Mist* and *Northern Star*.

A Japanese tourist, backed up against a pile of bright orange net, was taking pictures of a couple of bearded fishermen stacking crab pots.

Near the center of things stood a large monument, a big column encrusted with various species of fish. She recognized Dungeness crab and salmon. "A big flat creature with two eyes on one side of its head" was how Carla had described halibut—a similar smaller creature, she supposed, was a sole. There also seemed to be a sturgeon and an octopus and lots of other fish she couldn't identify. She stepped back nervously, imagining Norm rushing out and demanding she name all the fish there.

At the top of the pillar, in the style of Lord Nelson, though on a much smaller scale, stood the statue of a smiling, boyish-looking fisherman in a waterproof jacket with stiff hair in points that presumably had been shaped by the wind, pulling up a fish on a rope. He looked a bit clunky. Jane thought the artist had done a better job on the fish.

A plaque announced that this was the Fisherman Memorial. Off to one side, Jane watched a middle-aged woman in sweat pants, a parka and a chiffon head scarf bend down and leave a mason jar with some early spring flowers—saxifrage and quince still in bud—against a low wall. A few florists' bouquets in cellophane were already lying there. The woman stood back for a moment and then walked away, car keys in hand.

When she had gone, Jane went over to the wall herself. It listed the names of local commercial fishermen who had died at sea, year by year, starting in the late nineteenth century and ending with the previous year. The water around the area was so cold that if anyone fell in, they'd die in minutes. She imagined the recent ones had drowned in Alaskan waters, where most of the fishing was done nowadays.

She checked her watch and made her way back to Chinook's. The sign outside was a huge salmon. Inside was a big, noisy restaurant with big windows looking out over the boats, and a trendy-looking hostess in a tight suit and heels. The idea of young men dying in icy water seemed very distant.

She found Norm at a table in the bar, with two large men who were obviously brothers. Both were relaxed-looking guys with the tough and unflappable look of bar bouncers. One had dark hair and a dark beard with some gray in it and wore a T-shirt that had an attractive illustration of a salmon and lettering underneath that read "There's No Nookie Like Chinookie." The other had a tractor cap and a seventies-style mustache and sideburns. His T-shirt read "Say No to Drugs. Don't Eat Farmed Fish." When Carla had said they were poor representatives of the industry, she might have been referring to their loutish appearance. T-shirts that talked, Jane felt, tended to knock about ten points off the wearer's perceived IQ. Wearing that tractor cap in a restaurant sliced it down a few more points.

The three men were already drinking beer, some sales material from Norm's arsenal spread out in front of them. Norm, looking thin and weedy next to the burly Putnams, seemed to have adopted a hearty, one-of-the-boys manner that didn't seem entirely convincing to Jane.

"Hey, we're businessmen just like you guys," he was saying as she sidled up. "We like to show our customers a good time. That's why we have that hospitality suite."

"Yeah," said the man with beard, leering. "I appreciate the thought, but I can get laid all by myself, Norm."

Jane resisted the urge to point out that according to his T-shirt, he was willing to settle for a hot date with a cold fish. The other brother giggled.

Norm saw Jane, gave a decidedly guilty start, rose and introduced her. One was named Bob and one was named Don.

Jane wasn't quite sure which was which but decided it didn't matter.

"So you got rid of Carla," said Chinookie, nodding with satisfaction.

"She was a troublemaker," said Say No. "I'm glad she's outta here. You don't need her kind on the magazine, Norm."

Jane ordered a white wine and wondered just how much of their company she was going to have to take. The fact that Norm was at the very least joking about being some kind of a procurer for his advertisers made her feel a little squeamish. The way Chinookie was checking her out made her wonder if he didn't think she was available with a half-page ad. He did a standard and not very well-disguised head-to-toe-and-back body scan while she was standing and even took the trouble to lean back a little in his chair and watch her cross her legs under the table after she sat down. Maybe he'd spent too much time at sea.

She slapped the tape recorder on the table and said brightly, "Let's talk halibut!"

"The way that resource is managed sucks," said Chinookie with a dark look. "The way I see it, fish is the last food you have to go out and kill to eat. In the wild. There's no way a lot of pencil-necked geek biologists should be telling guys like us, that have the balls to go out after it, who can go out and who has to stay tied up at the dock. Let the strong survive, that's what I say."

Jane nodded. "So you don't like the management proposals from the council," she said.

"Hell no," said Say No. "Let anyone who wants to go out after it. The fish don't belong to a bunch of bureaucrats. They belong to whoever gets there first. It's in scripture," he said.

"That's interesting," Jane said warily.

Norm looked a little wary too as Say No leaned forward on his meaty elbows. "You think it's just a coincidence that a couple of the apostles were fishermen? God was trying to tell us something. And what about that deal with the loaves and fishes? Jesus didn't run out, right? That's God's way of telling us there are enough fish." He leaned back triumphantly. "It's right there in Genesis. God gave man dominion over the fish of the sea. Man! Not the International Pacific Halibut Commission."

Jane nodded and tried to look as if she were mulling over this theory of fishery management, meanwhile racking her brain for another of Carla's canned questions so as to cut him off at the pass.

"What about long term?" she said. "You know, the Norwegians are commercially farming halibut. Could that eventually affect the price of Alaska halibut?"

Chinookie snorted. "It's another species. Atlantic halibut. The Japanese will never go for it. They like Pacific species."

"Besides," said Say No, "fish farming is disgusting. We're supposed to go out and catch the stuff and risk our necks. Not grow it in tanks. It's right here in Exodus. Chapter seven, verse eighteen. 'The fish that is in the river shall die, and the river shall stink.' "

Jane smiled a little nervously. Norm coughed and looked into his beer, and Chinookie put a big hairy hand over his brother's in a surprisingly tender gesture. "Don't mind Don," he said. "He gets a little carried away sometimes."

Don certainly sounded like someone who had got his chubby hands on a Concordance during a bad acid trip. Or maybe a bad fishing trip.

Bob smiled indulgently. "We never went to Sunday school when we were kids, but he got hooked on this Bible stuff from watching these TV preachers." He rolled his eyes just a little, as if to indicate he wasn't buying into it but was willing to humor his brother.

Jane nodded sympathetically. If Don had been to Sunday school, maybe his theology and biblical scholarship would be a little more carefully thought out.

Bob continued in his soothing voice, something Jane thought he might have developed from managing a lunatic relative for so long. "Everyone in the wild salmon business has seen a noble way of life threatened by farmed Atlantic salmon flooding the market. It's hurt some mighty good people up in Alaska. We're pretty touchy about aquaculture." He gave a nice little smile. "I guess you know salmon farming's a hanging offense in the state of Alaska."

Don looked at his brother with a big idiot's grin. He looked as if he really believed the death penalty would be carried out.

Bob went on: "But we realize times are changing. That's why I support generic salmon marketing with the farmers. They aren't going to go away."

Jane revised her opinion of Bob. Maybe there was a little more to him than a testosterone-driven Hemingway wannabe, catching fish with his bare hands and biting their heads off. And he seemed rather sweetly protective of his brother.

She asked Bob a question about pricing and availability of halibut in the near future, let him drone on into the tape recorder and pretended to listen. She hoped Don hadn't stumbled across something prophetic in the book of Revelations about fish prices.

When Bob came to a halt, Jane hit the tape recorder with a decisive *thwack*, hoping she had enough there for Carla but deciding, nevertheless, that she'd put in as much effort with these guys as she could stand.

"Thank you so much for your time," she said. "You've given our readers lots to think about, halibutwise. I hope you'll like the piece I write."

"We better," Don said with a nasty, gloating expression.

"You'll love it," Norm interrupted with a frightened edge to his voice. "In fact, we'll fax you a draft so you can check it for accuracy."

Jane doubted they taught this technique at the Columbia School of Journalism, but she just nodded and said, "Absolutely."

"Now let's talk about that half page," said Norm.

"I'll let you gentlemen discuss that by yourselves," Jane

said like a bright young thing who knew her place and accepted cheerfully that the business side was all too important and high-powered for her. "But first, Norm, have you got that ticket and itinerary?"

Norm produced it from a nest of papers in his briefcase and seemed grateful to see her go.

In the car she checked the materials he'd given her. The tickets said Carla Elroy. She'd have to change that. And it was tourist class. Too bad. There was a changeover in Copenhagen, but she'd heard there was some fabulous duty-free shopping there.

The itinerary listed lots of odd-sounding towns, tours of various fish plants and interviews with a bunch of people with strange letters in their names—little circles over the A's, slashes through the O's.

There was also, she noted happily, a visit to Bergen. That was where Trygve Knutsen held forth. Surely it wouldn't be too hard to wangle her way in to see him.

She felt a familiar sense of elation as she pulled out of the parking lot, the sense of triumph she had when she had lied successfully. True, Norman Carver and the Putnam brothers weren't particularly crafty adversaries, but they all seemed to believe she was a fish journalist, something she hadn't even known existed until quite recently.

Now she had her ticket to what might prove to be a good case. She headed toward Carla's to drop off the tape and hoped this would be her last task before setting out on her own line of investigation.

But it hadn't been a complete waste of time. While she had dreaded this meeting, and the Putnams, the Tweedledum and Tweedledee of halibut, had proved to be less than inspiring companions, she had learned something of interest. It sounded very possible to her that Norm Carver used that hotel suite to provide female companionship as a sales incentive scheme. Was that what Marcia had been doing there? Entertaining a client? She knew who might know.

CHAPTER EIGHT

When Jane had dropped off the tape in Carla's mailbox (she wasn't up to any more fishy conversation or a visit to that murky, aquatic basement apartment), she went to a phone booth outside a BP gas station and once again called Marcia's colleague Stacy, the other Highland lass at the Seattle Seafood Show.

"Hi," said the familiar Minnie Mouse recorded voice. "I can't answer the phone right now, but if this is Steve, I'll be doing a demo at the Thriftway on Queen Anne. Come and see me there if you can. I was sort of thinking you would have called by now. How come you didn't?"

Jane sighed and resisted the temptation to say, after the beep, "He didn't call because he didn't have anything specific to say, and your basic need for constant telephonic reassurance is something he mistakenly interprets as pointless nagging." Jane had reached an age where she often felt compelled to counsel younger women to change their expectations in line with male reality.

Instead she hung up and drove back across the Ballard Bridge to Queen Anne Hill, where she found Thriftway with no problem. While she hoped Steve would show up there at some point, she hoped it wasn't now.

She wouldn't have recognized Stacy, who was now marketing to upscale daytime shoppers instead of fish executives at an out-of-town convention. The wet-lipped makeup job, French can-can hosiery and killer pumps were gone, replaced by a Sunday school teacher flowered print dress and a big white apron. Stacy looked well scrubbed and wholesome and was handing out little morsels of pizza on toothpicks at the end of aisle three.

Jane had prepared herself with a shopping cart and thrown in a few items. Now she lingered to the side a little, feigning interest in a display of tortilla chips while Stacy squeaked at an older lady: "Yeah, they have a really neat texture, and they don't get like all mushy and gross like some microwavable pizzas. We've got some coupons for them, a whole dollar off for two, if you'd like. They're in frozen foods."

When the customer had drifted off with her coupons, Stacy turned to Jane and gave her a breathless canned pitch. "Care to try our new microwavable pizza?" she said. "Just five minutes from the frozen state to the table, and I think you'll find they're as good as the pizzas they deliver." She wrinkled her nose for emphasis. "And a lot faster."

Jane bit into one. "I think I saw you at the seafood show," she said.

"That's right," said Stacy. "You look sort of familiar. Were you demoing something there?"

"I was the lounge singer at the Meade Hotel," said Jane.

"I remember. You sang those really romantic old-fashioned songs. How ya doin'?"

"Pretty good," said Jane. "Wasn't it terrible about that other girl?"

Stacy nodded. "I know. God, it was so weird." She gave short shrift to a mother and her baby who had stopped in front of her card table. "Try one," she said absentmindedly, gesturing toward her plate and handing them little napkins before turning eagerly back to Jane. "The thing is, I was dressed just the same. I keep thinking it could have been me, maybe. I mean, if it was some psycho. There were plenty of creepy guys at that show."

"Is that what you think happened? Some psycho killed her?"

"I don't know. See, I was going to go home afterward, but Marcia wanted us to go out and have a drink. I was sort of mad at my boyfriend, so I thought I'd stay out late just to bug him."

"Good thinking. That's a better idea than trying to force them to call through guilt or something," said Jane, pleased of the opportunity to pretend Stacy had already grasped this important fact of courtship while in fact planting the idea.

"So anyway, we go into the party and she goes like, 'There are some nice guys who want to buy us a drink,' and I'm like, 'Okay, why not?' And then she ends up with this guy who was really drunk, and before I know it she leaves with him. I ended up with some catfish salesman from Mississippi who was a perfect gentleman, thank God, and he took me to dinner with some of his buddies and then put me in a cab to go home, and next thing I hear is she's been found dead."

"Was she a friend of yours?" said Jane, eating a piece of pizza, which was too salty.

"No. I'd never worked with her before. She was new to the agency. Anyway, I did find out where she lived, because my car broke down that day, and when I called the agency to see if they'd pay for a cab, they set it up for me to go with her. I live on Capitol Hill, near Broadway, and so did she, so I like walked over to her house. She lived in this huge, rich house, I couldn't believe it."

Stacy was by now completely ignoring the shoppers who drifted by, and none of them were sufficiently bold to break up her conversation in search of a sample.

Jane opened her eyes wide, leaned forward and took on the dramatic, confiding manner of a woman Stacy's age. "You know what? I saw her body. The woman who found it went crazy and rushed over to where I was, and I went back and saw her."

Stacy was clearly thrilled. "Omigod, no way!" she said.

"It was awful," said Jane.

"Oh, you poor thing," Stacy said.

"Listen," said Jane, "would you mind if we talked about it? It really shook me up. I feel like if I knew more about her, about what happened that evening, it would be less freaky."

"No problem," said Stacy. "Do you live around here? I'll be off at nine."

"Great," said Jane, "I'll be back then. Maybe we can have a coffee or something."

"I'm really glad you came in," Stacy said. "It would help me a lot to talk about it, too."

Their morbid curiosity having been recast as co-therapy and thereby made respectable, the two women promised to meet at nine right outside the store.

Jane had an hour to kill, so she went to Tower Books at the bottom of Queen Anne Hill and headed for the travel section to read about Norway. The end papers of one fat book about all of Scandinavia showed a map of the region. She looked for some of the names that had appeared on her itinerary.

Everywhere she was going seemed to be along the west coast. A little town called Tromsø and an archipelago called the Lofoten Islands were both above the Arctic Circle. Trondheim was farther south, at the end of a long fjord. Bergen, she noted, was on the same parallel as the Shetland Islands.

She already had a vague impression of the place, borne out by the guidebooks she skimmed standing there in the aisle. Clean as a whistle. Lots of gorgeous scenery. Land of the midnight sun (except at this time of year it would be land of the midday gloom, she supposed). Plenty of fish to eat. No tipping. Everyone spoke English. A good place to buy furs and modern jewelry, with enamel work a specialty.

That eliminated shopping. Jane was hardly in the market for furs or jewelry, her fashion forays being presently limited to the Nordstrom rack, where all the markdowns went. Not to mention the bargain jeans, T-shirt and slinky dress emporium she favored in lean times, home of the perpetual ten-dollar sale, which she thought of affectionately as the "teen tart store."

The guidebooks were full of stunning photographs of fjords, charming little towns and mountain meadows. All the pictures had obviously been taken in the height of summer. Jane had a bleak vision of herself shivering in hotel rooms and browsing among dusty carved trolls in chilly souvenir shops. While snow was undeniably beautiful, she hated being cold.

She read a capsule description of the Norwegian character. "While traditionally considered cool and reserved, Norwegians often come alive at night, and love a party," it said. That sounded like Knutsen all right. And farther along: "A remarkably law-abiding people, Norwegians enjoy living in a country with one of the world's lowest crime rates. Violent crime is practically unknown."

She sighed. Here she was, barreling off to a cold place with a reputation for dull cooking, no shopping in sight, her days filled with watching fish being headed and gutted. And the guidebook was telling her the chances of her finding a demented killer there were minimal.

At nine Jane found Stacy outside the store, standing in front of a huge display of bright yellow daffodils, shivering a little in her floral dress and light raincoat and looking a little sad in contrast with the garish flowers.

Jane suggested a coffee across the street, and Stacy stood on tiptoe to check out the place before agreeing. Once inside, she made a point of sitting so she could look out the window over at the entrance to Thriftway. Jane wondered for a second why she seemed so distracted, then realized that, of course, Stacy was living in a state of perpetual hopefulness and had her eye out for the missing-in-action boyfriend.

When they were settled with their coffees, however, Stacy got back on track. Jane rewarded her with a description of the body. Just the bare details, the position of the limbs, the paleness of the skin, the clothes she was wearing.

"You're kidding!" said Stacy. "She'd changed?"

"That's right." Jane sipped her coffee. "I wonder when she did that?"

"She was wearing that stupid Scotch outfit when she left with that guy. His name was Trigger or something."

"Did she have a lot to drink?"

Stacy shook her head. "That was the weird part. She drank Perrier and lime. I can't see going off with that guy unless you were pretty shit-faced, no offense."

"Where did they go?"

"I don't know. She was kind of snuggling up against him, like rubbing his leg and stuff, and he slobbered something in her ear and she was all like giggly. It was like she was drinking, you know. She held on to her glass like it was really booze, and acted sort of out of it."

"He didn't notice she wasn't actually drinking?"

"Are you kidding? He was so far gone he was totally clueless."

"Maybe they went up to his room," said Jane. But where had she changed into that plain sweatshirt and jeans?

"I think they went in her car," Stacy said now. "Because she dangled her car keys in front of him before they left. They must have gone in her car." Her gaze drifted over Jane's shoulder.

"What was she like?" Jane tried to catch Stacy's eye. "What kind of a person was she?"

"Really strange," said Stacy, who politely met Jane's gaze once more. "We talked about modeling, because that's what my career goal is. Like a lot of girls who work for the agency. I told her I was going to try and be a spokesmodel on *Great American Star Search*."

Jane looked blank.

"You know," prompted Stacy. "It's on TV. With Ed McMahon. You can win a lot of money. You have to do an evening gown thing, and then you announce the next acts and stuff."

Jane got a vision of poor Stacy squeaking into the camera in a beaded gown.

"Anyway," Stacy went on, "she didn't know anything about modeling. Like how you have to have head shots and stuff. I couldn't figure out what she was doing there. She sure hated fish."

"Did she seem really interested in this guy, this"—Jane remembered not to use his actual name—"this Trigger guy?"

"Yeah, in a totally sleazy way. It was really weird. Because when we left her house her boyfriend gave her a big kiss, like they were really in love. He gazed into her eyes and gave her this serious look, and she gave him this sweet little smile. I thought they were totally in love. It was so sweet. They stood there for a minute like she was going off on a trip or something."

Stacy sighed, presumably at the thought of separated lovers, and her desperate eyes flitted back across the street.

Jane tried to imagine Curtis Jeffers in a passionate embrace, and failed. "And she was wearing that plaid outfit?"

"That's right. I guess she couldn't have taken that drunk guy home, because her boyfriend was probably there. I wonder where they went and where she changed? I don't get it. Because someone saw Trigger or whatever his name is back in the hotel hours later. Without her. So maybe she ditched him."

"Who saw him later? Did you?"

"No, this guy in the bar. Magnum something. He had a weird accent."

"What kind of an accent?"

"Like Uncle Scrooge on those *Duck Tales* cartoons," said Stacy. "My little sister watches that."

"You mean like from Scotland?"

"Yeah," said Stacy. "That's it."

"Magnus Anderson?"

"I think that's the guy. He came up to me and the catfish guy. It was quite a while later because we ended up having dinner at Benihana's of Tokyo." Stacy looked momentarily smug, as if she'd pulled a fast one on her boyfriend. "Anyway, this catfish guy was waiting for me to get into a cab, and this Magnum guy comes up and he's talking and he says something about poor old Trigger. Like someone just saw him in the hotel looking all wrecked up. This Magnum guy said something about him getting into some kinky stuff. He seemed to think it was funny."

"Kinky stuff?"

"That's right. The catfish guy was joking around with him, and he said something about how Trigger came back with his kinky gear. That was it. Kinky gear. Then I got in the cab and went home."

She sipped her coffee and seemed to grow impatient. "I didn't think much about it until the cops got in touch with me and asked me all about this stuff. Then it really hit me. Someone killed her."

"What did the police ask you?"

"What she was like and when I saw her last and if I thought she was a hooker. I said no, she seemed weird, though. And they asked if I noticed anything strange about the evening. I told them what I could remember, but I was really shook up."

"Did they ask you about this Trigger guy?"

"I told them they left the table together, and they wanted to know if I knew for sure they went in her car. I said she held up the keys. They were all cold and didn't give me any idea what they were thinking. I was crying because I was scared, thinking it could have been me."

"Of course you were upset," said Jane. "What a strange thing. I mean, it's hard to get an idea of what Marcia was thinking that night."

"It was," said Stacy. "Really strange. And the part that really weirded me out was when she opened her purse and took out the car keys and I happened to glance in there. I told the police about that." Just then Stacy half rose in her chair, and her face lit up.

"Omigod," she said rapturously. "I gotta go. There's my

boyfriend." She managed a birdlike, "Thanks for the coffee," as she scraped her chair away from the table.

"What did you see in her purse?" said Jane.

"A gun," Stacy said. "She was running around town carrying a gun."

Through the rain-spattered window, Jane watched Stacy on the sidewalk. She jumped up and down and waved her arms, her raincoat flapping crazily as she yelled, "Steve!" across the street.

Steve was tall and thin with a neat haircut, and he wore jeans and a baseball jacket. He jammed his hands in the pockets of the jacket and strolled toward Stacy across the Thriftway parking lot.

Jane watched them embrace and stroll off together arm in arm down the wet sidewalk. Her face was turned toward him, and he bent down and kissed her.

She finished her coffee and remembered from the map she'd seen earlier just how close the Shetland Isles were to Norway. Maybe she'd make a quick stop there on her way. She thought she had Magnus Anderson's card at home. It would be easier to ask him in person just what it was he'd thought Trygve Knutsen had been up to that night.

CHAPTER NINE

Jane woke up in her narrow bed in the hotel in Tromsø. The down comforter was all twisted, and her arms and legs were sticking out. She had probably thrashed around in her sleep, trying to cool off. Despite her worst fears, the hotel was overheated, not cold at all.

She went to the window overlooking the harbor and opened it a crack. A satisfying slice of clean, cold air blasted into the room. Her watch said four-thirty. Jet-lagged and still half asleep, she wondered whether it was A.M. or P.M. It didn't matter, really. And of course it was impossible to tell by looking outside. At this time of year, this far north, the sun could manage only a low, lazy circle near the horizon.

The view of the harbor from Jane's window looked like a photographic negative. Steep mountains covered with white snow stood out, luminous and pearly, against the dark sky and the black, flat water of the harbor. There were small, twinkly lights on in the big trawlers moored below and in the little houses on the steep slopes of the mountains across the water.

There wasn't much activity out there—although a few cars were moving across a sweeping concrete bridge off to her left. But then it was Sunday, and the woman who'd met her at the airport after her trek from Seattle to Copenhagen to Oslo and then up here had told her everything was closed and made arrangements to pick her up for dinner later. Jane wondered if she'd slept through their dinner appointment.

Maybe she could get CNN on TV, and some cheerful American voices would tell her what Greenwich mean time it was. Norway was one time zone away from Britain, so that would be easy to compute.

A wind had come up, and the window frame started to rattle. She closed the window and then, for good measure, the heavy curtains. The view was beautiful but somehow unsettling.

She had a brief struggle finding the power button on the television in the corner of the room but finally got the screen to jump to life. Little electronic letters on a white screen read "Welcome Mrs. la Silver" along with an invitation to learn about the hotel's automated checkout system.

Impatiently she picked up the remote control. After a few tries with various arrows pointing in different directions, she found a subtitled American detective show, a soccer game, a French music video and a group of dour-looking men in sweaters involved in some panel discussion in Norwegian or Swedish, she couldn't tell which.

The next time she hit the arrow, she got a view of two very pale people slamming laboriously to a sexual climax in one of those white laminated beds sold in America in Scandinavian furniture stores. A pudding-faced blonde blinked a lot as she gave forth clearly bogus cries of bliss. Her silent partner kept at her in a steady, workmanlike way. Jane felt rather sorry for him because of the expression of worried concentration on his face. The camera pulled back to reveal his white buttocks bobbing cartoonishly between her splayed knees and the soles of four dirty bare feet. Apparently the studio floor hadn't been swept for years. Nobody's toes were curled up with delight, either.

"*Ja, Ja,*" said the woman with what seemed to Jane just a trace of impatience, just as a big notice jumped onto the screen with directions in Norwegian and English for ordering the rest of the film and putting it on the room bill.

She hit what she thought was the button to go on to the next channel but instead got another black rectangle covering the middle of the image. This one read "Thank You Mrs. la Silver. This movie charge will appear on your room bill."

Panic set in as she had visions of this document being scrutinized by smirking bookkeepers at the Norwegian seafood agency sponsoring her trip. Beneath the notice (Jane felt her misspelled name was simply adding insult to injury) the blonde gave a yowl not unlike that of a Siamese cat, and a responding guttural grunt became audible, presumably from the man. Jane jabbed randomly at the remote control. Maybe the fish people would send a sharp note to Norm Carver, saying they wouldn't pay for *Inga and Sven Go All the Way*, or whatever it was she was watching.

The black notice disappeared suddenly. Sven was now on his back, crossing his ankles neatly and reaching for a pack of Marlboros, with the quietly satisfied look of a man who had just stacked a cord of wood or cleaned out the gutters. Inga was simpering and pouring her big soft breasts into a turquoise lace brassiere.

Jane managed to find the power button and turned off the whole thing, then picked up the phone and called reception.

"I've made a terrible mistake," she said. "I didn't understand the remote control, and I didn't mean to order the movie. I was trying to get rid of it."

The softly accented male voice put her on hold a moment, then came back on the line. "It is all right," he said. "You should be getting the erotic film now. Is there a problem with the picture?"

"But I don't want it," she said. "And I don't want it on my bill, either."

"If you watch it for five minutes," said the voice with a polite but slightly impatient air, as if he'd been through all this before, "you have to decide whether or not to order it."

"I am not interested in seeing any movie, erotic or other-

wise," she said firmly. "I made a mistake, and I want it off
my bill." She took a deep breath. "As far as I'm concerned,
you can take the whole television out of my room if it's
going to behave with a mind of its own."

She was tempted to tell him that Sven and Inga's exertions
were about as erotic as an aerobics session but realized he'd
think she was complaining about the movie's inability to
arouse her.

"Oh," he said, "you mean you want to cancel?"

"Yes," she said, beginning to feel resigned to the Kafkaes-
que nature of the encounter yet unable to resist adding: "And
I never wanted the film to begin with." She took a deep
breath and added, "Perhaps you could tell me if it's morning
or afternoon."

"It is sixteen thirty-three," he said as if speaking to a lunatic.

"Thank you. And how do I call room service?" A light
meal would cheer her up, and maybe a pot of coffee.

"There is no room service," he said. "It's Sunday."

She found a Coke and a chocolate bar in the mini-bar.
Next on the agenda, she knew, was dinner with the fresh-
faced woman from the fish agency who had met her at the
airport. Ragnhild somebody. She checked her itinerary.

Dinner with Ragnhild tonight, followed by a visit to a cod-
packing plant in the morning. Jane sighed. Why hadn't some
suave Chilean been a suspect for her to track down? South of
the equator it was summer.

An hour or so later Jane stood in the frigid gloom outside
the hotel. Apparently Norwegians didn't bother with snow
removal. This was the case in Seattle, too, where it snowed
once or twice a year and everybody just stayed home until it
melted. Here, the streets were covered with a sheet of
packed, shiny ice. The street was empty. Across from her
hotel were some charming wooden houses, painted pretty
colors: yellow, a soft green and an orangy red. They looked
like the steep-gabled wooden houses in Seattle.

A big Volvo wagon drove by on the ice, making a crunching sound. Its yellow headlights lit up three thuggish-looking young men farther up the street. Their footsteps made no sound.

A taxi arrived, delivering Ragnhild, who wore a shiny sealskin coat and high heels on which she negotiated the ice pack like a goat, walking Jane across to the restaurant.

"Watch for the ice," she said, confusing Jane by pointing up, not down. Jane saw that she was walking directly beneath a row of jagged icicles, some as big as an arm, suspended from the overhanging gables above the sidewalk. Overcome with the idea that those pretty little houses in soft colors could hurl a deadly weapon at her head, Jane stepped sideways and promptly slipped on the ice.

She landed stretched fully out on her back on the sidewalk, her head reverberating from the impact on the hard ice. She opened her eyes woozily and realized that she was staring up at the icicles and that the back of her head was very cold.

Ragnhild let out a little cry. She grabbed Jane and, with surprising strength, yanked her to her feet. Jane clung gratefully to the sealskin coat, remembering from the touch of the coarse fur that her grandmother had had a similar coat.

She assured Ragnhild that she was all right, and they continued down the street. "I think you have to spend a lifetime learning to walk on ice," said Jane. "I don't know how you do it."

"Some little old ladies are wearing shoes with things like nails in them, in case they break a bone in the hip like old ladies do," said Ragnhild in a way that was meant to be kindly but succeeded in making Jane feel like a helpless old crock. She imagined herself careening off the ice-covered deck of a boat on her ghastly high seas outings as outlined in the itinerary and plunging to her death in the icy seas. As soon as she met Knutsen, she'd pretend she had to go home to America for some fake emergency. She began to think of one now. Nothing short of the death of a loved one, she felt, would do.

Once in the restaurant, however, she began to feel better. It was in an old house with a creaky winding staircase and lots of woodwork painted a creamy white. She looked into the inviting room at the top of the stairs as they stood at the entrance waiting for someone to take their coats. There were some heavy pewter plates and brass candlesticks sitting on the ledge along the wainscoting and a few reasonably good impressionistic landscapes in oil in tarnished gilt frames around the room. A big one above the fireplace showed a smudge of red fox darting across snow under inky green tree branches in a clearing beneath a blue-gray sky.

Ragnhild handed over her coat. She was wearing a soft black dress underneath, with some big silver jewelry. Her fine hair was gray and primly arranged, and she had very white, fine-grained skin and pale eyes that gave her a strangely bloodless look. "Are you quite all right?"

"Yes, yes," said Jane. "Silly of me." She waved her hand to show she didn't want to talk about it anymore. To change the subject, she added: "What a nice coat! My grandmother had one like that."

Ragnhild smiled gratefully. "My husband was telling me not to wear this because you are American," she said. "You do not want us to hunt the seals."

Jane handed over her own raincoat. It looked skimpy and cold next to Ragnhild's fur. "Why? Are they endangered?"

"No," said Ragnhild, curling her lip. "They are cute. That is why we are supposed to stop hunting them after centuries. Because they have little cute faces." She pinched her own ethereal face into an approximation of wrinkled-nose Disney winsomeness. The effect was a little alarming.

They were taken to their table. Ragnhild sat down, flapped her napkin and said with a knowing look, "But of course, with your knowledge of fisheries, you know what will happen if we stop hunting of the seals."

Jane made a noncommittal "mmm" sound and grabbed the menu, hoping she wasn't expected to provide the answer.

"They would have the seals and whales eating all our cod." Ragnhild shook her head sadly. "Not just the Americans, of course. But we thought you were our friends, and then you talk about all these boycotts."

"It must be irritating having other people telling you what to do," said Jane. "I'm afraid Americans tend to think the world would be a happier place if everyone did everything just as we do."

Ragnhild let out an extravagant, relieved sigh and said, "I see I can be honest with you. But when we are trying to explain it to other Americans, they don't seem to understand. I think we are too polite about it. It is not our nature to make a big fuss."

"No," said Jane. "Of course not." There were plenty of Norwegians in Seattle. They weren't known for raising their voices or waving their arms around.

Ragnhild stuck out her jaw stubbornly. "We could be telling you not to eat deer. It's like eating Bambi. And what is the difference between a whale or a cow? It's sometimes hard to tell the difference from whale beef and real beef. Do you let the Hindus come and tell you to close all your hamburger restaurants because you're eating sacred cows?"

Jane smiled and tried to look sympathetic. "I suppose people are afraid the world is running out of whales."

"We have eighty-five thousand minke whales off our coast," Ragnhild said heatedly. "And we want to harvest a few for our own use."

Jane nodded and pretended again to read the Norwegian menu. She wondered if whale was on it.

Ragnhild shook her head sadly. "We Norwegians have never had much, so we've always been careful. How many buffaloes are left in America?"

Jane felt on firm ground here. She wasn't supposed to know anything about hoofed animals. "I have no idea," she said.

"Tell them!" said Ragnhild, getting shrill. "Tell them in America that we're fed up. When we had the Olympics we were told the Americans wouldn't like us to eat reindeer, either. They think of this one with the red nose. What is he called?"

"Rudolph," said Jane.

"These fanatics have already ruined our fur business."

"What should we eat?" said Jane, handing over the menu.

"The moose should be good," said Ragnhild.

"I had moose last night," said Jane, who felt very much like a nice piece of broiled chicken.

She ended up with a first course of reindeer, which was remarkably tasty, not gamey but nutty in flavor, served with a piquant brown sauce; then came cod with melted butter, tasty except for the disconcerting fact that the cod's decapitated head, its eye removed, lay in slack-jawed profile on the side of the plate. Jane assumed this was for visual interest and made no attempt to eat it, but when her companion looked down at her plate with a little frown, she was afraid she was going to be scolded for leaving it untouched.

Instead Ragnhild said, "It is a pity the tongue isn't there, but we sell those to the Japanese."

Jane recklessly drank quite a bit of good French wine, telling herself she deserved its analgesic effects after all she'd been through. She also wondered if she was thereby increasing her chance of another painful and humiliating fall on the way back.

"You must also see Tromsø in the summer," said Ragnhild. "Our gardens are full of huge roses because the sun is up all day. It is called the Paris of the North, you know."

"Really?" said Jane, tempted to ask sarcastically if Paris were also called the Tromsø of France. "I like the one in France, so I'm sure I'd like it," she added more tactfully, but with just a hint of teasing.

"So do I," said Ragnhild. "I go to the big food show there every other year. We always have a large display."

"So you travel a lot?" said Jane.

"Yes," said Ragnhild. "All over the world. I like this very much."

"Were you at the seafood show in Seattle?" asked Jane, hoping Ragnhild hadn't seen her belting out a few torchy numbers in the Fountain Room now that she was supposed to be a fish journalist.

"No, we had just a small delegation. Some of our salmon people were there because the salmon exporters were having a meeting."

"Yes," said Jane, trying to look as if she were searching for a name. "It seems I met a Trygve Knutsen."

Ragnhild laughed merrily. "Ah, yes, Trygve," she said.

"I was hoping to interview him in Bergen."

"I am sure this is possible," said Ragnhild, dropping her voice to a more intimate tone. "And how was Trygve? Did he behave himself?"

"I suppose so," said Jane. "Although I guess people tend to let down their hair on the road."

Ragnhild nodded thoughtfully. "You say this, too? About letting your hair down? We have this also in Norwegian."

"Doesn't Trygve always behave himself?" Jane asked.

Ragnhild leaned over confidentially. "You know how this is. Traveling can lead to all kinds of things. But I am very happy with my husband, so I take it easy."

"Of course," said Jane, wondering if Ragnhild were assuming she was a slut on the road. She looked guiltily at her own wineglass. "I suppose the key is not to drink too much."

"Oh, my colleagues and I get drunk together, of course," Ragnhild said matter-of-factly. She held up a finger like a schoolmistress. "But that's all. A woman has to watch her reputation."

Jane poured herself another glass of wine. Apparently the cultural drinking norms were a little different here.

"Trygve, though, he thinks he is a big ladies' man. Do not get in an elevator alone with that one," she said with a little smirk. "But then, I think men like that are usually harmless, don't you think?"

CHAPTER TEN

The next day Jane struggled through the plant tour in Tromsø, putting on gum boots, a lab coat and a thing like a shower cap and walking over wet concrete floors, looking at glassy-eyed cod (unattractive fish with spiky, whiskerlike appendages on their faces) run through heading and gutting machines. Using news footage of British royals visiting factories as a model, she admired everything with polite courtesy and feigned interest in the water-jet, computer-activated filleting machine; the device that scanned for para-sites; the perfectly calibrated weighing devices; the sluice that took away fish guts to be made into fish meal some-where. She made meaningless notes in her reporter's note-book and nodded sagely at a blur of statistics about the plant's capacity, its remarkable quality control system, its state-of-the-art packaging system, and its fabulous spiral freezing system.

She nodded again when informed of the different stan-dards for the European Community, the Japanese market, the Food and Drug Administration in the U.S. and some UN agency or other. The key to quality control, she learned, was temperature control, and computers made sure the cod never got warm. The workers, she noted, wore thick sweaters un-derneath their white uniforms.

A visit to the lab to squint at bacteria through microscopes gave her a brief respite from the bone-chilling cold and the wet—people seemed to be hosing off everything constantly. But the visit to the freezer, where the lonely freezing manager kept chatting to her for twenty minutes behind the cloud of frost crystals that floated in the air in front of him, practically killed her. The inside of her nose froze first, a strange, dry asthmatic sensation.

The freezer guy went on about which boxes were going to Japan and which to Germany and which to Denmark and France, and Jane tried to breathe through her mouth. She thought it would give her sinuses a break. But then the inside of her mouth flash-froze, a dry, sharp, panic-inducing sensation that made her realize how comforting it was to feel one's tongue and the roof of one's mouth, warm and wet, almost like kissing oneself, and how she had never realized it before now.

Finally she was taken to the factory's elegant dining room and fed a well-prepared meal of more cod with some good local beer, potatoes, carrots and coffee and pastry. She left carrying her notebook with its meaningless squiggles, a clutch of business cards (Carla could call all these people to "verify" a few facts, they had decided) and pounds of glossy brochures about fish that she figured Carla could use to cobble together the article.

Ragnhild, who was some kind of fish bureaucrat (Jane couldn't keep the various governmental and quasi-governmental agencies straight), plied her with more brochures back at the hotel, along with a silk scarf covered with stylized salmon, a sterling silver pin shaped like a fish, a key chain with the logo of her agency, a calendar, and a cookbook.

Deploying these items in her luggage proved difficult. Jane had decided that since shopping was out, she didn't need to leave the usual space for expansion in her luggage and had crammed everything into a small suitcase, not counting on the fact that she'd be inundated with fish stuff. She thought with a sinking heart that she would start sprouting the extra hand luggage—plastic bags and cheap tote bags from airports—that transformed her look from that of the sophisticated traveler to that of the demented bag lady.

She did feel pretty slick, however, in that she had arranged for Ragnhild to fax Trygve Knutsen's office in Bergen and more or less demand an interview with him. It was all set for two days from now.

There were still, however, the Lofoten Islands to get through. She found this leg of the trip the most alarming. It involved venturing out into icy seas on a cod boat. Some of the pamphlets she'd received in Tromsø had given her pause.

Apparently the citizens of Lofoten had been selling cod to the rest of the world for over a thousand years. The most disturbing detail from the brochures, however, was the quaint fact that the old-time fishermen, to prevent the arctic wind going through their woolen mittens, would dip their hands into the sea and form a glaze of ice to keep out the elements. Presumably they had some high-tech space age Scandinavian gloves today, and she wouldn't have to wear igloos on her hands. But her stint in the freezer at the processing plant and the casual aplomb with which her hosts had lounged around in the polar atmosphere, conversing as if they were at a cafe, didn't augur well for conditions on the fishing boat.

From the air, the Lofoten Islands looked otherworldly: a collection of steep, jagged crags jutting out of the dense, gray water in a belligerent, Wagnerian way, all cast in an eerie light. Jane wouldn't have been the least surprised to see a flock of Valkyries winging their way over these peaks, braids streaking behind them, their bellicose soprano cries floating through the clear air.

A young man with sandy hair and an engaging, open sort of face met her at the small airport. His name was Per-Olav, and he seemed to work for some sort of fisherman's cooperative. He kept apologizing in excellent English that his boss was at a meeting in Oslo, so he'd be escorting her around.

"I hope I'm showing you what you want to see," he said fretfully. "We'll go see the dried cod this morning, but I'm still working hard getting a fishing boat for you to go out with tomorrow. I'm afraid it is difficult. The weather is very bad and dangerous." He looked awfully sorry to be letting her down. Jane tried not to appear overjoyed.

He rolled a cigarette nervously and added with an eager smile, as if he were now giving her the good news, "But we were able to arrange for you to spend the night in a traditional fisherman's hut out at the end of a dock."

Jane had visions of wet plank floors shiny with centuries of fish scales, arctic winds whistling through the chinks and a thin blanket smelling of cod-liver oil. Per-Olav seemed to notice her anxiety.

"The Italians and the Germans rent them in the summer for vacation cottages," he told her. "They are really very nice. They pay nine hundred kroner a night to stay there in summer."

"I'm sure they're lovely, but I'm devastated I can't go out on the cod boat," she said, managing two outrageous lies in one sentence.

Per-Olav looked a little nervous. "It would be dangerous, and you would get very sick. But if you think—"

"Thank you very much," she said, doing her best to sound like a dowager empress, "but I will fly back to Bergen. This would be a better use of my time." Her appointment with Knutsen wasn't for two days. She remembered how close Shetland was on the map. She'd zip over there and find out just what Magnus Anderson was talking about when he'd said Trygve had been up to something kinky.

Some hours later, after a short, bumpy flight down to Bergen, she got herself on a U.K. Air flight to Aberdeen over a choppy gray North Sea interspersed with desolate-looking oil derricks and, finally, a run up to Shetland on British Airways. By the third flight she was a wreck.

She had called Magnus from Aberdeen and left what she hoped was a perky, casual message on his machine. "I don't know if you remember me, but we met in Seattle, and I sang a Patsy Cline number for you. The salmon was terrific."

God, she felt like a fool. He was so affable, he probably gave his card to everyone he ever met, secure in the knowledge that the chances of their coming to somewhere as remote as the Shetland Isles was minimal. Besides, for all she knew, he was on the road.

Then she remembered that her alternative was a cod boat in bad weather. All in all, she supposed she'd rather hunker down in a hotel in Shetland for the night than take her chances on open, storm-tossed arctic seas.

She was getting tired of airplane seats, but at least this time she had an aisle. She was still wearing the jeans, long woolen underwear and down jacket in which she'd arrived that morning in Lofoten and felt overheated, incredibly unattractive and grimy. She closed her eyes after takeoff, and when she opened them just a crack at the clinking sound that signaled the approach of the drinks cart, she was startled to see a tall, elegantly groomed man with a gaunt, serious face staring at her from across the aisle with apparent interest.

I don't look as bad as I feel, she thought, opening her eyes a little more and smiling.

He didn't smile back but looked away. She chided herself for thinking he'd been checking her out. She thought she had seen him before, him or someone who looked a lot like him. Maybe it had been in the Bergen airport.

He had his tray table down and was slamming away on a laptop computer. She studied his face in profile. It was really a very interesting face—like some Renaissance portrait, with a strong nose and chin and a curved flat plane beneath the high cheekbone. He had fine dark hair and an intense look about him. He was definitely European, but probably not British. She wasn't sure why she knew this. It had something to do with tailoring, she imagined.

She ordered a large Scotch, sat up and ran a hand through her hair. In the seat next to her, a man in a tweed sports jacket with fake suede elbow patches ordered the same and said to her with an American twang: "What the heck are you going to Shetland for?" He gave her a big, complacent smile, settling in for what he evidently assumed would be a long, friendly conversation. He seemed amiable enough—a bald, florid-looking man with a large diamond ring—but Jane wasn't in the mood to chat. No one but an American would demand to know her business like that, she thought. In the States, she wouldn't have minded so much; it went with the territory. But in Europe it seemed an imposition. She supposed he felt he could chum up to her because they were both Americans surrounded by cold, unfriendly Europeans. His question did, however, remind her that she had to come up with some story to explain her presence in Shetland.

"Just visiting a friend," she said, feeling a bit of a traitor to her country by giving him a squelching little frosty look. She rummaged around in one of her plastic bags and came up with the only reading material she could use as a screen. It was a large brochure with facts and figures about Norwegian fish exports.

"I'm in the oil business myself," he said.

"Oh," said Jane, frowning in concentration over a picture of a salmon lying in state in a Styrofoam box full of ice.

"Ever been to Shetland before?" He didn't wait for an answer. "I thought Aberdeen was the end of the road, but Shetland is just about the ends of the earth," he went on. "I guess you know they have a big oil terminal up there at Sullom Voe."

"Mmm," she said.

He looked over her shoulder. "Looks like you're in the fish business," he said in his loud, cheery voice, rattling ice cubes.

"That's right," she said, putting the brochure on her knees and leaning over to look for earphones. That and closed eyes might be her only defense. There didn't seem to be any earphones, and the brochure slid from her lap into the aisle.

She unbuckled her seat belt and reached for it, but a long brown hand beat her to it. The man across the aisle handed the brochure back to her.

"Thank you," she said, looking into his intelligent gray-blue eyes.

"You are welcome," he said without a discernible accent, but with a little nod that confirmed her suspicion he was continental. It was the kind of nod that might have been accompanied by a Teutonic click of the heels.

"Remember the *Exxon Valdez*?" her seatmate was saying now.

"That oil spill in Alaska?" said Jane, who had decided she was irrevocably trapped.

"They've renamed her the *SeaRiver Mediterranean.* She's up there now, taking on a hundred and ninety-four thousand tons of crude for delivery to the U.S."

"Really?" said Jane. Maybe she should tell Magnus she was singing in Britain somewhere and had come up for the weekend to get away from it all. It seemed a little lame. She imagined herself in some rowdy pub in Blackpool, singing "The White Cliffs of Dover" while football hooligans scuffled in the corners. She had to say she was a singer, though. After all, that's how he'd met her.

The American cleared his throat and launched into his monologue again. "That's metric tons, of course. Interesting, the way the salmon up there in Alaska were smart enough just to swim around all that oil, but I guess you know all about that, being in the fish business."

"Yes," said Jane. Maybe she could say she was on her way to Norway and took a side trip through Shetland. That had the advantage of being partly true. Or could she risk telling Magnus the truth? If it got back to *Seafood Now,* she could be in trouble. But so what? She'd got what she wanted from them, the trip to Norway. However, Magnus and Trygve Knutsen knew each other. What if she told him what she was doing and he tipped off Knutsen?"

"I don't eat much fish myself," the man said. "Just a little catfish once in a while. Fried up real nice."

She wondered how small a place Shetland was and had a hideous vision of this garrulous American running into her somewhere with Anderson and asking her in a loud voice how things were in the fish business. She took a sip of her Scotch and decided she was getting paranoid. What she needed was a good night's sleep. She'd call Anderson tomorrow, and by then she'd have a convincing explanation for her presence. All she had to do was worm out of him what he knew about Knutsen, fly back to Bergen and see what she could get out of the Norwegian himself.

Jane's seatmate was still hovering at her side as they filed off. She'd managed to deflect his questions about her, which hadn't been too tough, as he had lots of his own material he wanted to share. His stories about his adventures in the oil business went back several generations ("My granddaddy, he was a wildcatter . . .") and covered his international adventures, or lack thereof ("I never saw a woman the whole time I was in Saudi. They're all wrapped up from head to toe. Doesn't seem natural. Hey, I'm a normal, red-blooded American man, you know?"), as well as his stateside experiences ("Those people up in Alaska, they're a tough bunch of sourdoughs, let me tell you. Seems like every tough son of a bitch who doesn't end up in Texas ends up there!").

The last thing she expected was to see Magnus Anderson mooting her plane. But there he was, in a big flapping raincoat, smiling and scanning the arriving passengers. Surely he wasn't meeting her. There were a score of flights a day from Aberdeen, and she hadn't told him which one she'd be on.

She had to ditch her new friend, who might blather on about fish in front of Magnus. She ducked behind a group of men in bright red jumpsuits who looked as if they were on some paramilitary mission. "These boys are heading straight for the choppers that'll take 'em out to the derricks," the American informed her.

"Is that where you're going, too?" she asked hopefully.

"No, I'll be checking into the hotel in Lerwick and heading up to Sullom Voe in the morning," he said. "Maybe we could get together for a drink. You could tell me about the fish business. I've really enjoyed talking to you."

Magnus had caught her eye and was waving at her, looking surprised.

She had to get rid of the oil man immediately. "I cannot have a drink with you," she said sternly. "I don't hold with drinking. And I'm not in the fish business. I'm here on a religious mission to convert Shetland to a bible-based Christian fellowship. I am," she said, suddenly inspired by one of the Putnam brothers, "a fisher of men."

"But you had a Scotch on the plane," he said.

"Strictly medicinal purposes," she said. "I'm terrified of flying."

"Yeah?" he said doubtfully. "Well, ma'am, your secret is safe with me." He gestured over to Magnus. "Is that one of the brothers? Maybe you should have a tic tac or something."

They had arrived at the baggage claim area. Jane watched gratefully as the oil man sidled away into the knot of men in red jumpsuits. She looked around and saw Magnus shaking hands with the tall, dark man who had sat across from her on the plane.

Magnus excused himself and came over to her. "I got your message," he said. "It's great to see you. I'm a bit tied up with business just now, as you can see. . . ." He indicated the dark man, who was now yanking an aluminum suitcase off the baggage belt. "Maybe we can meet tomorrow. Actually, I'm having some folk to tea. Can you join us?"

"That would be lovely," said Jane. "When's teatime?"

Magnus smiled. "When we say tea it's what you probably call dinner," he said. "Round about seven? Will you sing for us?"

"I'll sing if you want me to."

"Brilliant. And where are you stopping? I can put you up at my house."

His soft voice seemed even quieter than it had been in Seattle. She realized it sounded as if she were shouting at him. She lowered it a decibel or two. "That's very kind, but I'm all set at the Shetland Hotel," she said.

"I'm driving Gunther over there now," he said. "Come along with us."

He tried to take her plastic bag, which she realized with horror bore the logo of the Norwegian fish agency.

"Oh, look, there's my suitcase," she said, pointing to the arriving baggage. Magnus dutifully went after it and came back with it and Gunther, whom he introduced. His last name was Kessler.

Herr Kessler offered her a dry, cool hand, staring unsmiling into her face, and Magnus said to him: "Jane's visiting from Seattle. We're giving her a lift to the hotel." To Jane he added, "Gunther's giving us a hand with a little problem."

"A problem?" she said sympathetically. "With your salmon?"

"I'm in refrigeration," said Kessler. He turned to Magnus. "If it's all the same to you, I shall hire a car. Perhaps we can meet at the hotel." He nodded to them both and went over to the one car rental counter.

Jane watched him take out his wallet and passport. It was red with a little cross. Gunther Kessler was Swiss.

"What brings you here, then?" said Magnus as they had settled themselves in his small Japanese car.

"Well," she said gaily, "I'm going to Bergen on Monday, and I noticed how close you were, and I thought why not spend a weekend in Shetland. I've always heard how lovely it is. As lovely as your salmon, by the way, which I enjoyed very much."

"We get very few visitors this time of year," he said.

"I understand the bird life is fascinating," she said rather desperately. She had noticed a large poster of a puffin in the airport.

"Birds!" he said eagerly. "Are you interested in ornithology, then?"

"Well, a little," she said. She knew less about birds than she did about fish. She was fond of Robert Benchley's remark about birds being all right in profile, but "did you ever see one of the sons of bitches head on?"

"People come from all over the world to see our birds," he said proudly. "If you've time, I can show you a cliff full of them. It's on the way."

They drove up a winding road through grassy, hilly fields divided by dry-stone walls and dotted with stone cottages and strange-looking sheep with narrow, goatlike faces. Fifteen minutes later they reached a parking place on top of a bluff.

Outside of the car, the wind practically knocked Jane flat. Magnus strode purposefully in front of her up a little path, his hair streaming back from his face, his raincoat flapping, until they reached the top of a towering cliff with a view of the white-capped sea and an adjacent huge, irregular rock wall. It was teeming with birds of various kinds. More birds swooped in front of the rock face, letting out cries, bleats and squawks barely audible against the wind and the crash of surf below.

Magnus beamed happily at the cliff. "This rock is home to gannets, guillemots, kittiwakes and puffins. And we've great colonies of auks. Of course, we have our own names for the birds. In Shetland we call a puffin a tammie norie. The terns are called tirricks, and the arctic skuas are skootie alans."

Jane nodded as if she were committing all this to memory.

"Many of the seabirds have no need of land except to nest, you know," he said. "There aren't a great many now. The time to come is May and June."

"The sky is wonderful," said Jane, looking out to sea after a suitably polite pause to appreciate the bird life. It was a huge sky, soft gray with dark, bluish clouds touched at the edges with peach and gold. The sun was obscured except for a fan of pale lemon–colored rays slanting down to the sea like a symbol of the divine presence in an old painting.

"Very fine crepuscular rays," Magnus commented approvingly. "Of course, they're very common here." He was one of those rare individuals who seemed to be completely enchanted with his home turf. Jane wasn't sure whether she was charmed or slightly irritated by his Chamber of Commerce take.

Back in the car on the way to her hotel, she reminded herself why she was here and managed to find a way to get to topic A.

"Birds are fascinating," she said. "But I can only admire them from afar. I can't imagine letting them sit on me like funny old people in parks covered with pigeons." She paused. "Or wanting to talk to them, like St. Anthony. Maybe I mean St. Francis. They always show him with a bird or two on him, don't they?"

Magnus said that keeping your distance was fine and that it was very important for people to stay away from nesting birds. "The Victorians spent a great deal of time collecting eggs," he said, shaking his head at their bad behavior.

Jane wrenched things back to her own agenda. "Terrible," she said. "You know, St. Francis reminds me of that young woman who died at the seafood show. Her name was Marcia St. Francis. Did you know about that?"

"Yes, I heard." Magnus shook his head sadly. "And we'd been told that Seattle is a safe place. But with all those guns about, I suppose no one is safe in America. How many people do you know who've been shot?" he said. "I imagine it's pretty common."

Jane couldn't think of anyone she knew who'd been shot, and said so. "The police still don't know who did it," she added. "Or much about the woman. But I ran into the other girl who was dressed up in those awful Scottish outfits. She said Marcia had come back from some kind of a date with one of the salmon people. That Norwegian."

"Old Trygve," said Magnus with a smile. "I can tell you, he was horrified. Went straight back to Norway and swore he'd never set foot in America again."

Jane wondered how the hell she'd get Magnus to tell her what his remark about kinky gear had meant. It would have been easier, perhaps, if Magnus hadn't heard the girl had been killed.

She decided to let him think that she already knew. "Yes," she said. "I heard something about it. Some jokes about kinky gear or something, but I can't remember exactly. . . ."

Magnus startled Jane by blushing. She'd seen him turn red once before, when Carla had been grilling him. "Trygve left with her drunk and came back sober and ashamed looking. I ran into him in the elevator. He tried to put his hand in his pocket—" He broke off as if embarrassed and said, "Poor old Trygve."

Jane remembered Knutsen with his hand in the pocket of his bathrobe. If she hadn't been focusing on the fact that he wore one slipper, she might have noticed that his hand in the pocket looked a little too studiously casual, considering the circumstances.

Magnus slowed down to let a trio of sheep cross the road safely. "He told me American lasses were daft."

Suddenly he looked over at her, apparently flustered by his own remark. "Nothing pairsonal, mind you. That's just what old Trygve said."

CHAPTER ELEVEN

Her window at the Shetland Hotel was dirty. Everything else
in the place was perfectly clean and nice, so she supposed
the fierce winds on these islands made it impossible to keep
windows clean. The room overlooked a working port, a large
expanse with cranes and shipping containers, and a terminal
where a massive blue-and-white ferry lolled. A few desolate-
looking pedestrians in anoraks and jeans walked along the
road in front in a sort of resigned way. Jane felt vaguely sad
herself.

After a room service dinner she went to bed early, listening to BBC Radio Two in bed. She slept in very late the next
morning.

What woke her was the telephone. For a moment she
thought she was back in Norway and this was her early
morning wake-up call for a visit to a fish plant or a cod
trawler.

Instead it was Magnus, who said that he was spending the
morning taking Gunther Kessler to some salmon pens. For a
moment Jane feared he'd ask her along. More fish in the
company of that lugubrious Swiss sounded grim.

Magnus apologized again for not being able to get away.
"It's part of my duties as liaison with the International
Salmon Exporters Association," he said with a sigh. He told

her he would come by in the late afternoon and then take her up to his place for tea.

"The other guests are coming later," he said, "but I need to get back and see if I have any faxes and prepare things. You don't mind, do you?"

"You're sure it's no trouble?" she said, pleased. The more time she had with him, the better chance she had to pump him about Knutsen.

She ate a hearty breakfast in the hotel dining room, served by some sweet, translucent-skinned Shetlanders with soft voices—a nice high-cholesterol meal of bacon and eggs with Earl Grey tea. The meal was marred only by the fake-American Muzak reminding her of the boom box that had busted up her last act.

After breakfast she consulted a map she found in her room and set out in search of a bookstore, bucking wind and a light rain that reminded her of Seattle. She wasn't going to be caught with nothing but fish brochures again.

Lerwick was a little gray-stone town of peak-roofed houses with small windows overlooking a harbor. Squatting in the middle of it all was sturdy, pugnacious Fort Charlotte and an old hotel flying the Union Jack. Lerwick looked as though it could have belonged to any of the past five or six centuries.

The street names spoke of Scandinavia—King Haakon Street, King Erik Street, and strange saints whom she imagined taming Vikings—St. Olaf, St. Sunniva, St. Magnus. Along the water's edge were stone houses coming straight out of the water, as if the town had spilled into the harbor. Behind the fort she found what she guessed was the old part of the town, interlaced as it was by cobbled lanes too narrow for anything more than a wheelbarrow.

She found the Market Cross and Commercial Street, a stone-paved plaza surrounded by small shops, and eventually a bookstore, where she bought some paperback novels and a history of Shetland. She had halfway hoped to find a shop that could sell her Britain's famed WonderBra but didn't find one. She'd have to wait until this alleged technical marvel crossed the Atlantic.

By the time Magnus picked her up back at the hotel, she had managed to learn a little about the place. Stone Age settlers had neatly divided it up with the kind of stone walls, called dykes, that still marked fields. There were traces of these early farms underneath the layers of peat that covered the islands. By the Iron Age the Shetlanders were building brochs, dry-stone fortifications, which were still standing around here and there. Later, small, dark, Christian Picts were overrun by big, fair barbarian Vikings. Norway managed to hold on to the place for the next five hundred years or so, with the Scots squabbling over it once in a while. After the Danes swallowed up Norway, they took possession. The bankrupt King Christian pawned the islands to Scotland for 8,000 florins in 1469 to pay for a dowry and told the inhabitants to be obedient to the kings of Scotland and pay their taxes until he redeemed his pledge—which he never got around to doing. The place had been left in the hock shop for centuries.

She closed the book and checked her watch. Catching up on local history had been a charming escape. It all seemed so far away from Marcia St. Francis, dead in the bathtub in the Meade Hotel.

Which was where Jane had overheard Magnus Anderson complaining to that Chilean about King Christian's careless behavior, centuries after the fact. Time seemed to stretch out in this place.

Magnus arrived at twilight to pick her up, and they drove out of Lerwick, past modern houses and gas stations into a treeless landscape composed of very few elements—hills, peat, heather, grass, sky, sea and stone—but managed to combine and recombine in what seemed like an infinite number of ways. Hills changed from green to gold to a dark peaty brown. Coming around a curve in the road would afford a sudden view of a serene gleaming blue inlet or a cluster of islands in the distance; the light illuminated the land, then cast it in shadow again as the clouds moved across the vast sky; the landscape changed from a forbidding hill to a gentle slope leading to the sea, or it sheared off from a grassy field to a rocky precipice.

"You don't find it bleak?" he asked her.

"Not at all," she said, wanting him to know how much she liked the place. "It's very sculptural."

The stone walls ran everywhere, and at intervals in the barren landscape there were stone houses—new, with flouncy white curtains at the windows, or abandoned, roofs rotted away, peaks pointing upward, sometimes just walls or piles of rubble.

They passed a pretty little pond in a grassy field. Magnus said, "A Viking princess drooned in that pond," with a stunning casualness. Jane wasn't sure whether this was an affectation or not. Magnus seemed to come up with some amazingly picturesque stuff. In any case, she was beginning to feel the spell of the place.

She certainly wasn't prepared for Magnus's house. First of all, it was accessible only by rowboat. He parked the car and rowed them across a small, glassy body of water he called a "voe." On the other side of the water, Jane faced what looked like a small castle.

One part was clearly older, a square, two-story stone house. There was also a Victorian addition, with turrets and stained-glass windows. It stood there, looking proud and stately on its own little island, surrounded by sheep and some rickety outbuildings.

"My God," said Jane. "It looks like something out of one of those nostalgic British TV shows. Does it have a name?"

"Bellevue," he said, handing her out of the boat. "A French name in a place like this! It's a Norman conceit of one of my ancestors."

"Your ancestors?" Somehow she would have imagined Magnus's ancestors as Picts huddling in brochs or as yeoman Viking farmers.

"On my mother's side," he said. "He was only a cousin,

but when he died the other heirs lived in Canada and New Zealand and didn't want to bother themselves with it, so it came down to me. It's shameful, really. I never thought I'd be the laird. A lot of Scottish sheep thieves is what they were."

"You're the laird?" said Jane.

"Yes," he said, clearly embarrassed. "But I will say my old cousin wasn't so bad. The tenants even bought him a tombstone."

"That's sweet," said Jane. "Perhaps they'll do the same for you if you don't have them whipped for poaching or violate their daughters."

"The rents are all fixed," Magnus said with a shrug. "And if I could sell the place to someone, I'd be glad to do it." He led her up a stone path grown over with grass. "It's a bit ironic, really, when I've always been the champion of an independent Shetland, to find myself cast as one of the oppressors."

A few sheep stared at them as they made their way up toward the house.

"Does the title go with the property?" asked Jane.

"That's right," he said. "If you know any rich Americans, they can have it for a hundred thousand pound."

An island, a manor house or whatever it was and the chance to call yourself a laird for less than the price of a luxury condominium seemed like a pretty good deal to Jane. Magnus sighed and told her the place needed work and went into a litany of repairs—drains, wiring, plumbing, the roof and more. Having sunk a lot of the money from her first paying case into Uncle Harold's old house back in Seattle, Jane knew just how overwhelming all that renovation could be.

They entered a side door. Magnus explained that he lived mostly in the kitchen, which was a big room with thick green paint on the walls, orangy-looking wooden doors and wainscoting, appliances from the fifties, narrow tiled counters and a worn linoleum floor.

The kitchen seemed warm enough—there were some old-

fashioned radiators around—so presumably Magnus didn't
have to heat with peat. On a solid old table at one side of the
room was a fax machine. Magnus scooped up a handful of
faxes and read them while Jane looked out a small window
to the serene voe and the soft curves of the hills beyond. The
stillness of the place was more than an absence of sound or
other stimuli. It had a quality of its own—something deep
and cool, slightly mysterious but benevolent.

"Oh," said Magnus, "here's a nice order from Santa Mon-
ica."

Jane was taken aback. In her present mood she found it
impossible to fathom that this place and Southern California
could exist on the same planet, let alone be in instant communication.

It reminded her why she was here herself.

"I read a book about Shetland today," she said. "It had a
wonderful quote in it from some old Scottish minister in the
eighteenth century. He said he'd never met people more interested in gossip than Shetlanders."

Magnus laughed. "That's still absolutely true."

"Well, you were awfully reticent when I asked you about
Trygve," she said. "All you told me was he had his hand in
his pocket, then you stopped."

Magnus looked slightly crafty. She'd never seen him that
way before. "Dinna tell no one," he said, "but Trygve wasn't
quick enough in that lift. Before he put his hand in his
pocket, I marked he had a handcuff hanging from his wrist."

"Sounds a bit kinky," said Jane.

Magnus blushed again. "That's what I thought. And then
his telling me American lasses were daft . . ."

A handcuff hanging from Knutsen's wrist as he came back
from a date with Marcia. Of course, it brought up visions of
some kind of sex orgy. Maybe if the Meade Hotel had offered *Sven and Inga Go All the Way* on a pay-per-view basis,
Knutsen could have spent a quiet night with a room service
meal.

Magnus put on a Patsy Cline CD, and Jane helped him

prepare a big meal of pasta. About a dozen guests arrived at intervals, and they all made themselves at home in the kitchen, opening bottles of wine and nibbling on things. There was a whole slew of accents—one English couple in their mid-thirties seemed to her to be the British equivalent of people who might have grown up in a Connecticut suburb and escaped to a blueberry farm in Maine with trust fund money. Jane talked to a schoolteacher named Margaret who'd grown up in Glasgow, a cozy-looking woman with a long challis skirt and a hand-knit cardigan, and a young native named Peter who told her that most Shetlanders who'd left the island to go to the University of Edinburgh never came back, but that he'd been lucky enough to find a job with the Shetland Council.

There was an aristocratic-looking salmon farmer and his glamorous French wife, Marie-Claire, who told Jane in whispered French that she often went mad in the winters here but regained her sanity every summer, and a fiftyish lady who was a cousin of Magnus and worked in the library, who said she'd been abroad only once in her life—to Scotland. Jane also talked to a man who'd been born in Zimbabwe when it was still Rhodesia and ended up in Shetland as quality control officer in a fish plant. Jane turned the conversation away from fish as fast as she could.

While all this mingling was going on, volunteers were ferrying guests back and forth in the rowboat. The last guest to arrive, still wearing his business suit and looking over-dressed, was Gunther Kessler.

Everybody ate in the kitchen, by now warmer and full of the smell of smoke and food. The other guests were animated and lively and had a nice way of making Jane feel welcome.

After dinner they went into the living room, a big Victorian stage set of a room with stained-glass windows, a walk-in fireplace, lots of oppressive, heavily varnished wooden sideboards and cupboards, some worn old plush furniture and ancestral portraits that looked as though they'd been done in the early nineteenth century. Magnus said he hadn't

the faintest idea who these people were and wasn't sure if he
was related to them or not. They had simply always hung
here and would still be there when and if he managed to unload the property.

"This Victorian bit is a horror," he said cheerfully.
"Would you like to see the original part of the house?"

Jane followed him up a narrow staircase to what was
mostly a long hall with a series of small bedrooms off it. The
rooms were furnished with old dressers and sagging beds.
The walls were whitewashed and the wooden floors agree-
ably uneven. There was a slight dampness in the air. She
imagined a lot of pale, lonely young girls with chilblains
growing up in these rooms, combing out their hair by candle-
light and wondering if they would ever meet anyone of their
own station to marry. Just a trip into Lerwick in those days
must have been a major undertaking.

From below they suddenly heard a violin tuning up and
some accordion chords. On the way back down, Magnus explained that Shetland fiddle music was unique in the world.
"It's a distinctive style, less rigid than Scottish fiddle music,
with what we call ringing strings, playing two strings at
once, and lots of grace notes and turns."

It did indeed sound very busy and lively. Jane hoped
Magnus would forget he'd asked her to sing. Her Meade
Hotel lounge act seemed pretty tacky compared with all this
folklore. But unfortunately he remembered, and after con-
sultation with the accordion player and a heartfelt introduc-
tion from Magnus, she found herself standing by the
fireplace singing "La Vie en Rose" to the roomful of people.

They all looked odd in this stuffy Victorian room, sitting
around in lots of sweaters and jeans like children partying in
the living room under the gaze of the ancestral portraits
while Mom and Dad were out of town. Over by the fireplace
stood Gunther Kessler, holding his wineglass stiffly. Jane
had been aware of him at the edges of the group all evening.
As she looked over at him in her friendly, visual sweep of
the room—part of her standard moves, although with "Vie

en Rose" one could also lean against something in a world-weary way and close one's eyes—she saw his glass stop midway to his lips. She realized it was a gesture of recognition. He hadn't known where he had seen her before, but now that she was singing, he recognized her.

Something about the eye contact they made—her singing, him standing across the room with a drink—gave her a feeling of déjà vu herself. Was she imagining it? Or had he been in Seattle at the Meade Hotel during that seafood convention?

CHAPTER TWELVE

There was some hearty applause and a few requests, but it was always a good idea to quit while people were still appreciative.

Magnus came up to Jane and told her what a fine job she'd done, and handed her another glass of wine. Kessler approached.

"A lovely party," he said to Magnus, "but I have a report to write, and I must go." He turned to Jane. "Would you like a lift back to the hotel?"

"She can stay here," said Magnus. "A lot of people are. You can always have as much drink as you like at my house because you never have to drive home."

Jane had noticed the damp in the wing full of bedrooms and didn't like the idea of a large hangover breakfast gathering the following morning when she could have room service. "Actually," she said, "I should probably take Mr. Kessler up on his kind offer. I have an early flight tomorrow."

"She's off to Bergen to sing for the Norwegians," said Magnus. He turned to her, and she noticed his pale skin was pinkened with wine. "Bergen was once our capital," he went on. "The cultural center of this part of the world, before the soothmoothers came."

"Soothmoothers?" said Jane.

"Foreigners," he said with a scowl. Jane had the sudden idea his patriotic Shetland sentiments emerged more strongly after a few belts. "Literally, it means people who talk with accents from the south."

"Oh," said Jane. "South mouthers."

He nodded a little impatiently, as if to say "That's what I just said."

Jane thanked him for everything, throwing in a few gushy sentiments about Shetland for his benefit. "I must come back in the summer," she said.

Magnus nodded. "When the bird life is at its most interesting," he said.

Kessler was silent as one of the other guests rowed them across the narrow stretch of water to his rented car. They had driven about a mile when he said, "So, you are interested in birds?"

"Well, a little," she said. Terrific, another ornithologist. "I don't know much about them, but Magnus told me this place is famous for its birds."

"And you are also interested in fish?" he said. He was artfully working the high and low beams as they traveled along the winding roads in the dark.

She shrugged, then realized he couldn't see the gesture in the darkness. "I learned a little about the business when I was in Seattle. There was a seafood convention at the hotel where I sang."

"Yes. I remember you there, but on the plane I noticed you were reading about fish. Salmon."

Jane felt her heart sink. "As a matter of fact, I'm visiting someone in Norway. Someone I met at the fish convention. I was brushing up a little on his business before I visited." There. That should stifle his curiosity.

"So, you are going to be singing in Bergen also?" he asked.

"Yes," she said. That's what Magnus had told him, so she'd have to stick with it. Why was he interrogating her, anyway?

"Where?" he said. "I know Bergen a little."

She decided not to answer. "Yes, I imagine you do," she said, "being in the fish business yourself. Refrigeration, wasn't it?"

"That's right," he said.

He didn't ask her again where she was singing, thank God. Or anything else. They drove the rest of the way in silence. Nevertheless, he had managed to unnerve her. To her slight shame, she usually enjoyed lying, but Kessler had somehow managed to make her feel guilty. And the story she had come up with about meeting some Norwegian at a convention and then brushing up on the salmon business to impress him made her feel slightly shabby.

She didn't know if it was simply Gunther Kessler's stiffness—refrigeration seemed a very apt business for him—but she got the impression he didn't quite approve of her. He saw her, no doubt, as a louche lady making her living singing in saloons and looking for a meal ticket. Which, come to think of it, was pretty much true, except that her meal ticket wasn't a prosperous conventioneer, but a chance at getting some of her uncle Harold's money under the terms of his eccentric will by finding and solving a pro bono case. Why should she care what Gunther Kessler thought, anyway? As soon as they got back to the Shetland Hotel, she'd never see him again, she thought.

But she did see him again. The next morning. On the plane to Bergen. She was unaccountably resentful. When she'd told him she was headed there, he hadn't said a word about his own plans. She wondered if he'd ask again where she was singing so he could go hear her. Gunther Kessler was beginning to give her the creeps.

"What a surprise," she said rather coolly as she walked past him down the aisle to her own seat.

"Hello," he said, lowering his newspaper. This time he gave her a little smile, and she realized it was the first time she'd seen him smile.

She spent part of the flight worrying about the ubiquitous

Swiss. But why was she worrying? In Shetland she had found out part of what she wanted to know about Trygve Knutsen. Now she was going to come face-to-face with him and try to find out the rest. None of this had anything to do with Gunther Kessler, and if the story she told him didn't quite make sense, what difference did it make?

It would be more useful to plan just what she would say to Knutsen. She still didn't know if he would recognize her as the lounge singer at the Meade Hotel. She counted on the fact that he had been very drunk and that meeting someone in a different context was always confusing. Gunther Kessler seemed to have much more on the ball, but only when she sang had he been able to place her.

She kicked a few scenarios around in her head, from the disingenuous ("Wasn't it terrible about that girl who was killed? And it happened right in the room next to yours, didn't it?") to the confrontational—Perry Mason style ("And isn't it a fact, Mr. Knutsen, that after a lust-crazed night of bondage games, something went seriously wrong and now a girl is dead?"). In the latter version, as in the old TV show, Knutsen broke down sobbing and confessed (*"Ja, ja,* it is true!").

Finally Jane dismissed all these ideas as ridiculous. There wasn't any way she could have a fixed plan, because Knutsen would presumably be sober, and she had no idea what he was like in that state. She would have to take the situation as she found it and play it by ear. This pleased her. She always liked to improvise.

At the Bergen airport she found Kessler next to her in the passport control line. "I suppose your friend is meeting you," he said.

Worried that he'd offer to share a taxi or something, she smiled and nodded, wondering when she'd ever be rid of him. He seemed interested in her in a way that managed to be both mysterious and slightly unpleasant.

When she pushed her baggage cart into the main waiting area, he was again at her side. In desperation she gave a little wave to a tall, good-looking blond man who seemed to be waving toward someone near her.

"Your friend?" said Kessler, raising an eyebrow and smiling just a fraction, in what she thought might be his version of a leer.

"Yes," she said, perversely pleased she'd picked such a handsome fake lover. Now, surely, Kessler would back off. She congratulated herself on her quick thinking.

Unfortunately the tall man she'd fingered turned out to be meeting Kessler and came over and greeted him. The three of them stood there awkwardly for a moment, and the Norwegian said to the Swiss, "I got your fax this morning. I am glad I was able to meet this flight. Actually it was better for me than later."

Kessler gave one of his Teutonic little nods—presumably of thanks—and said to the man, "I didn't know you were at that seafood show in Seattle. And met the charming Miss da Silva there."

Kessler in gallant mode was a bit startling. His accent sounded suddenly kind of cute.

"I'm sorry?" The blond man looked back and forth between Kessler and Jane, obviously wondering what the hell was going on.

"No, *I'm* sorry," Jane said with a big smile. "Across a crowded room I guess all Norwegians look alike. This is, of course, not my friend."

Great. Now Kessler thought she couldn't even recognize the man she was coming to spend the week with. "I'm a little nearsighted without my glasses," she added, trying to preserve what little dignity she had left.

"We may all look alike to you," said the tall Norwegian, "but if I had the pleasure of meeting you before, I know I would have remembered." The poor man looked tremendously relieved that he hadn't committed some social gaffe.

Jane backed off and made a flustered but speedy exit. She abandoned the cart around a corner, wrestled off her bag and retreated to the nearest ladies' room to regroup. Surely

Kessler wouldn't follow her in there. She'd give him and his Viking companion enough time to leave the airport before she emerged and trusted that Bergen was a big enough town that she could avoid him from now on.

One thing was interesting: Kessler had changed his flight. Could he have done it to get on the same flight as Jane? But why?

She took a cab through snow-covered woodsy scenery to her hotel. When she'd barreled off from Lofoten, she'd been purposely vague about her arrival time back in Norway. That way she could avoid being met by another gracious fish bureaucrat.

Now she felt deliciously alone in her nice anonymous hotel room. She avoided the television set as though it were an unexploded bomb, and after a brief collapse on the bed, rummaged among her papers for her itinerary.

She was due shortly at a nearby hotel for a breakfast meeting. She took a short, slippery, packed-ice walk alongside the harbor. The water was incredibly still, and the old, solid brick buildings were reflected in it in a way that managed to be both stately and somehow festive.

Breakfast was a sumptuous Norwegian smorgasbord: a selection of breads and cheeses, eggs—boiled and scrambled—big Icelandic shrimp in their shells bristling with orange roe, pickled herring, salmon caviar, lettuce and tomato slices, waffles and jam. Jane staggered through an interview with a cod importer, taping everything for Carla, picking up more brochures and hoping her questions weren't too dumb.

Back at the hotel, she was slightly chagrined to see that her minders had caught up with her. There was a message from someone named Solveig, who was coming by to escort her to the Fisheries offices later that afternoon.

Once in her room, Jane set about to try to make sure Knutsen didn't remember her from the Fountain Room. First of all she removed the minimal makeup she wore most of the time. When she sang, she went all out—lipstick and mascara, foundation and blusher—and that's how he'd seen her. Next she brushed her hair back from her forehead and fastened it with a couple of clips. She tried using an eyebrow pencil to add a widow's peak to her newly exposed brow but decided it looked too peculiar and washed it off again.

Maybe she should have brought some Kmart glasses. She could look like the repressed woman in a corny old movie who at some point removes her glasses, lets down her hair and causes the hero to gasp, "Why, Miss Jones!"

She supposed that as she was impersonating a fish journalist, she should have worn earrings shaped like halibut or something; then she remembered that Ragnhild up in Tromsø had given her a fish-shaped pin. She attached this to the lapel of her jacket and arranged the silk scarf with salmon swimming upstream under her jacket in a kind of matronly pouf she'd seen on Carla when they had first met.

She looked herself over in the full-length mirror. She didn't think she'd fool anyone she knew, but then Knutsen didn't really know her. She experimented a little with posture, it being one of her theories that the two most effective things a woman could do to look attractive were to stand up straight and to smile, and she was especially careful to do both on stage. It followed that doing just the opposite would create a radical change in appearance.

She rounded her shoulders, let her chest cave into her ribs and scowled. The change was quite remarkable. She looked truly pathetic. The whole wretched life of this new persona unreeled itself in Jane's mind, going back to early self-esteem problems in adolescence, subsequent disappointments in career and personal relationships and, finally, years of self-indulgent therapy and crabby bitterness. Hardly the kind of person who could bully the truth out of Knutsen.

Oh, the hell with it, she thought. She unclipped her hair and put on a little mascara and lipstick. So what if he recognized her? Let him be confused. She'd have him cornered in his office, and she'd just demand to know what he remembered about Marcia's last night on earth.

Chapter Thirteen

Her escort, Solveig, turned out to be a large, freckled young woman with pale orange hair. They met in the lobby, where she presented Jane with a few pounds of brochures, a calendar, another oven mitt, and a huge glossy cookbook.

Jane thanked her warmly and took it all over to the desk for pickup (and possibly disposal) later.

They then took a taxi to the Fisheries Directorate, a name that conjured up in Jane's mind a scene from a children's book, where bureaucratic fish wearing cartoon spectacles sat behind desks and shuffled papers, blowing bubbles and making policy.

Solveig seemed sweet and rather passive, which was good news because Jane was already scheming to eliminate her from the room when she interviewed Knutsen.

Whatever happened during the interview, Jane was determined to blow off any more hospitality or further meetings. Her flight left in the morning; she would declare herself off duty until then.

"We are having it very lucky," said Solveig. "There is a meeting of the International Salmon Marketing Committee here in Bergen this evening, so you can write about this, too, perhaps."

"I doubt it," Jane said firmly. She remembered something

Carla had said back at the Meade Hotel. "Those meetings are generally closed."

"Well," said Solveig, taking on a look of stubbornness Jane hadn't anticipated—there was something ominous about the clench of her wide jaw—"they will be wanting to announce a new marketing campaign, and I think they will be glad to be talking about it."

"I'm terribly sorry, but—"

"We have faxed your magazine," said Solveig. "And the meeting is in your hotel, so it is very convenient."

Jane tried to think of another way out—ever since her failure at the airport with Kessler, she'd felt off her game—but just then the taxi pulled up in front of a handsome glass building, and Solveig was paying the driver and getting a receipt with the decisive air of one who had not only finished a discussion, but won. Lest there be any doubt, Solveig turned to her and said, "Amanda Braithwaite says you should write about this. You know Amanda, of course?"

Jane thought about winging it, then decided not to bother. "Never heard of her," she said.

"She is an English lady. Very experienced in food marketing. She will be handling the campaign. You will be meeting her at the hotel tonight." Solveig smiled and added, "Of course Mr. Carver, your editor, knows her. She is buying advertising from your magazine."

Good old Norm. Jane supposed if this Amanda Braithwaite wanted to be featured in a fashion layout, modeling fish wearables, she could have that, too. Further struggle seemed pointless. Jane reasoned that she had to eat anyway. She might as well bring along the trusty tape recorder and come up with something Carla could fashion into a sidebar.

The Fisheries offices were housed in a stunning modern building that incorporated some ancient wooden beams and brick walls. Solveig led her to Knutsen's office overlooking the harbor, and they waited outside for a moment. Jane managed to ditch Solveig by demanding in a high-handed way that she confirm her plane reservations and make sure she would get her frequent flyer miles. As Jane didn't collect miles on SAS, she figured that would stall her a little. Solveig crept away, outwardly passive once again.

Finally Knutsen came to the door, wearing a Mr. Rogers–style cardigan of thick gray wool over a white shirt and tie. He didn't look like a thrill killer at all. He smoked a pipe, which he held up questioningly as he said, "You don't mind, I hope?" with a look of genuine concern.

"Not at all," said Jane, who rather liked the smell of pipe tobacco.

"Ah, Americans," he said, all twinkly. "You don't like people to smoke or drink too much. . . ."

"Or eat whales or wear fur," said Jane, laughing. "I know. We can be very annoying and self-righteous sometimes."

He held up a finger in the manner of a winsome professor, "We will get along fine," he said in a cozy little singsong accent. He waved a hand at the chair in front of his desk, waited politely until she was seated, then sat down himself and smiled at her with a pleasant, expectant look. "What can I do for you?" he said. "What do you need to know?"

Jane made a great show of fumbling with her tape recorder while she decided what the hell to ask before she started grilling him about Marcia St. Francis. "I'm sorry I missed your speech in Seattle . . . ," she began.

"I tell you what," he said, "I was just going through the things I brought back from Seattle, and I have a tape of the speech. Why not take it with you?"

"That would be wonderful," said Jane. "You don't need it?"

"I always come back from these conferences with all kinds of tapes and papers, and I never go over them again. Least of all my own." He pawed around in a drawer.

"All I have to say about all the problems of the world of salmon marketing are in the speech," he said with a self-deprecating little smile, handing her a cassette with a courtly nod.

"Did we meet in Seattle?" he asked, squinting at her a little. "I know I met some woman from your magazine, and you do look familiar, but I thought her name was different."

"Perhaps you met my colleague," said Jane. "Carla Elroy? You've spoken with her on the phone before, I know."

"Yes, but I am sure I have met you, too," he said, looking genuinely confused.

"These conventions can be very overwhelming," said Jane. "A lot happens, and people are jet-lagged and socializing a lot."

"That's for sure," said Knutsen, touching his forehead.

Jane imagined he was remembering his hangover and thought for a moment she had an entrée. Yes, she could say, you were pretty drunk yourself. Remember lurching around the Fountain Room? But she couldn't bring herself to do it just yet.

"Tell me about the marketing campaign you've just put together," she said. "I understand Amanda Braithwaite is involved." Solveig had expected her to know who this person was. Presumably Knutsen did, too.

"Ja," he said, leaning back and blowing a crown of blue smoke that floated across the big window overlooking the harbor, like a baby cloud trapped somehow on the wrong side of the glass. "As I am sure you know, farmed salmon has been in a terrible state for years. We Norwegians developed the technology, and before we knew it the world was covered with salmon farms and there was overproduction. We have been too generous with our knowledge."

Jane nodded and checked to see that her tape was moving. It was.

"And then of course we have had trade problems, duties, legal problems. Everyone knows that if we get people to eat more salmon, there is plenty of business for all of us. Instead we are fighting each other the whole time.

"Now it seems we can have a—what do you call this, when you stop fighting a war?"

"A truce?" said Jane.

"Ja, ja. If we can spend on marketing a little of what we

have been spending dragging each other before the GATT and the EC and the Department of Commerce, we can get people to eat more salmon. It is not so difficult. Everyone loves salmon."

"Of course," said Jane.

"So Amanda is putting together a campaign, and we are discussing for the first time the campaign itself, not only how we will pay. Before we are talking only about the budget, but I think this is a better way. Amanda is a very intelligent woman. She has worked very hard. Perhaps we can all agree. We even have"—he leaned over as if imparting startling information—"the Alaskans involved! The wild salmon people. I never thought I would see this."

"I never thought I would see the Berlin wall fall in my lifetime," Jane said solemnly.

"Exactly!" He tapped with his pipe on a big glass ashtray, and a lot of tarry tobacco fell out in a smoldering mass.

"What kind of a campaign are we talking about?" said Jane.

"I'll tell you one thing," Knutsen said, scraping away at his pipe with a knife. "In this country we prefer to promote the fish on its merits. Not by using a lot of young, half-naked girls in black stockings, like I saw in Seattle." An expression of moral repugnance crossed his features.

Oh, really? Jane thought to herself. You seemed to be getting into it when I saw you last, lurching around the Fountain Room requesting "Yust Von of Dose Tings" and trying to cop a feel here and there, not to mention the handcuffs, you nasty hypocrite.

"Listen," she said, "I knew one of those half-naked girls. She ended up dead. In the room next to yours."

His excavation in the bowl of his pipe ceased, and he set it down very carefully in the ashtray and folded his hands in front of him as if in prayer, all the while gazing across at her. His light blue eyes uncrinkled and grew suddenly exposed— fuller, paler and glazed over. She wondered if it were grief or disingenuousness. Or fear.

"I am so sorry," he said. "A terrible thing. I was very shocked. All these guns you people have . . ."

"You knew her, didn't you?" said Jane. "You went off with her that evening. People saw you leaving together."

Knutsen stood up and stepped back from his desk. "I ask you please not to discuss this," he said.

"Too bad," said Jane. "The girl's parents have a right to know what happened to their daughter. You're the only person who knows, and you've refused to help."

"I spoke with the police in Seattle about this poor girl," he said stiffly, reaching for the phone. "If you don't have more questions about the marketing campaign, then . . ."

"Don't touch that," said Jane. "Not unless you want me to tell the world about those handcuffs you were wearing that evening."

Knutsen's eyes retreated into leathery folds. "You were there," he said. "I saw you. You were singing. Cole Porter."

Jane remembered the two-dollar tip he'd given her and wondered how she could have been suckered in by that avuncular cardigan and the pipe.

His hands had balled into fists. Jane suddenly got up and leaned across his desk. "Look, I'm not here to upset you," she said in a softer voice, the voice women used when trying to calm down men who were feeling cornered. "I don't want to embarrass you. Just tell me what happened so I can tell her family. Then we can forget all about it. If you've told the police, you can tell me."

Unspoken was the threat that if he didn't, she'd retail the story about his kinky evening in Seattle around the industry.

He sat down heavily. She sat, too, slowly, so as not to startle him. "What are you doing here?" he said. "Who are you? They told me you are a journalist. Now I remember you singing in a bar."

"I am a private investigator, working for the family," she said brusquely.

"Then why do you pretend to be these other things?" he

said. "Why didn't you just call me up and ask your questions?"

"I tried," she said. "You refused to speak with me."

"So that was you? Well, it is natural," he said. "Why should I speak to you?" He looked remarkably helpless.

Jane suppressed her pity and came down hard. "So I won't tell everyone in the industry how you were involved with her. How you came back with that thing on your wrist."

"But I was drunk!" he said, as if that explained everything. Perhaps it did. "I drank a lot of whiskey, and then this girl . . . I am sorry she is dead, but you see, she was very strange. She rubbed up against me in the bar and asked me to go with her. I am a normal man. A normal man who was very drunk."

"Where did you go?" said Jane.

"I don't know. A house somewhere. And before I know what is happening, she has this thing clamped around me, like in some American film. I am telling you honestly, I was terrified." He seemed to be pleading with her. "I am in a strange country, a country that we hear is full of murderers and crazy people, and I am chained to a . . . what do you call it, a heating thing."

"A stove?"

"No, no. The thing the hot water goes through." Impatiently he grabbed a fountain pen and drew a squiggle.

"A radiator?" said Jane.

"Yes."

"Then what happened?"

"I am telling you, that isn't the sort of thing that excites me," he said indignantly, adding with a sort of Scandinavian frankness: "Making love is fine without a lot of silly dramatic nonsense."

Jane tried and failed to repress a picture of Knutsen in the throes of passion—a good old-fashioned hydraulic lover like Sven in that video.

His story, whatever the truth of it, was rolling right out

now. Jane decided a little nonjudgmental sympathy was in order to keep it coming.

"How upsetting," she said. "These conventions can get wild, of course, but for someone to manacle you to a radiator!"

"It was terrible!" he said indignantly. Jane almost imagined him writing an irate letter to the *Seattle Times* or the Convention and Visitors Bureau.

"What happened after that?" she asked, wondering if she'd get a blow-by-blow description of any drunken attempts to fight his way through Marcia's fishnet tights with one hand tied to the radiator.

"I passed out," he said, as if this were the most reasonable thing to do. "I had a lot to drink. Usually I just drink beer, but I had been drinking whiskey. In the bar and before, in that little refrigerator in the room."

Suddenly he put a hand to his head. "God, I can't believe I'm telling you this. If my wife knew . . . if my colleagues . . ." He bristled a little. Clearly this was what he feared the most. Ridicule from his colleagues.

"I won't discuss this with anyone," Jane promised. "And I won't tell the family your name. They may not want to know how strange Marcia was. These details will remain between us. What happened when you came around again?"

He gazed out the window at the clear water of the harbor. It had begun to snow. "I was horrified. I looked over at my hand. Then I realized the stupid girl had attached me to a sort of control."

"A knob?"

"Yes, a big knob. So I just unscrewed the knob with my free hand. It was easy."

"Then what did you do?"

"There was no one in the house. I was going to call a taxi, but I didn't know the address, so I walked outside and far away I saw that space needle thing. I began to walk downtown, and soon enough I saw a taxi and whistled for it, and it stopped and took me back to the hotel. They had left me my wallet, thank goodness."

"They?"

"Yes," he said. "Just before I passed out, I heard her talking to someone else."

"A man or a woman?"

"A man. He was in the next room. It was then I thought I might be killed, but I was spared. I passed out while they were talking."

"Why do you think this happened to you?" she said.

"The girl was crazy. Some kind of a sexual lunatic," he said, as if he had to fend them off every day. "A nymphomaniac."

"And who do you think the man was?" said Jane.

"Who knows?" he said. "An accomplice. Or maybe another sexual victim?" He shrugged. He seemed to have pulled himself together. "I was no good to her. I was passed out." He pulled himself up in his chair and said with dignity: "Anybody who had drunk as much as I had would be in the same state."

"Oh, of course," said Jane, who could think of absolutely no situation on earth when questioning male virility would be productive.

Despite his initial reluctance, Knutsen now seemed eager to share his ordeal. "Back at the hotel I had a horrible time getting the handcuffs off. It was humiliating. I tried with a pocket knife and a corkscrew. Then the police came and wanted to know something about a dead girl in the next room. They said there had been an accident. A shooting."

Knutsen threw up his hands. "I decided then and there to get out of America and come right home. I arranged for an earlier flight."

"So when the police came, you kept your hand in your pocket to hide the handcuffs," she said. "How did you get it off, finally?"

Remarkably, Knutsen seemed to have forgotten that she

had blackmailed him into telling her all this. Now he was leaning across the desk with wide eyes.

"I had to ask the concierge to send up a locksmith. It was terrible. This young man came up and took it off. I told him it was all just a silly joke. He said he'd come across this before."

Jane could imagine the locksmith leering at another bungled bondage stunt. "And what did the police ask you?" she said.

"If I had heard a shot. Which I had not. And they wanted to know about the door that led from my room to the suite. The hospitality suite of your magazine. That's all they asked me."

"The connecting door?" she said.

"Earlier there had been a cocktail party there, and I had arranged to have the door open," he said. "The editor . . ."

"Norman Carver?" said Jane.

"That's right. He said he could use the extra space. The party kind of spread out. And I had some friends in, too, so it worked out. We got our drinks from his bar." He frowned. "The mini-bar is so expensive. Almost as bad as buying a drink in Norway."

"So the door was open?"

"I wasn't sure, and I told them so. You see, I wasn't too interested. Because I didn't realize until later that the girl who'd been shot was the same girl who tied me to the radiator."

"How did you find that out?"

"A friend told me. After I came back to Norway."

"And the police didn't want to detain you?"

"I showed them my diplomatic passport," said Knutsen, "and told them I needed to go home."

"And the police didn't know you'd been out with her?"

"I don't think so," he said. "But when I came back I got a phone call from the police in Seattle. They asked me about it."

"And what did you tell them?" said Jane.

"I told them the truth," he said. "That I left with her, went to her house, passed out and came back to the hotel alone."

"You left out the detail about the handcuff, though, right?" Jane couldn't imagine him volunteering that little touch.

"They didn't ask about that," Knutsen said with dignity. "They wanted to know what she was wearing and if I'd seen her change clothes. They said they would be in touch. Naturally, I am hoping to avoid any more unpleasantness. I would like to forget all about this business."

"Naturally," said Jane. "What a horrible experience."

"The police didn't ask to test your hands for powder burns," she said. If they had, they would, of course, have found the handcuff there. Then she remembered he seemed to have come straight from the shower. A test would have been inconclusive.

"No, nothing like that, thank God."

"And you lost your slipper," she said.

"I looked all over for that damned thing," he said, looking just as puzzled as he had over Marcia St. Francis's odd behavior. "I never did find it."

By the time Jane left his office, she couldn't quite see how or why Trygve Knutsen would have killed Marcia St. Francis. If she had been wearing the same outfit, there might have been some sort of trail. But clearly Marcia had gone somewhere else, changed, come back to the hotel and ended up in the *Seafood Now* suite.

Knutsen seemed to be genuinely bemused by the strange events that had taken place in Seattle that night. If he'd been making up a story, the one he'd come up with was unnecessarily bizarre.

Jane was confused, too. What was Marcia up to, luring him to a house, chaining him to a radiator, then changing into a remarkably unseductive outfit and returning to the hotel? Jane felt that she was seeing only a small part of the picture. The missing bit was what motivated Marcia. Jane found it hard to believe that she was a predatory sex fiend.

As for Trygve Knutsen, he seemed quite straightforward,

amazingly forthcoming and actually rather amiable once she had him going. Then she reminded herself that she had met a couple of killers before. They had seemed nice enough, too. That was exactly what she had found most frightening about them.

CHAPTER FOURTEEN

"There's no need for you to come back with me in the cab," Jane said firmly to Solveig. They were standing under the falling snow on the curb outside the Fisheries Directorate.

Resentful because she had been bullied into attending that night's salmon market reception, Jane was beginning to take a perverse pleasure in thwarting whatever further plans of Solveig's she could. What she wanted to say was, "I've had it up to here with you and your damn fish, so back off." Instead she tried to look pleasant but firm.

"All right," said Solveig, "But I will see you later at the hotel." She lifted her powerful jaw and narrowed her pale eyes. "In the meantime, I am arranging your dinner hour."

Jane had a ghastly flash of a whale blubber dinner with a stubborn Solveig watching to make sure she cleaned her plate.

Just then the taxi pulled up, and Jane darted toward it, risking another fall on the slippery pavement. "We'll talk later," she said over her shoulder.

"Keep the taxi receipt," said Solveig, coming after her. "We shall be reimbursing you."

Feeling like a hunted animal, Jane got into the cab, slammed the door and waved and smiled at Solveig through the window while repeating, "I hate you, I hate you, I hate you," through clenched teeth.

There's no reason for that woman to get to me so, she thought when she got back to her hotel room. She was only doing her job. Still, Jane toyed with the idea of pleading appendicitis or something to get out of the evening's event. It seemed more exhausting to think up an excuse than not to go, but the triumph of foiling Solveig might make the effort well worthwhile.

Jane hadn't had lunch, so she poked around in the minibar and came up with a chocolate bar and some cheese. She took off her shoes, lay down on the bed and made a half-hearted attempt to eat her snacks.

Finally she gave up and set the food on the bedside table. Her head on the pillow, staring at the cheese and chocolate nestling unappealingly in their wrappers, she thought about Trygve Knutsen.

A name badge could bring out the animal in a lot of people, she knew. Could he have been so drunk he'd killed Marcia with her own gun, enraged because she'd handcuffed him to a radiator? And then blacked out?

Jane drifted off to a jet-lagged traveler's afternoon nap. Tomorrow she'd be on her way home, and maybe she could find out more about Marcia. And maybe Jack Lawson would be in town. Jane realized she hadn't thought about him once on this trip.

When she woke, it was to the shrill ring and flashing red light of the bedside phone. It took her a second to realize where she was, a disorienting feeling that often came upon her when she woke after sleeping during the day.

Solveig was on the line. "Why aren't you down here at the reception?" she demanded.

Jane didn't feel up to a story about a burst appendix or even a migraine. "I'm sorry," she said. "I fell asleep. I'll be right down."

Groggily she went through her suitcase and found a dark dress to wear. She had the impression this affair was a big deal, perhaps because it was billed as "a reception." At least there would be something to eat. Probably salmon. Jane had always been fond of seafood, but after this trip she found herself craving red meat. She could hardly wait to get back to Dick's Drive-In on Broadway, where she would order a couple of deluxe hamburgers and a mess of Dick's home-made fries.

She made her way to the room where the reception was being held. It was dimly lit and full of men in suits standing around, glasses in hand. The lighting was dim because a tall, stout woman with curly blond hair and a pink tweed suit was standing on a podium, showing slides of pie charts. Jane recognized her as the backslapping Englishwoman in blue who had worked the room back at the Meade Hotel. This presumably was Amanda Braithwaite.

"As you see," she said in a middle-class English accent, "even this modest increase in per capita consumption, a modest goal and surely *well* within our reach, will, in markets the size of Europe and North America, enable us to move many more tons of product."

Her eyes becoming accustomed to the light, Jane tuned out the woman's bossy voice and looked around the room. There was a large buffet, with lots of salmon—some of it smoked, some of it in puff pastry, some of it poached and dusted with dill. Jane's fantasy meal switched from Dick's deluxe hamburgers to rare roast beef sliced thin, maybe a French dip with some nice meaty, garlicky juice.

Amanda Braithwaite clicked a control in her hand—the other hand held a pointer—and a carousel lurched to the next slide. A happy, upscale family beamed down at a plate of rosy salmon. "Like all successful creative concepts, ours is simple. We've got to let people know salmon is *accessible*. Research shows people like it, but consumer attitudes are still lagging behind. Consumers don't realize that the development of farmed salmon means our product is available all year round." She tapped at the screen with the pointer and said accusingly, "It's an absolutely *appalling* situation and the result of years of promotional neglect on the part of the industry."

Jane glanced around the room. The men in suits were looking vaguely guilty, as if their dentist had just scolded them for not flossing properly.

"A *quite* appalling situation," Amanda Braithwaite repeated, clicking her tongue, frowning at them all. She let this sink in before she hit the advance button to reveal a slide with all kinds of boxes and arrows. "Here's the way the funding will be deployed," she said, her persona shifting slightly—from the pull-up-your-socks schoolmistress to an army officer briefing the troops before the assault on Normandy.

Looking around, Jane recognized some faces. Several of these people had been at that other reception back in the Meade Hotel, brooding in corners while she had serenaded them with "Autumn Leaves."

Thank goodness it was dark in here. When the lights went on, maybe she could fade away. She was about at the end of her rope, worrying about the fact that these guys had first seen her as a lounge singer and now she was supposed to be a fish journalist.

Knutsen was there, too—having changed from his cozy cardigan to a dull suit. To her horror, she saw he was talking to Gunther Kessler. What the hell was he doing here? Wasn't he in refrigeration? Jane had learned enough about the fish business by now to wonder just what the glum Swiss was doing at a marketing conference. And to ask herself why he had been looking at salmon pens in Shetland with Magnus.

The sooner she got out of the fish business, the better. Gunther Kessler was an unpleasant reminder of how incredibly unslick she could be.

When she turned away from him, hoping to avoid his eye, she found herself staring at the tall, good-looking Norwegian she'd fingered as her squeeze at the airport. It seemed that every time she turned around, she was brought face-to-face with another rip in her frayed and shredded cover story. To make matters worse, the Viking god was staring right at her. She was relieved to hear an American voice at her elbow.

"Well, it's Jane da Silva from *Seafood Now*."

It took her a moment to recognize one of the Alaskan Putnam brothers—she wasn't sure whether it was Don or Bob. He looked a lot better here than he had at Chinook's. For one thing, his burly frame was now encased in a good-looking suit instead of a T-shirt.

"How are you?" she whispered, offering him her hand as Amanda barked on about a salmon recipe program with which she intended to reach every household in the northern hemisphere.

"Are you involved in this salmon marketing thing?" Jane asked. "I thought salmon farming was a hanging offense in Alaska."

"If you can't beat 'em, join 'em," he said amiably, leaning over to whisper in her ear. "The fact is, I'm trying to get some of our guys interested in working with the farmed guys and promote salmon across the board. I'm here as a friendly observer."

On the podium, Amanda Braithwaite cleared her throat elaborately and glared at him. "The recipes will be developed with high nutritional standards," she said sternly, "with both American *and* European weights and measures."

"They already handed out a lot of printed stuff with this whole presentation," he whispered to Jane, as if by way of explanation for his lack of interest.

They both stood there, chastised, and listened to details of the chef's competition, the print campaign in women's publications, the point-of-purchase display for supermarkets, the PR campaign to tell the world how safe and hygienic farmed salmon was and, if the Alaskans "came on board," the liaison program with "the wild sector." Jane found the last phrase rather evocative, conjuring up the image of a bunch of crazed, fur-clad Alaskans busting up a bar in Kodiak.

When the presentation came to a merciful close and the lights went up, Putnam asked her to dinner. "I know a terrific place here in Bergen along the waterfront," he said. She'd placed him now. Clearly he was the brother who hadn't spouted Bible phrases, but she still wasn't sure if his name was Don or Bob.

Remembering that Solveig had threatened dinner plans, Jane decided to accept. That would settle the Valkyrie's hash nicely, and whichever Putnam brother he was, he actually seemed quite pleasant.

"That sounds great," she said, but at that moment Solveig hustled up, handed her a huge press kit and announced that she had arranged for Jane to have an exclusive dinner interview with Amanda Braithwaite, who was already bustling over, a splotch of pink bouclé wool among the dark suits.

"I understand completely," said Putnam, backing off graciously. Jane decided he wasn't the sleazeball she'd first thought. It was partly his appearance that had given her that impression. The beard and the barrel chest had made him look tough, and the Chinookie T-shirt was definitely a fashion mistake. But in these surroundings he seemed a lot more couth. Maybe he was one of those chameleon types—Jane felt that she herself was one—who unconsciously took on some of the coloration of their environment.

As he faded away, Amanda Braithwaite descended on her, pumping her hand in a hearty way. "*Super* to meet you," she said enthusiastically. "I love your pieces in *Seafood Now*. Absolutely brilliant! Smashing stuff! I always look for your byline."

She'd have to look pretty hard, seeing as nothing had ever appeared under Jane's name in the magazine. Jane gave her a smile and said, "Thank you so much. Are there any articles you particularly enjoyed?"

"It's all wonderful," Amanda said without skipping a beat. "I do so hope you'll be writing about our campaign."

"Well, it's obviously a very important story," said Jane. Right up there with the second coming of Christ, she thought.

"We'd actually sort of been hoping to get the *cover,*" Amanda insinuated coyly.

Jane checked out her ensemble. The suit was bristling with

big pearl-and-gilt buttons. People who wore pink that hot liked attention. "What a great idea!" she said. "I think I'll suggest to Norm that we put *you* on the cover."

Amanda's face immediately blossomed and expanded. Fat pink cheeks rose like two hills to flank a wide, satisfied smile. "That would be jolly super," she breathed.

"Let me go up to my room and get my tape recorder," said Jane. Based on Amanda's wordy presentation and clearly healthy ego, dinner could be spent with Amanda monologizing into the machine while Jane nodded and looked alert and let her mind drift. Maybe Carla could get another story out of it. She could probably use the money.

"Terrific," said Amanda, hitching a quilted Chanel purse onto her shoulder. "I'll bag us a decent table in the restaurant. See you there." She turned imperiously to Solveig. "Do you think you could possibly arrange for my presentation materials to be taken to my room? That would be most helpful. Thank you so much. Good night!"

Solveig, who'd evidently thought she would be having dinner with them, looked considerably put out, but she had clearly met her match. At the sight of her Norse taskmistress scuttling away to do Amanda's bidding, Jane found herself warming to the Englishwoman.

She checked out the remaining guests, who were streaming away with expressions of relief on their faces, and tried to plan an escape route that would allow her to avoid anyone she had ever met, especially Gunther Kessler and his friend the Viking god.

Kessler seemed to have disappeared, thank goodness. The Viking god was over by the podium, talking to Solveig, who was gathering up the slides. Jane was disconcerted to see that he was staring at her. Solveig looked over her shoulder and followed his glance, then seemed to reply to some question he had asked.

In the elevator she fantasized briefly about locking herself in her room with the Do Not Disturb sign on the knob and simply refusing to come out. She had a vision of Solveig

hammering on the door and another, more alarming one of
Amanda Braithwaite putting a beefy shoulder to it and burst-
ing into the room, brandishing a hockey stick to herd her to
dinner.

She put the plastic key card into the lock and opened the
door, then gasped, feeling a stab of prickles all over her body
before she understood what had caused the physical rush of
alarm.

Gunther Kessler was standing next to her unmade bed,
bending over her suitcase and calmly riffling through the
contents.

CHAPTER FIFTEEN

Kessler looked up at her. She would have found it less frightening if he'd had the grace to look unnerved at being caught.

She stood there in the doorway, reluctant either to enter the room or to surrender it to him. "What the hell do you think you are doing?" she demanded angrily.

"I am searching your room," he said, putting down the lid of her suitcase with the confident air of a customs inspector.

"You're going through my things," she said, letting him hear the note of revulsion in her voice. Horrible visions of him making off with bits of her underwear came to her.

"It is nothing personal, I assure you," he said with the same infuriating sangfroid.

She stepped into the room. She hated the idea that he could just come in and take over and leave her standing in her own doorway. But she made sure to leave the door wide open.

"I was told you were going to dinner with that Englishwoman," he explained patiently, as if this unpleasantness were all her fault. "If you hadn't come up, you would never have known and you wouldn't be distressed now."

"Oh, I see! And that makes it all right?" She wanted to tell him to get out, but the idea of his walking past her was creepy. Besides, she wanted to know just what he was up to. And why had he been stalking her in the first place? The fact that she could now presumably get him arrested might give her some leverage when it came to satisfying her curiosity.

Kessler was now glancing over at the bedside table. He looked with a frown at the remains of her chocolate and cheese. He was exploiting her indecision to conduct a visual sweep of the room, and it made her furious.

"Tell me in five seconds what the hell you are doing, or I will call security," she said.

"That might work to my advantage," he pointed out thoughtfully. "If there is an inquiry, perhaps I will find out who you are and what you are doing here in Norway. In Shetland. In Seattle. Pretending to be part of the fish business, then denying it. Stories about lovers in Bergen and singing engagements." He smirked. "It all sounds very fishy."

"At least I haven't been going around breaking into people's hotel rooms," she snapped. "Is that part of being a refrigeration specialist? I suppose you are planting promotional brochures about freezing equipment in my luggage." She stepped toward the phone.

He gave her a quirky little half smile. "If you call security," he said very quietly, "I suppose I'll tell them you invited me here."

"You bastard!" she hissed. "Get the hell out of here right now." Even as she said it, she realized she had been outmaneuvered. He'd managed, in his cold-blooded, nasty way, to make her angry. And because she was angry, she'd abandoned her attempt to discover just what he was doing.

As she stood there glaring at him, she heard a doorknob rattle in the corridor behind her. She looked around guiltily.

The Putnam brother was standing there.

He took in Jane, Kessler, the open door, her clenched fist.

"Hi, Jane," he said quietly but firmly. "Are you all right? I heard your voice."

"I found this guy in my room, going through my things," she said.

"Want me to throw him out?" Putnam said very calmly.

"Or do you want me to hold on to him while we call the cops?" He gave Kessler the eye. "I've seen this character around," he said. "Who is he?"

"That's what I'd like to know," said Jane.

"Okay." He strolled into the room. "Watch the door," he told Jane. "So just what are you doing in her room?" he said to Kessler, striding across the carpet.

Jane felt herself relax a little.

"I'm searching her belongings," Kessler said. "I'm sorry. . . ."

"You're sorry!" repeated Jane.

Kessler shrugged. "It's part of an investigation." He began to reach into his inside jacket pocket. "I have a card."

Before he had a chance to reach it, Putnam was all over him, wrapping his arms around him in a bearlike embrace. Both men started breathing heavily. Jane suddenly felt the whole thing was ridiculous.

"Go ahead," Kessler said, wheezing. "Take my card out yourself."

"He might have been going for a gun," Putnam said to Jane. He was shifting Kessler around, with Gunther's apparent cooperation, until he was holding him around the chest from behind.

"A gun? Nonsense," Kessler said indignantly. "This isn't America."

"Take out his wallet, Jane," said Putnam.

She stepped forward, and while Kessler held his hands up and looked down at her with another of his horrible smirks, she lifted his jacket away from his body by the lapel and reached into his inside pocket. She hated doing it. It was too intimate. She could feel the starch in his shirt and the heat of his body coming through the fabric.

"So who is this?" demanded Kessler. "One of your colleagues? Maybe he plays the piano for you. Or helps you do whatever it is you do in the fish business."

"I suppose there's an explanation for this," said Putnam in a world-weary way. "But I can't imagine what the heck it might be."

Jane got hold of a wallet and a card case, took them out of
the silk pocket and stepped back. She flipped open the case.
Inside was a whole set of creamy business cards. She
plucked one out, read that Gunther Kessler was a representative of a Swiss security firm based in Zurich and flung the
card case on the bed. Then she flipped open the wallet.
Kessler hadn't volunteered that, but if he was going to go
through her suitcase, she might as well check out his wallet.
It contained Norwegian crowns, Swiss francs and American
dollars, a few Scottish pounds and a mass of credit cards as
well as a Swiss government ID card in five languages with a
picture of Gunther Kessler.

She felt in the back of the wallet and touched a small
square package and the ring of a condom through foil. Just to
humiliate him, she flung that out on the bed, too. "Very
Swiss," she said. "Now you'll be safe if you ever get lucky."

Putnam smiled, but she didn't. Kessler shook off the
Alaskan, who let him go and stepped back a pace.

"Okay," said Kessler. "There's not much point in continu-
ing with this, is there?"

"Sure there is," said Jane, hoping Putnam was still game
to prolong the encounter. He seemed to be. "What are you
investigating? And why me? And who is your client?"

"That is confidential," said Kessler. "If you don't know,
then you have nothing to fear."

"You might have something to fear," said Putnam. "If you
don't tell the lady what she wants to know."

"Don't be ridiculous," Kessler said with a sort of a sniff.
He was looking into the mirror and adjusting his tie. Jane noticed he was also using the mirror to keep an eye on both of
them at the same time. "This is all very unfortunate," he said
as if he were talking about a missing memo or a shipment
that went awry. "Let us forget all about it."

"Absolutely not," said Jane. "If you have any direct questions about your investigation, go ahead and ask them. After
a damn good apology. And an explanation."

"Where I come from," said Putnam, sliding into the old

hot and cold routine, "we'd take care of a guy like you real fast."

Kessler turned and looked at Putnam haughtily. "You have seen too many cheap American films. You have begun to believe your own stupid myths. You are a bunch of loutish cowboys."

He said it rather elegantly, but right then loutish cowboys seemed to Jane like a pretty good thing.

"Welcome to the West," said Putnam, making a fist, pulling it back and preparing to flatten the Swiss.

He wasn't fast enough, though. Kessler managed a tricky maneuver in which he turned sideways, used two of his arms to stop one of Putnam's and twisted it down in a way that Jane thought would pop out the elbow.

"Stop it!" she shouted.

Kessler was braced with his feet a few feet apart, keeping up the pressure. To her astonishment, Jane found herself kicking the spot right under Kessler's right kneecap, something she'd read about somewhere in some article about women's self-defense.

"*Ai!*" he screamed.

"Get out of here right now," said Jane, brushing back the hair from her forehead. The last thing she wanted was a full-scale brawl in her hotel room.

"Fine," said Kessler, apparently recovered from her kick. "Please do not try to strike me, either of you." He gathered up his card case and his wallet. "You can keep that," he said, gesturing to the condom before he sauntered out the door. "You might need it."

"Hey, that was pretty exciting," said Putnam, rubbing his elbow. "Thanks for giving him that kick. The sneaky bastard seems to know some weird martial arts moves."

He made it sound as if there were something downright un-American about using anything other than a good, old-fashioned haymaker.

"Thank you so much!" said Jane. "I didn't mean for you to

have to come in here and struggle with the guy. Is your elbow all right?"

"It's okay," said Putnam. Jane wasn't completely convinced. "No big deal. I can't resist a lady in distress. Just who is that guy, anyway?"

"It looks like he's some kind of a detective," said Jane, handing Putnam the business card. "Why he's interested in me, I can't imagine."

"Well, you're pretty interesting," said Putnam, frowning at the German on the card.

Jane suddenly wished she weren't standing with this man in her hotel room with an unmade bed and a condom lying in plain view. She ran a hand through her hair. "I have to go," she said. "Amanda Braithwaite must be wondering what happened to me. I can't thank you enough."

"Call me if you have any more problems," he said. "I'm right across the hall. Twenty-four-hour service. You sure you don't want to complain to the management?"

"Too much hassle. The police might be involved, and I'm planning to fly out of here tomorrow morning."

He shrugged. "Whatever. You seem to be a pretty tough lady, but if I were you, I'd keep that door chained tonight. He's gotta be pretty slick if he can get into a locked hotel room."

CHAPTER SIXTEEN

Amanda Braithwaite was sitting at a corner table behind the dregs of a large gin and tonic when Jane arrived, slightly breathless.

"Oh, here you are, finally. Almost gave you up," Amanda said, scowling.

"I *am* sorry," Jane said, sounding more polite than actually sorry. "An important call from the States came in."

"Oh, I *know* how that goes," Amanda sympathized, handed her a menu. "Everything always seems to fall apart whenever I leave the office. The little sprogs they hire just can't seem to handle *anything* on their own. It's *so* pathetic. No initiative. That's the whole problem with Britain today."

For a PR expert who wanted to have an article written about her and her firm, Amanda seemed more than a little tactless. She'd practically said she had a lousy staff.

"Tell me about it," Jane said with phony exasperation, sensing a way to shorten her time with Amanda. "In fact, I'll have to excuse myself fairly early. I'll be spending the night sending out a lot of faxes."

"Same here," said Amanda, apparently unwilling to let anyone seem to be working harder. "Let's skip the starter and get on to the main course. I'm up to my ears myself! Now that the presentation is over, I have to make sure that all the bodies are signed up and get the final draft of our agreement okayed by the key players. Talk about problems!"

"It can't have been easy getting all those salmon guys together," said Jane, adding, "Even the wild sector," with a serious expression. This was apparently a big deal. Earlier in his office, Knutsen hadn't even smiled when she'd compared the generic salmon marketing campaign to the end of the cold war.

Amanda nodded earnestly. "Putting together this campaign," she said, "has been the biggest challenge of my whole career."

"A great quote. I should get this on tape," said Jane. She suddenly wondered whether Kessler was back in her room, poking around. Nothing about that creep would surprise her. How *had* he got in? Unless she was in the room, with the chain on, he could get back in again. She'd been stupid not to think about that. Maybe she *should* have called the hotel management.

Meanwhile Amanda blathered on about the vital need for increased salmon consumption in the entire Western world and hinted that once she'd accomplished that task, it was on to the former Warsaw Pact nations and then Asia. "We're talking tremendous potential here, simply tremendous. If we could get every single Chinaman to eat just one salmon meal a year . . ."

First, thought Jane, she'd have to avoid calling Chinese consumers "Chinamen."

A waiter came up, and Amanda broke off impatiently to order before going back into her pitch, this time bringing it all around to her own role.

"Scads of other agencies wanted the portfolio, of course. The difference is, I had a track record in food. I started out as a food technician. Recipe development, nutritional content of foods, the whole shebang.

"I broke through professionally during that egg scare we had in Britain. Salmonella. Worst-possible scenario for egg consumption." She had a gleam in her eye. Probably likes mad cow disease, too, Jane thought.

"That egg scare was my window of opportunity." Amanda was the kind of Thatcherite eighties Brit who used American business clichés to sound tough and competent. "I have a flair for consumer education. And for marketing as well," she went on.

Marketing yourself, anyway, thought Jane. Amanda's large pink presence exuded confidence. Jane glanced over at the recorder as the tape went around and around and Amanda started in again.

"When this campaign gets off the ground, production will increase by leaps and bounds. Ditto the promotion budget, with all the salmon producers chipping in their percentage levy. This is a revolutionary concept. I see salmon as a major commodity, promoted like toothpaste or any other consumer product! The sky is the limit! You can grow tons of this stuff. Tons! Not to mention economies of scale. Producers worldwide are getting more and more efficient, as the little players get squeezed out and the big boys come in and take over. We can feed the world!"

"With that level of enthusiasm, I can see how you got the account," said Jane.

"Ha!" Amanda said aggressively. "You think it was easy? The salmon producers didn't know their asses from their elbows when I moved in. They were living in the past. First I had to educate them, bring them up to speed, make them see that without promotion they'd all die. They just didn't have a grasp of the Darwinian facts of business life."

Jane imagined her companion rising from the table like someone in an old film and shouting, "Fools, fools. They said I was insane!"

Amanda reached over and clicked off the tape recorder. "Off the record," she said, lifting an eyebrow dramatically. "The only way they got their act together was when they perceived an external threat."

"Really? What threat?" said Jane in a bored tone.

"There have been certain rumors," Amanda said archly. "Nothing I can't handle now I have the account, of course, but it concentrated their tiny minds."

Jane recalled that Carla had alluded to that when she'd grilled Magnus Anderson back in Seattle. A real journalist would have pounced on this tantalizing little clue, she realized. Instead she marveled at Amanda's lack of discretion. For a moment she had started to buy in to Amanda's idea that she could conquer the world and get everyone on the planet to eat nothing but salmon. Now it occurred to her that this woman was possibly the world's klutziest flack.

Leaving the machine off as the waiter brought them their plates, Jane asked casually, "Have you run into this Swiss guy? Gunther Kessler, his name is. He seems to be big in salmon."

"I haven't been able to make out who he is, exactly," said Amanda, looking unsure about something for the first time. "He's never part of the official program. It's all rather mysterious. Needless to say, the Swiss don't farm salmon. He may be a banker or something."

"He told me he's in refrigeration," said Jane.

Amanda looked puzzled. "Sounds a bit peripheral."

"He has something to do with that tall Norwegian, the tall blond one who was at the reception. Who's he?"

"They're *all* tall and blond," said Amanda.

"This one looks like a hero from the sagas. He's got a bit of a tan, and he was wearing a double-breasted suit."

"Ooh, him," said Amanda, suddenly girlish. "That's Hans-Christian Haakonsen. Yum! He's an assistant fisheries minister. Big chief stuff. He's in with all the cabinet, and the king and queen, for all I know."

She leaned over the table. "It all just goes to show how big-time this campaign is!"

"That must be very gratifying for you," said Jane, wondering what the hell a Swiss detective with the demeanor of a sociopath was doing hobnobbing with cabinet-level fish bureaucrats, posing as some sort of a refrigerator salesman.

Even more, what he was doing poking around in her suitcase.

Gunther Kessler wasn't lurking there when she got back to her room, but her message light was blinking red. The desk clerk told her someone had found her passport and turned it in to the desk. The clerk sounded critical, as if she'd been careless to leave it lying around. She realized she'd left it in her room with her airline ticket, feeling that Norway was such an honest place. She should have kept it in her purse. When she went down to fetch it, she asked who had turned it in.

"A Swiss gentleman," said the clerk.

Jane arranged for an early wake-up call and a shuttle to the airport, trying not to let the clerk see how upset she was. She supposed she should be grateful he'd returned it to her. But then, she realized, he'd done that just to show her he could act with impunity. Just to let her know that despite being muscled around by Putnam and kicked in the knee by her, he could have the last word.

CHAPTER SEVENTEEN

Back in Seattle, it took two large Nordstrom shopping bags, relics from more prosperous days, to hold all the fish materials Jane had collected on her trip. She drove the bags over to Carla's apartment and delivered them with a feeling of immense relief.

Carla dove at them like a kid on Christmas morning, then spread the brochures around her happily. "They have great promotional materials!" she said. "And there's lots of statistics here."

"You can keep the other stuff, too," said Jane. "The head scarf and the fridge magnets. There's a kind of sweet silver fish pin."

Carla looked grateful, and her pale fingers caressed an oven mitt. "Did you have a great time?" she asked wistfully. "How was the hands-on cod harvest experience?"

"Bad weather kept the boats at the dock," said Jane.

"What a shame," Carla said with feeling.

"Bad luck, wasn't it. So how's the job search going?"

"I'm up for a tech writer position at the College of Fisheries at the university," she said. "I'd like that. No advertisers."

"Sounds good," said Jane. "A state job. Security. A great medical plan. Retirement." All the things she didn't have. "Grab it." Then, worried, she added, "But you will write the

Norway article, won't you? Even if you find something right away?"

"Of course," said Carla. "I'm looking forward to it."

"Good. Here are the tapes. I've written on the labels who's speaking on all of them. And I have everyone's business cards so you can spell their names right. I interviewed a lot of people. Including Amanda Braithwaite. Do you know her? They added this salmon promotion thing to my itinerary. There's a press kit in here, maybe you can write that up as a smaller piece."

"Amanda Braithwaite!" exclaimed Carla. "Wow. She's a terrific fish marketer."

"Yeah, well, she landed the generic salmon campaign."

"That's so exciting," said Carla. "The industry has needed to get together and promote itself for years."

"I know," Jane said. "All that infighting has been so counterproductive. Even the wild sector is involved. One of the Putnams was over there. Just a small increase in consumption would really stabilize things."

Jane realized with a cold chill that she was talking with real feeling about the fish business. She had better stop herself before she got pulled in further. She might end up at the Women's Seafood Network monthly dinner, networking and bristling with fish jewelry and eventually growing a set of gills.

"Well," she said briskly, "I'll let you get to work. Call me if you have any problems or want me to get in touch with any of these people to ask follow-up questions or anything."

The sooner she got that article delivered and got herself out of the fish business, the better, as far as she was concerned. Her priority now was to focus on Marcia.

She supposed too that she should give the Hunters some kind of interim report. Unfortunately she had learned much more about cod and salmon than she had about Marcia St. Francis, who remained a complete mystery in Jane's mind. Neither did she relish telling Phil and Barb Hunter that the man they suspected claimed to have been chained to a radiator in some sort of kinky sex stunt by their dead daughter.

In the end, Jane decided she'd put off talking with them until she'd interviewed their other daughter. Besides learning something about Marcia, she could also feel her out about how the parents might take this bizarre news.

She called Lisa, who knew all about Jane and sounded a little warier than her parents had. "I suppose if you really could find out anything, it would help them. The police haven't done a thing as far as I can tell."

A few days later they met in Lisa's house in Kent, the kind of place realtors called a "starter home"—a small square box painted yellow with white trim, sitting in a larger square of lawn, a concrete path leading to the door, on a street full of identical houses in different pastels.

Lisa looked about thirty, a little plump, with a round, open-looking face, made up very carefully with black mascara and pink lipstick. She wore jeans and a light blue sweatshirt and tiny diamond studs in her ears. On her left hand she had a bigger diamond in a complicated setting next to a wedding band.

They drank weak coffee in a small, neat kitchen, and Lisa told Jane that she hadn't seen her sister for ages before she died. "Ever since that boyfriend of hers, Curtis. She just dropped out of sight. We were never that close, really. She's five years younger. . . ." Lisa still hadn't switched consistently to the past tense when speaking of her sister.

"I've met Curtis," said Jane. "I didn't know quite what to make of him."

"That's more than I did. She used to call once in a while when she was at the U. But we had different shifts. I was working nights. Anyway, she told me she met this guy and that he was Mr. Right. She said he was a genius and so sensitive, and really exciting and so kind."

Jane hadn't exactly seen Curtis as Mr. Charisma, but she knew there was no accounting for sexual attraction.

"I invited them to a barbecue once, but she said he was a

vegetarian, and she'd become one, too. I said no problem, we'd make a big salad or whatever. Or they could bring tofu or whatever he eats, but she said they'd pass. I was kind of hurt."

"So you never did meet him?"

"No. To be honest, it bugged me the way she acted about the barbecue. It was like she expected me to change the menu for them. I didn't call her for a long time after that. Then I thought maybe the vegetarian thing was some kind of excuse, that she didn't want to see me, and that hurt me even more."

"When's the last time you saw her?" asked Jane.

"About two weeks before she died. She just showed up at work. I work in a convenience store about a mile or so from here. It was about two in the morning, and she just walked in. Said she was in the neighborhood, which I thought was weird. Anyway, I went and got her some coffee, and we sat there behind the counter and chatted for a while."

"How did she seem?" said Jane.

"Real normal. I asked her about Curtis, and she said he was fine, and she made kind of dumb small talk. By then she had sort of cut herself off from my parents, and I asked her about that. She just said that she had changed and they never would, and that if she had to choose between them and Curtis, she'd have to choose him. I didn't get it. She'd always gotten along with my parents."

"Seems harsh," said Jane.

"Oh, but Diane *was* kind of harsh," Lisa said. "There was always only one right way."

"Did you know she'd changed her name?"

"No. Not until the police told us." She leaned toward Jane. "I never told my parents about the vegetarian thing. I didn't think it was a big deal. I know a lot of vegetarians, especially since I moved here. But it would have hurt their feelings. I mean, beef consumption is way down because of this health stuff. It's been tough for their business."

"Curtis told them they had blood on their hands," said Jane. "I bet he meant beef blood."

"God, what a thing to say to a couple of people who just lost their daughter," Lisa said bitterly. "I'd like to get my hands on that creep."

"Is there anything else you didn't tell your parents?" said Jane.

Lisa was quiet for a minute, then she went over to a drawer in the counter and took out a pack of cigarettes and an ashtray, sat back down, carefully lit one and exhaled. The whole ritual seemed to be accompanying some kind of decision-making process. Jane kept silent and waited.

Finally Lisa said, "I should have told the police, but I wasn't sure. And I sure didn't tell my parents, because they're already worried about my job. But I think maybe Diane stole my gun."

"Your gun?" said Jane.

"The store is in an okay neighborhood and all, but at first I was nervous, so I went out and bought myself a gun. My boss wouldn't like it, so I never asked his permission. I kept it under the counter, way in the back. There's a drawer that's sort of mine." She gave a sly little smile. "I put it in a Tampax box. I figured he'd never look in there."

"And when did you find it missing?" asked Jane.

"I think it was about a week or so after Diane came by. I was messing around in my drawer and I pushed the box aside and it was too light.

"I never thought it was her that took it. Not in a million years. You see, there are lots of people working there during the day, and there's lots of turnover." She wrinkled her nose. "Some of the clerks are pretty scuzzy, to be honest. I figured one of them took it, but I didn't want to say anything because I wasn't supposed to have it in the first place. I mean, it was legal and all, but my boss wouldn't have liked it. He says if we get held up just hand everything over, but I was afraid of some psycho. Plus, growing up on a ranch and all, I'm not afraid of guns."

Lisa took a deep breath. "When the police asked my parents if Diane had a gun, the idea that she might have taken it occurred to me. I'd left her there alone for a sec while I got us some coffee from across the room.

"Now that I think about it, I don't think any of those scuzzy clerks would have looked in a Tampax box, do you? I mean, they were all guys, the ones I suspected."

"But Diane knew about it?"

"Yeah. I told her. I told her not to tell my parents because they were already freaked about my working there." She ground out the cigarette. "It's not for much longer. Just until my husband finishes school and starts working full-time again. He went back to school and we had house payments, so I took a second job at night. It works out okay. He studies while I'm at work."

"What kind of a gun was it?" asked Jane.

"A little black thirty-eight-caliber revolver with a rubber grip. Lightweight. I think it was called a Rossi. I bought it used at a gun store for a hundred and fifty dollars. The bullets cost eighteen bucks."

Lisa looked suddenly horrified and began to shake a little. "Everyone was worried about me, but then Diane got shot," she said. "The police say the bullet went into a million pieces inside her, but they added them all up and they're pretty sure it was a thirty-eight."

There were four messages on Jane's machine when she got home. One was from Carla. "The story's done," she said. "I think you'll be interested in my angle on repositioning cod for an upscale market." Jane decided not to bother to read Carla's opus. Carla's voice continued: "Can you find out if Norman wants that salmon sidebar, too? And there's another thing. There's something really weird on one of the tapes you gave me. It isn't what your label says at all."

The second call was from Jack Lawson. "Where've you been?" he said. "I've been trying to call you. I'll get back in touch soon. The album's going great." Jane sighed.

The third message was from Norman Carver. "Have you

got that Norwegian cod copy? There's a bunch of faxes here for you. Oh, and some German-sounding guy called for you. I gave him your home number. I hope that's okay." Jane felt a horrible little stab of fear. She had thought she was rid of Gunther Kessler.

The fourth message was a hang-up. Maybe it was Kessler. She tried not to panic and reminded herself that he was probably back in Europe, investigating whatever it was he was supposed to be investigating. Still, before she left the house she chided herself for not having called a home security company yet. She imagined finding the sinister Swiss in her house when she got back from delivering Carla's copy to Norman.

Carla had a big envelope ready, with a hard copy of the story as well as a computer disk. "Did you find out about the salmon sidebar?" she said. "I'm still in the running for that tech writer job, but they told me it might be weeks before they decide. I could use the work, to be honest."

Jane assured Carla she'd pitch the idea to Norm, even though she didn't really want to. She felt sorry for poor Carla and grateful to her for providing her with a cover, but she had also been looking forward to telling Norm to take his job and shove it.

"And here's that weird tape," said Carla. "I don't get it at all. It's creepy."

"What's on it?" said Jane. She recognized the label she'd made herself: "Knutsen. Seattle Speech."

Carla shrugged. "I just listened to a chunk in the middle. It wasn't about fish," she said in the same tone she might have used to say "It wasn't in English."

In the car on her way over to Norman's office, Jane popped the tape into her car stereo, rewound it and began to listen.

A reedy male voice began to declaim in a dreary monotone. "Trygve Knutsen, Assistant Fisheries Ministry of the kingdom of Norway, is our prisoner," said the voice. "He is

being held by soldiers of the Army in Solidarity with Animal
Victims, Cetaceans Division.

"His safe return depends on the actions of his government. Our nonnegotiable demands include: number one—an
immediate moratorium on all whaling in Norwegian waters;
number two—a public apology from the Norwegian government to all cetaceans and the humans in solidarity with
them; number three—the publication of the following statement in the Norwegian newspaper *Aftenposten*, the latter to
be translated into Norwegian.

"When these demands are met, Knutsen will be released
unharmed in a neutral area. The prisoner is being treated hu-
manely and is receiving a healthy, animal-free diet. He has
already expressed regret at the vicious genocide of minke
whales in waters controlled by his government and under-
stands that the temporary inconvenience of his imprisonment
is a small price to pay in order to save innocent lives. But be
forewarned, we are steadfast in our purpose, and the prisoner
will not be released until all conditions are met.

"To prove that we are holding the prisoner, we will send,
in due course, a personal object we have taken from him to
the Norwegian embassy in Washington, D.C."

The Fremont bridge was up. Distracted, Jane had to brake
hard as she entered the line of waiting cars.

She was quite sure that the voice was Curtis Jeffers. He
cleared his throat like a nervous after-dinner speaker and
went on to read the statement he wanted published in Norway.

"All life has certain inalienable rights," he began, and
launched into a rambling treatise based loosely on the phi-
losophy of the Enlightenment as applied to animals, the
whole thing laced with quasi-legalisms and the threatening
pseudomilitary language of 1960s student bombers. "We
have taken up arms in defense of the innocent lives of the
planet," he said. "If necessary, we will sacrifice our own
lives to prevent genocide. Let the oppressors, the torturers,
the killers, all with blood on their hands, be forewarned.

And remember, the innocents who are being slaughtered and cut into pieces all over the globe every second of the day, receive no such warning. We will not rest," he ended, his voice quavering with emotion, "until all that walks on the land or swims in the sea or flies in the air can live freely and without fear of the only truly vicious species—until the day when all the creatures of the planet live in harmony— when every life, regardless of specificity, is lived to the fullest and each creature is free to love and to achieve his or her full creative and spiritual potential."

The monologue was cut off by a muffled bellowing sound in the background. The bellow was repeated. This time Jane could make out Trygve Knutsen's accented and drunken voice yelling, "Yust what de fock is going on?"

CHAPTER EIGHTEEN

When traffic started to move again, Jane found herself shaking. She was pretty sure that the army Curtis had talked about consisted of himself and his gullible girlfriend. "To take up arms" meant stealing a handgun from a Tampax box in a convenience store in Kent. "The prisoner" was a drunk and confused foreigner who thought he was about to get lucky with a cheap pickup. And the idiots hadn't even been clever enough to attach him properly to the radiator. It would all have been a farce, except for the fact that Marcia was dead.

One thing was clear. Trygve Knutsen had never listened to this tape. He certainly hadn't meant to hand it to her. In fact, she remembered him saying he hadn't listened to it. Somehow he'd mistaken this cassette for one with his speech on it. She had to find out how.

And, she realized, she'd have to hand over this recording to the Seattle police. But not before she made a copy.

A flurry of previously mysterious details now made sense. Back in the ladies' room at the Meade Hotel, Marcia had scrubbed away at her hands and said with real anger how much she loathed handling fish. To her they were the corpses of slaughtered innocents. She must have been working at the seafood show in hopes of meeting, then luring, her victim into captivity. In fact, Jane remembered Knutsen was a last

minute substitute for the fisheries minister. He would have
been a bigger fish to fry.

Stacy's description of Marcia's touching farewell with
Curtis clicked into focus, too. Stacy had said he'd kissed her
good-bye as if she were going away on a long trip. In his
mind she was embarking on a heroic mission into enemy territory. Even Curtis's own ramblings made sense now that
Jane had the context. To Curtis, Trygve Knutsen was indeed
a killer—of whales and seals. Presumably he'd told Carla
she had blood on her hands because she worked for a
seafood magazine.

Jane felt particularly dense not to have picked up on the
name change. Diana was the goddess of the hunt. Both Diane
Hunter's names had to do with killing animals, while St.
Francis was their protector and patron saint. Marcia, Jane
thought, must have something to do with Mars and martial
things. Marcia no doubt saw herself as a soldier fighting for
a holy cause. She could imagine the poor ditz going over a
"name your baby" book in search of a new, animal-friendly
handle.

She had plenty to tell the Hunters now. "Your daughter cut
you off because you raise cattle for people to eat. She came
under the sway of a fanatic." She might soften things somewhat by adding: "If she had lived, she might have come to
see things in better balance."

But Marcia hadn't lived. While Jane finally thought she
understood what had motivated her, she still didn't know
who had killed her or why. A loony episode had turned into a
tragedy. What were those stupid kids doing running around
with a gun, anyway? Were they prepared to shoot Knutsen if
he tried to escape? Or to kill themselves in some kamikaze
gesture? Marcia hadn't done that, though. The gun that had
killed her had not been found at the scene.

As Jane pulled into the parking lot at the offices of
Seafood Now magazine, she began to wonder if the board
would go for this case and give her the trust income. She'd
provided the Hunters with investigative services they couldn't

afford—including a trip to Norway—and found out about
their daughter's clandestine life. She felt a heady little rush,
thinking about the life this case might buy her. No more
lucky gigs leaning against white pianos.

It was a struggle to pull herself together and face Norman.
She had hoped he'd be out kissing up to advertisers, but he
was in, hunkered down in his office, surrounded by his
chaotic mass of paperwork. She handed him the envelope
with Carla's article.

"Listen," he said, flinging it aside, "I just got a fax from
Amanda Braithwaite. She could be a potentially big advertiser. She wants you to cover some salmon thing here in
town. It's the first wave of her campaign. Some cooking
demo or something."

Jane started to say, "No way," but remembered Carla. Instead she said, "I interviewed Amanda over in Norway. I
could use that interview and tie it in to this event, whatever it
is." She figured Carla could trot over and check out this
cooking thing. Along with the Amanda tape, she'd have
everything she needed to pry a few more bucks out of Norm.

"By the way, Amanda seems to be expecting the cover,"
she added. Maybe Norm had promised it to someone else,
and she could enjoy watching him squirm.

"She's got it!" said Norm excitedly. "I figure she's good
for a full color insert if we promise her the cover. I'll go with
you to the demo and take a photographer and art direct something we can put on the cover. And we can use a big banner
over the art. 'Salmon Struts It Stuff.' "

Jane's heart sank. If Norm was going to be there, she
couldn't send Carla, she'd have to go herself. Hell. Yet another fishy event. She'd been suckered in because she felt
sorry for Carla. She swore to herself this was the last thing
she'd do for *Seafood Now*. Already she felt it might be quite
a while before she ordered fish in a restaurant again.

Norm rooted around in the teetering piles of paper on his
desk. "This is a pretty fancy thing they're putting on," he
said. "Some kind of TV link-up between several cities." He

shook his head sadly. "I hate to see advertising budgets get gutted by these events. They could have spent the money on pages."

Underneath the phone he found a couple of ivory-colored engraved invitations. "I'm glad she sent that fax," he said. "I'd forgotten about these." He kept one and handed the other to Jane. It said that she and a guest were invited to a salmon tasting and extravaganza at the Four Seasons Hotel the following Wednesday at five o'clock. She sighed, feeling resigned to her fate.

On her way home, Jane bought a blank cassette tape. She stuck the original ransom tape and the blank in her stereo system and made a copy, thankful that her furry intruder had left the system for her to use.

Then she called the Seattle police and told them she had something in her possession relating to the murder of Diane Hunter. She was told a detective would call her back.

Finally she called the Hunters and told them what she had discovered. Barb was on one extension and Phil was on the other.

They were horrified to learn that Marcia had been involved in kidnapping, but equally horrified that she'd become an animal rights crusader. In cattle country that was no doubt high treason.

Jane said she thought it was all Curtis's idea. She didn't know if that was true or not. Actually, Curtis seemed to have done very little other than make the pompous tape. It was Marcia who'd got the gun, lured Knutsen to her house and manacled him.

"This animal thing—it explains a lot," said Barb. "We had no idea."

"If she hadn't cared so much about you," said Jane, "she might have been able to tell you. It sounds like she couldn't figure out how to reconcile the two parts of her life, so she made a complete break. Given time, she might have learned how to deal with it all."

"She raised little calves for the Four-H," said her father,

"and then she turns into one of these animal nuts? It's that bastard she got mixed up with. I hope the cops take care of him."

"But she cried and cried when those calves were sold, didn't she?" said Barb. "She begged to keep them, but we told her they weren't raised as pets. We tried to explain it to her."

"I still have no idea who killed her," said Jane. "This Norwegian could have done it, I suppose. In fear, or something. But he'd already escaped by then. There's a lot that's still unclear. I'll try to talk to him tonight—when it's morning in Norway—and see if he can explain where this tape came from." She also told them that she planned to hand over the tape to the police. It had been a difficult phone call, and she was relieved when she could hang up.

A Seattle police detective arrived to pick up the tape. Detective Olson was a breezy young man in a sports jacket and slacks, with a splashy hand-painted tie and a large high school ring, the same one who had interviewed Jane that first night, after the body was found.

When Jane had first started Uncle Harold's work, she had assumed, based on movies and TV and the mysteries she'd read, that the police would be terribly threatened by an amateur conducting an investigation into a criminal case. She had learned very quickly that they couldn't have cared less. They just kept on gathering facts and putting a case together, and because they were working several cases simultaneously, they didn't have time to wonder what anyone else was doing.

While her first instinct was to impress Olson with her brilliant detective work and to pump him breathlessly for information about the case, she was now sophisticated enough to know that the police always controlled the agenda in any interview and that they weren't about to surrender control of the situation to any well-meaning civilian. She vowed not to gush on or to volunteer a lot of information, but to answer simply but fully and wait for the next question.

"I think this is important," she said, handing him the cassette. "I believe this tape was made by Diane Hunter's boyfriend. I got it from Trygve Knutsen, the Norwegian fisheries official who was staying in the room next to the one where the body was found."

Olson's eyebrows shot up, but all he said was, "Tell me why you think it's her boyfriend."

"I recognize the voice," said Jane.

"I didn't realize you knew the victim," he said, narrowing his eyes. "Or her boyfriend. How are you associated with them?"

Jane took a deep breath. "Diane's parents sought me out to ask me about how I found her body in the bathtub. They were naturally distraught, and they told me they wanted to know more about Diane's life. I offered to help them find out what I could, being here in Seattle and all, and I talked to the boyfriend."

"But you never knew the Hunters before this, did you?"

"No. I got to know them because I was there after Carla found the body."

"Okay. So you volunteered to help them. As a compassionate gesture."

"That's right. They're from out of town and so forth. They seemed overwhelmed."

"So what did you and the boyfriend talk about?"

"Nothing. He wouldn't talk to me. Told me to go away. I just told him her parents had asked me to find out about her life in Seattle. He basically threw me off the porch."

"Okay. And you say Mr. Knutsen gave you the tape?"

"Yes. He told me it was a tape of a speech he gave at the convention." Here Jane was tempted to tell him that she was posing as a fish journalist, but she stopped herself.

"So you spoke with the Norwegian, too," he said. "When was this?"

"Last week."

"Here in Seattle?" said Olson.

"No, in Norway. Her parents asked me to. I was going to be there anyway."

Olson's eyebrows shot up again, but he didn't ask her anything more. "I'll listen to this, and I may get back to you with more questions."

Jane tried not to feel let down. In the movies, of course, the policeman would have sat next to her on the sofa, listened to the cassette on her tape machine, grabbed her by the shoulders and shouted, "That's fabulous. You've answered so many of our questions! Let's go arrest Curtis Jeffers for kidnapping and conspiracy, and then we'll find out who killed Marcia!"

Instead he stuffed the cassette in his pocket and strolled out. Trying not to feel disappointed, Jane turned her attention to the next task before her, which necessitated counting nine hours ahead on her fingers. Knutsen would get to the office around midnight, Seattle time. The police hadn't asked her not to get in touch with him, so she decided to go ahead and call tonight. She wanted to know herself just where this tape had come from.

Knutsen answered with a frightened-sounding "Hello" and seemed relieved when she said she was calling about her article. "The tape you gave me wasn't your speech at all," she said.

"No? I'm sure that's the right one," he said. "Unless the taping service made a mistake."

"The taping service?"

"All these events are recorded. The taping service sells you a cassette if you are wanting one. I ordered it, and it was delivered to my room. It was on my bureau when I packed. I was sure that is what it was."

"I'll check with them," said Jane. "Sorry to bother you."

"So you are really writing about fish?" he asked, sounding more confused than ever.

"Yes," she said in reassuring tones. "You will be able to read all about the salmon campaign."

"I am glad," said Knutsen, adding hastily, "I am afraid I must go," before she had a chance to start in on Marcia or his nocturnal ramblings at the seafood show. Jane hung up feeling certain that Trygve Knutsen had no idea what was on the tape and probably no idea that he'd been the victim of eco-terrorists.

However, what he had said did give Jane an explanation for Marcia's presence back at the hotel. It sounded as if she had come back, after imprisoning Knutsen and changing her clothes, in order to leave the ransom tape. Presumably she'd taken the key to his room from him after he'd passed out.

What happened after that was more speculative. Could Knutsen have escaped, become enraged, found Marcia in his room, attacked her and turned Marcia's own gun on her in some kind of a struggle? But why would he have become enraged? Because his sexual pride was hurt? Because he felt so strongly about Norway's right to harvest its minke whale population? But in that case, how had Marcia ended up next door?

It was late. She was very sleepy. She got ready for bed, wondering if she should tackle Curtis Jeffers in the morning, if possible before the police got to him. That little weasel had a lot to answer for, she decided. Then she remembered his talk about taking up arms. Curtis was pretty scary.

Maybe she should just put together a report on what she had for presentation to the board. She'd provided a distraught family with background on their daughter's life. Answered some nagging questions about their estrangement. Allowed them to get on with their grief. Surely that's what Uncle Harold would have wanted her to do—provide them with investigative services they wouldn't otherwise be able to afford.

It might be enough for the board. But it wasn't enough for Jane. Until the Hunters knew why their daughter had died, she couldn't feel she'd closed the case. But she had no idea how she would ever find out what had happened to Marcia.

CHAPTER NINETEEN

The phone woke her the next morning at eight. Gunther Kessler was on the line.

"What do you want?" she demanded.

"To apologize," he said. "To apologize and to offer you a business proposition."

Jane remembered how badly she had wanted to find out just what Kessler was up to. She didn't accept the apology, but she said, "What did you have in mind?"

"I have learned that you work more or less as a detective."

"How have you learned that?" she asked sharply.

"And I have cleared you of all suspicion in the matter I am investigating."

"How gratifying," she said.

He cleared his throat. "My firm is an excellent one, and we pay well. Occasionally we use freelance operatives who are in a position to get themselves in places we can't. Are you interested in discussing this further?"

"Frankly," said Jane, "I'm not that keen on doing business with someone who goes through my things and treats me like dirt. Just who the hell do you think you are?"

"Mrs. da Silva," Kessler said very politely, "I think you should at least hear me out. First of all, I think you could use the money." Great, she thought, he'd probably checked her Visa balance. "Secondly, I'd like to make up for our recent

unpleasantness by offering you a commission and treating
you with professional respect. To be honest, this case has
been very maddening, and I sometimes become a little ruth-
less when I can't come up with a solution. I'm sure you can
appreciate that."

"All right," said Jane. "All right, we can talk. But no
promises." While Kessler had been sweet-talking her in his
ponderous, overrehearsed way, she had suddenly flashed on
one of the instant rosy scenarios for which she was such a
sucker. His glitzy security firm hired her on a freelance
basis and liked her work. For the first time she would be
paid to investigate something, really paid, and by a client,
not that fusty old board. She would get her foot in the door
and maybe something to start a résumé with. And later, if
all else failed, she could moonlight as an investigator, not a
lounge singer. Who knows? she thought. If she did a good
job, maybe this could get her back to Europe. She figured it
was at least worth a conversation.

She also had another, more disquieting thought. Kessler
had spotted her as a complete phony right away. Why would
he want to hire such a klutz? Jane thought it would be poor
salesmanship to bring that up.

They arranged to meet in the Georgian Room at his hotel,
the Four Seasons Olympic, that evening. She spent the day
wondering if there was some way she could get screwed in
this deal, and with a sense of suspense about just what he
wanted her to do.

With a sinking heart she realized that this very likely had
something to do with fish. Unless, of course, they wanted to
plant her as a lounge singer somewhere. This conjured up a
more amusing picture. She saw herself in a low dive in Ran-
goon or Tangiers or maybe somewhere in the South Seas,
spying on the customers while she belted out torch songs
below a lazy ceiling fan. All filmed in glossy black and
white, of course. She had already begun to plan her wardrobe
for this adventure—bias-cut satin and tarty shoes—when she
brought herself up short. A sentimental attraction to the

clichés of yesteryear was what had messed up her life and
gotten her into becoming a saloon singer in the first place. A
saloon singer pushing forty, she reminded herself grimly,
overly dependent on the kindness of strangers.

Just for the heck of it, she called the Seattle Public Library
quick information service and asked them to check on Gunther Kessler's firm. They transferred her to Business and
Technology, which leafed through some directory and told
her it was a legitimate, privately held company with branch
offices in Paris, Milan, London and Brussels. They even provided her with a phone number of the head office in Zurich.

It was still early enough to call them at the end of their
business day. When she asked for Gunther Kessler, they put
her on hold for a while, then said they would take a message. She said she'd call back and hung up. It sounded as if
Kessler was legit—assuming that was his real name. She
wondered how his bosses would like his pawing through innocent people's luggage. It seemed pretty sleazy for such
an apparently classy firm. If he gave her any more trouble,
she'd figure out a way to make trouble for him.

The Four Seasons Olympic was one of her favorite places
in Seattle—a big, old-fashioned ornate hotel with soaring
ceilings, large potted palms and nice thick carpets. Native
Seattleites still called it the Olympic, while newcomers and
travel agents called it the Four Seasons.

Kessler was already in the restaurant when she arrived. He
rose, touching his lapel in the gesture of a maître d', and
nodded with a grave expression. The idea that she was sitting
down to share a good meal and a bottle of wine with him,
after having kicked him in the knee when they'd last met,
struck her as quite ridiculous. It was his old-world formality
that allowed her to carry it off.

He handed her the menu like someone on a festive date.
"There are a couple of things I'd like to ask you before we
go any further," Jane said.

She put the menu to one side, the gesture meant to imply
that she would stalk out then and there if she didn't like the

answers. Actually she was afraid that if she saw the menu, her resolve would be weakened. The food at the Olympic was sensational.

"First, what makes you think I am some sort of an investigator?" she demanded, staring at him aggressively.

He looked away, narrowing his eyes. After a pause he said, "I learned this from someone in the Norwegian security apparatus. I can't reveal who."

"I see," she said, not really seeing at all. "Okay, now I want a full explanation of why you were searching my room in Bergen."

He sighed, as if they had been over this all before. "I am investigating a case of industrial sabotage. It has taken place in many countries. Your passport shows you haven't traveled to the countries in question. Further investigation showed your connection with the fish business is very recent. In fact, I interviewed a couple of people in Norway who said it was clear you didn't know the first thing about fish." He gave her a little smirk. "Finally, I learned today from the Norwegians just what you were up to."

Presumably this would keep him from spying on her anymore. "You did?"

Kessler nodded once. "Yes. Mr. Knutsen received a call from the Seattle police and learned that you had discovered he was the victim of some kind of terrorist plot. He immediately informed his superiors. The Norwegian government takes any illegal actions of antiwhaling and antifur groups very seriously. Their economy is being threatened by the activities of these groups, and there has also been direct sabotage—a whaling vessel was sunk last year by some California-based group.

"Knutsen told his story, and it became clear what your interest in his movements was. You apparently represented that dead girl's family in some way. The story checked out." He cleared his throat and moved a knife a millimeter to the left. "But in developing your cover, you've put yourself in a position to help us." He leaned forward. "We need you to get close to someone. Someone whom we suspect of being behind a campaign of sabotage.

"We want you to find out if there is a connection between the sabotage and this person. We will pay you very well to ask the questions we want asked. There will be a bonus of twenty thousand dollars if you can get this person to tell you on tape that he is responsible for this sabotage. We will take care of the technical aspects. A simple microphone taped under your clothes."

A waiter came by, and Kessler said, "I wonder if you would be at all interested in the chateaubriand for two."

"Yes, I would be," she said, looking forward to the béarnaise sauce. "Medium rare." They decided to start with hearts of palm salad, and Kessler ran a finger along the wine list and ordered something by number.

"Who is the client?" she asked him.

"The International Salmon Exporters."

"And what makes you think I'll agree?"

"To be blunt, I think you'd like the money," he said. "You are a widow, making your way in the world. It has not always been easy."

"So you've checked up on me?"

He shrugged. "It wasn't too difficult, as I'm sure you can appreciate. Once I learned who your husband was, it was much easier. Bernardo da Silva was quite famous. The Formula One driver. I remember him well."

Yes, thought Jane, and he would have made short work of you, too, going through my suitcase.

Kessler went on, "The Norwegians were interested, too, because of what you found out here in Seattle. They shared information with me. We also know you've been involved in other kinds of investigations—something to do with your family. This part is a little unclear, but not particularly important from our point of view. Anyway, you yourself would check out someone you considered doing business with, wouldn't you? After all, we're both in the business of collecting information."

That's right, thought Jane, except you are professionals with computers and expertise and contacts, and I am a blundering amateur. She dismissed his smarmy, flattering, "we're colleagues" routine with a slight sneer, so he wouldn't think she'd bought into it. "So who is this person you're interested in?" she said.

"Your gallant rescuer. Mr. Robert Putnam."

Jane was astounded. "What? After he rescued me from you, you think I'd turn on him like that?"

"You might." Kessler shrugged. "You don't really know him that well."

"How do you know that?" she asked sharply, irritated by his air of omniscience.

"I watched him speak to you at that presentation in Bergen. When he had no idea he was being observed. He was clearly a man who wanted to get to know you better. I can't imagine him faking that. Also his manner when he came to your rescue. That was very telling. I also checked with the hotel and discovered that the fact he was in the room across from yours was pure coincidence. I eliminated the idea you were in some collaboration, although until I spoke with the Norwegian, it did occur to me."

"What's he suppose to have done?" said Jane.

"Someone has been interfering with farmed salmon all over the world."

"What have they been doing to it?" said Jane.

"Never mind the specifics," Kessler said. "It will be more credible if you don't already know. It will take some time for you to develop a rapport with him. We will pay you a per diem rate, and I'll stay in touch. We will liaise closely."

"What makes you think I won't tell him immediately that you suspect him?"

Kessler smiled. "I think you would rather have twenty thousand dollars. But if you feel loyalty to him, go right ahead. Tell him. If he is guilty, he will stop the sabotage. That in itself will be telling, and will help solve my client's problem. I am not a policeman, trying to bring him to trial. I am someone who works to limit damage to my clients."

"Mr. Kessler," Jane said very firmly, "let's spell it out here. You think I'll sleep with him for twenty thousand dollars, don't you?"

He looked very slightly taken aback. "I don't know what you'd do. But I think he finds you charming, and I think you can probably be very persuasive with any man who feels that way."

Great. He hadn't decided if she were a slut or a tease.

"I don't know yet if I will accept," she said. This was a big fat lie. Twenty thousand would definitely buy her a lot of time away from the Fountain Room or its equivalent. It would also make her less dependent on the board of querulous old men who held her fate in their gnarled, worm-veined hands. Too bad the price she had to pay was dealing with the odious Kessler, who evidently realized only too well that she had her price. Still, the food and beverage manager at the Fountain Room hadn't been much better, and he'd paid a lot less.

"So you will think about it?" Kessler said.

Instead of answering, Jane asked a question of her own. "In your investigation have you come across any connection between your case and the death of Marcia St. Francis?"

"If there is a connection, I'm not sure what it is," he said.

"Is the sabotage related to animal rights?" asked Jane. "Are they letting salmon free?"

Kessler smiled. "Even fanatics would hesitate to do that. One of the ecologists' fears about salmon farming is that escaped fish, bred by man, will create some kind of genetic havoc with wild strains. In Alaska, for instance, where salmon farming is—"

"A hanging offense," said Jane. "That's what Mr. Putnam says." All in all, she thought the other brother, Don, was a better candidate for sabotage. He would clearly have seen interfering with fish farms as a mission from God.

The salad arrived, and Kessler looked it over with the

slightly worried air of a man who feared a bad meal more than anything else. He seemed satisfied, and his face relaxed, especially after he took his first bite. She wondered how much Kessler knew about Marcia and how much the Norwegian security apparatus, whatever that might be, had checked into it. If she could pump Kessler while he was paying her to pump Bob Putnam, she might make herself some money and firm up her case for the board at the same time.

Which was why, halfway through their chateaubriand, Jane agreed to accompany him to the opera the following night. "I have tickets to *La Bohème*," he said with his usual bossy stiffness. "You can give me your answer then." He then looked, for the very first time, just ever so slightly shy. "I don't know how good your opera is here, but Puccini is fairly indestructible, and I'm very fond of him."

"So am I," said Jane.

CHAPTER TWENTY

The next evening Jane was disquieted to discover that she was feeling defensive in a provincial, hometown way. She often found herself comparing Seattle to Europe, where she had spent so many years. Tonight she was seeing everything through Gunther Kessler's cold, cosmopolitan eyes and hoping (rather pathetically, she felt) that it would all meet with his approval.

Was this because she lived here now and wanted to believe that coming home hadn't been some sort of retreat? Or was it because Gunther Kessler had always been so damned patronizing on a personal level?

She hoped Gunther wouldn't be put off by the newness and the scale of the opera house. Built in the sixties, it was simple and streamlined. The carpeted lobby, with an open staircase leading up one flight to the row of doors that led to the orchestra seats, had the look of a pleasant airport waiting area. There was, she decided, something very Seattle about it all. No vulgar fountains or chandeliers, no pretending to be more than it actually was.

The audience, too, had a low-key look, quietly underdressed and with a relaxed manner that some visitors found bland, others refreshingly self-contained.

Jane had pegged old Gunther for a Wagnerian. This wasn't just cultural stereotyping, she told herself; there was definitely something Teutonic about him that went beyond his bearing and his accent. His fondness for Puccini had been more than a surprise, it had given her hope. Perhaps they could develop enough fellow feeling that she could worm out of him whatever he had learned about Marcia's death.

He didn't seem to blanch at the English supratitles, projected above the proscenium arch—Jane felt sure a lot of Europeans would have sneered at that, and the orchestra sounded solid to her ears, which cheered her up. Sitting next to him, she sensed him relax along with her as soon as it became clear the singers had good voices.

As act one unfolded, she forgot about Gunther Kessler entirely and became involved in the opera, listening to Mimi and Rodolfo get to know each other in the dark and the cold, fumbling charmingly, suspensefully, with candles, key and Mimi's frozen little hand. When Rodolfo opened the window, stage snow falling gently outside the casement and stage moonlight rushing in illuminating Mimi, and then began to sing "O soave fanciulla," Jane became aware of her companion again. There was a sense of heightened tension coming from the body just a few inches away from her side.

After Mimi's voice had joined Rodolfo's in mutual, newfound, impassioned love, and the audience, with the usual Seattle enthusiasm, had produced thunderous applause and a chorus of bravos, Jane found herself casting a sideways glance at Gunther. She was amazed and touched to see that his eyes, like hers, were glazed with tears.

Oh, hell! she thought. He's as big a sap as I am. By the time Mimi coughs her last, we'll probably fall into each other's arms, weeping. Jane knew that Italian opera could have an aphrodisiac effect on her, and even someone as unlikely as Gunther Kessler, if he were similarly afflicted and went ahead and lunged, could benefit from her weakness.

By the time the curtain fell on Rudolfo's despairing cries of "Mimi! Mimi!" Jane had managed to pull herself together. Those bohemians should have found themselves day jobs, she told herself, trying to overlook the fact that their plight reminded her unsettlingly of her own on the many occasions she had reached the financial edge. Of course, she reasoned, if it happened today, Mimi probably could have cleared up those lungs with modern antibiotics. But there was no cure for love. She left the opera house in a haze of melodious passion and heightened emotional intensity. Gunther, silent at her side, seemed equally moved.

What she saw as they left the building, however, changed her mood entirely. An antifur demonstration was going on. A group of outrageously costumed people with big signs were haranguing elderly ladies in old-fashioned mink jackets and a few younger women in more stylishly cut furs. The demonstrators were wearing ratty old thrift store fur coats daubed with crusty red paint, a street theater look that was meant to horrify. Presumably it was all right to wear fur if it prevented others from doing so.

A big, soft-faced woman swathed in distressed weasel snapped, "Killer!" at a frail, white-haired lady in a tailored Persian lamb jacket that looked as if it had been in the family for generations. Jane was alarmed to see the old lady startle and step back a pace, tottering a little on her patent-leather high heels. Gunther looked alarmed and sprang forward, but she regained her footing.

When Jane passed, the weasel woman smiled sweetly and said, "Thank you for not wearing fur."

Jane hissed back, "What I choose to wear is none of your damn business," and walked on.

Then she spotted the creature she'd encountered in her house, wearing the same ratty gray squirrel number, now smeared with red paint. But this time there wasn't a knobby head covered with a ski mask—just the sallow, fanatic face of Curtis Jeffers. He had a big stick with him, with smaller horizontal sticks attached to the top, like something from a religious procession. From the crosspieces hung a nasty-looking animal trap with sharp steel teeth from which dangled a grisly, red-streaked antique fur scarf made of the heads and tails of some kind of ferrety creature. Another exhibit was hanging there: a red-streaked sealskin slipper, just like the one Jane had seen on one of Trygve Knutsen's feet the night he was questioned by the police.

She stopped and stared. Curtis hadn't noticed her and was now jumping up and down, chanting, "You're wearing carcasses. You have blood on your hands." Why hadn't the police arrested him after she'd given them that ransom tape? Instead he was still carrying on bullying people. No doubt he thought anything he did for the cause, from rudeness to abducting people, was perfectly justified.

And how the hell had he gotten his hands on that slipper? Jane decided to tell the police about that. While she was at it, she could tell them she'd identified the coat belonging to the intruder she'd grappled with.

She turned to Gunther. "I have to make a phone call," she said, looking around for a booth.

He pointed into the outer lobby of the opera house. "There's one back there," he said.

"Keep an eye on the guy in the bloody fur with the stick," said Jane.

"No problem," Gunther said. "He's not the sort you can easily lose in a crowd." Curtis was now jumping up and down and keening, perhaps trying to duplicate the cries of a trapped animal.

Jane called 911. She didn't think for a minute she'd be able to do anything other than leave a message for Detective Olson.

Much to her delight, the dispatcher, after clacking audibly on a keyboard, said a patrol car would be by soon and asked Jane to stay where she was and make no attempt to communicate with "the individual in question."

Jane also asked if she could leave a specific message for Detective Olson. "Curtis Jeffers has a sealskin slipper that is exactly like one Trygve Knutsen lost the night he was abducted," she said. "He's standing in front of the opera house with it." The dispatcher asked her to spell Trygve Knutsen.

Shortly after she hung up, she heard sirens. She had rejoined Gunther, who was standing by a bed of azaleas with the air of a man waiting impatiently for his wife. Most of the crowd had dispersed, and the demonstrators were already packing up their signs and props.

When the police car pulled up, the woman who'd thanked Jane for not wearing fur looked pleased and excited. "Wow. They're going to arrest us? Awesome!"

One of the policemen got out of the car, came up to the group and said, "Any of you guys Curtis Jeffers?"

They all looked at each other. Curtis said, "Civil disobedience!" The furry little group immediately fell to the ground, and the policeman rolled his eyes.

Jane stepped forward. "He's the one," she said, pointing to the mound that was Curtis. His grisly exhibits lay beside him. "And that slipper may be a piece of evidence in a murder investigation."

"Okay," said the policeman, looking as if he were humoring her. "You the one who called?"

"Yes," she said. "It's Detective Olson's case."

He nodded and touched Curtis delicately with his toe. "Are you Curtis Jeffers?" he said.

"We have a perfect right," began Curtis, "to protest senseless slaughter—"

"I don't care about any of that," said the policeman. "I've been asked to take you downtown to answer a few questions. You coming along to help us out?"

"No," said Curtis, now sitting cross-legged on the concrete pavement and apparently trying to think of a way to get back up on his feet without looking silly. The other bundles of fur began to uncurl and blink with curiosity, as if coming out of hibernation.

"Okay," said the policeman, reaching for a pair of handcuffs on his belt. "I'm arresting you."

"What's the charge?" Curtis shouted.

"You have a whole mess of outstanding parking warrants. You've been ignoring those little postcards that keep coming to your house, Curtis. And today is the day of reckoning."

"I demand that you arrest me for defending innocent lives," said Curtis, standing up. For the first time, it seemed, he noticed Jane. He looked confused.

"You know what?" said the policeman with a big smile. "I'm a police officer. I arrest people, and I decide the charge, not you. Sorry it's not more glamorous."

Jane turned to Gunther. "We can go now," she said quietly.

Gunther, incredibly correct, didn't ask any questions. It rather irritated her that he wasn't curious, but she didn't volunteer anything, either. Let him think she could make a phone call and get someone arrested. She wondered if and when she'd be able to find out what the police got out of Curtis tonight.

Gunther suggested that they go for coffee or a drink. They ended up on Queen Anne Avenue, in a cozy little place with Mozart coming out of the speakers, and ordered a couple of coffees.

"For about a year now," said Gunther, "as I told you, someone has been interfering with farmed salmon around the world. All the salmon producers kept quiet about the problem, because they all suspected each other. Eventually, it came out that everyone was being affected: the Norwegians, the Chileans, the Scots, the Canadians and even some of the few American farms. That's when they stopped fighting each other and hired me.

"Whoever is doing this has to have had access to farms all over the world. That's why I was so interested in you. You had an entrée to various facilities and seemed not to be what you said you were."

"I'll see what I can find out," said Jane. "But if Putnam's responsible, I can't imagine him telling me or anyone else that he's been running around poisoning fish or anything."

"Probably not," said Gunther, gazing with interest at a pastry cart. "But his brother is another matter entirely." He looked back at her. "I think I would like a napoleon," he said. "How about you?"

"An éclair, please," said Jane. "Tell me why you think the Putnams have something to do with this."

"They're from the wild salmon sector. Robert has traveled to the countries involved and visited farms. He always talks about promoting salmon across the board, while his brother makes outrageous, threatening statements about salmon farming. There seems to be an element of religious mania." He leaned forward. "And the brother also appears to have a criminal background." He raised a hand imperiously and ordered the pastry from the waitress who came over.

When they were alone again he said, "Donald Putnam has spent time in prison for drug trafficking. And he has been arrested several times for assault. Yet his brother continues to associate with him and keeps him in the business."

"They're an odd pair all right," said Jane. "But tell me more about this sabotage. What seems to be the point of it? Is someone trying to kill all the farmed salmon in the world?"

Gunther shook his head. "All you need to know is that the fish is being made unmarketable. This causes financial hardship for the farmers. If the public learned of this, the long-term effect could be disastrous. Farmed salmon could be completely discredited."

Jane shrugged and tried not to look hurt that he didn't trust her with whatever nameless horrors were being perpetrated on salmon. "I'll see what I can find out," she said. "How do you suggest I go about this?"

"Tomorrow there is a big reception to launch the generic campaign. Putnam will be there, with his brother. I asked Amanda Braithwaite to make an effort to get you there, too."

"Yes, she sent a fax. I'll be there all right," said Jane. "I can start ingratiating myself with the Putnams right away."

"If I were you," Gunther said, gazing analytically at his napoleon as the waitress set down their pastries, "I would start by telling Robert what a terrific job he did rescuing you from me in Bergen, and how much you appreciate his cowboy style."

CHAPTER TWENTY-ONE

The Spanish ballroom at the Olympic Hotel was lined with more long tables bearing plates of fish. Jane felt she had spent a lot of time lately in rooms lined with fish-laden tables. She sighed, accepted her name tag from a woman at a card table by the entrance and got herself a glass of Chardonnay from the bar set up along one side of the room.

There was no sign of the Putnam brothers, but she was surprised to run into Carla, decked out in another bad power suit. This time it was kelly green with matching pumps. Carla explained that she was attending as a representative of the Women's Seafood Network. "I wouldn't have missed it for the world," she said. "It's a milestone in salmon promotion."

"Great," murmured Jane, who realized that she had completely forgotten to tell poor Carla about the salmon sidebar. "Go ahead and write this event up and I'll give it to Norm. I already fixed it. Tie in the Braithwaite interview on the tape I gave you."

Carla looked thrilled.

Jane sipped her wine and surveyed the room, looking for the Putnams. "Carla, didn't you say there was some kind of problem with farmed salmon? Some rumors or others?"

"That's right," said Carla. "Some pigmentation thing. No one knows if it's a disease or what."

"Pigmentation? You mean color?"

Carla nodded. "Of course, in farmed salmon, pigmentation is something you can control."

"What do you mean?"

"Fish farmers decide how red they want the flesh to be and add carotenoids to the feed in the final grow-out stage," said Carla, apparently startled that this wasn't common knowledge.

"Carotenoids?"

Carla nodded. "The reason wild salmon are pink is they eat tiny crustaceans with red shells. Farmed salmon get a dose of shrimp or krill, or sometimes a synthetic version that's chemically identical. Otherwise they'd be very pale. Like albinos."

"So albino fish have been cropping up?"

"I'm not sure what the problem is. There are just rumors that lots of fish have been destroyed because their pigmentation is all wrong, and no one knows why. Everyone in the industry has been denying it." Carla clicked her tongue. "Norm didn't want me to follow it up. Typical."

"Norm's coming tonight," said Jane. "With a photographer. Will it be too hard for you to face him?"

"This industry is big enough for both of us," Carla declared boldly. "He can't intimidate me." She tossed her head. "I've dealt with a lot worse than Norm."

Carla, Jane realized, knew an awful lot about the fish business. Maybe she had some goods on the Putnams. "Didn't you say Don Putnam gave you a hard time?" she asked.

"He threatened to smash my computer," said Carla. "Said he'd come after me and smash it in front of my eyes. I kind of hinted that I'd heard something about their company. A price-fixing thing. I think that's what bugged him, but he said he wanted to get me for writing an editorial explaining that aquaculture was the only answer to the problem of dwindling resources and increased global demand for seafood. He's nuts."

"I wonder why his brother puts up with him," said Jane.

"The word is," Carla said, "that Don went to prison on that drug rap, but Bob was in it, too." She shrugged. "A lot of fishermen arrive in Dutch or Kodiak, they have a big roll of cash and they've been clean and sober for a long time. Back when cocaine was big, Don Putnam was waiting for them at the dock. Maybe Bob can't unload him because Don knows where a few bodies are buried."

"Are they legit now?" Jane asked.

"When the whole thing blew, Bob made a big thing about going into rehab and cleaning up," said Carla. "More than a few people in the industry were into cocaine back then. It wasn't that unusual."

A crackling microphone indicated that the festivities were about to start. A large woman in a beaded chiffon gown standing at a lectern announced that she was privileged to introduce the winning chefs in the salmon competition. "But first," she gushed, "we'll hear from Amanda Braithwaite in New York and see what those artistes in the Big Apple came up with." Behind her, on a giant TV screen, appeared the round, eager face of Amanda Braithwaite.

"Welcome, everybody!" she shouted at the camera. "Welcome, San Francisco, Chicago and Seattle, to what I hope will be the first of many national and international salmon galas."

The camera pulled back to reveal a crowded room, with lots of people chatting and ignoring Amanda's remarks. With the time difference, Jane assumed the crowd there had got through a lot more Chardonnay than the sedate group who stared politely up at the screen here.

"I think I'll go mingle," Jane said to Carla. She set off in search of her quarry, finding instead Norm and a photographer. She waved to them and kept on going. On the screen Amanda was holding up a plate and saying something about a salmon Wellington with pureed root vegetables and guacamole sauce.

Over by the bar she found not Bob Putnam, but Don. He was wearing a coat and tie. A fishhook tie tack imprisoned a hand-painted number with a setting sun and a flock of birds ascending from a lagoon. "Hi," she said, "remember me?"

"Oh, yeah," he said. "You got Carla's old job. I'm glad she's gone. The industry doesn't need her kind."

Jane wondered if he actually would have smashed her computer if she hadn't been fired. "Gee, I'm surprised to see you here," she said. "A lot of this salmon is farmed."

He scowled. "My brother says we have to do business with these guys."

"You think there's anything wrong with their fish?" said Jane.

"Who knows what kind of chemicals they put in that shit?" he said.

"Have you heard anything about any problem with color?" she asked.

Don was about to answer, perhaps with quotations from scripture, when his brother approached.

"Hello, Bob," said Jane, giving him a big, warm smile. "I can't thank you enough for taking care of my intruder over there in Bergen."

Bob, looking genuinely concerned, said, "Did you know the guy is here in Seattle? When I was walking through the lobby of this hotel, I saw him talking to the desk clerk. I guess he's staying here. Has he been bothering you again?"

"Hey!" Don barked. "He better not. Because Bob already told him to leave you alone. He told me all about it. If I see him, I'll be all over him."

"Maybe you should have called the cops on him in Norway," said Bob.

"Screw the cops!" said Don. "We take care of our own shit."

Bob ignored this, as he did all the outrageous remarks his brother made. After years of hanging around with his brother, he had presumably developed the ability to tune out his ramblings. "Did you ever find out what he was investigating?" he said to Jane.

"I think he was checking into the murder that happened at the seafood show."

"You mean that little demo girl?" said Bob. "Who would hire him to check into a murder case in Seattle? The police take care of that stuff. And why on earth would he go through your stuff?"

He had a point. Once again Jane had come up with a lame cover story.

She shrugged and said, "I don't know. I was the one who reported it to the police. Maybe he thinks I know more than what I told them. Personally, I think he's just a creep."

Bob jerked a thumb toward the TV screen, where Amanda was kissing a chef and waving a fond farewell to the camera. "Remember her?" he said with an easy smile. "You stood me up to have dinner with her, and here she is again, via satellite."

"And now," Amanda was saying, "come in *Chicago!*"

The screen danced and flickered for a second, and then with a crackle of static, a man in a dinner jacket with a horrible maroon cummerbund and matching tie and handkerchief came on screen. Standing next to him were three chefs whose toques were cut off by the screen. They stood in an awkward row, holding up plates of food.

"A real cross-cultural application, using fresh local ingredients," gushed the host, reading from a three-by-five card. "Our first-prize winner: salmon with cornmeal, black bean sauce and whitefish roe, drizzled with a piquant sauce of wild huckleberry."

The camera lovingly caressed the bizarre winning entry, which on the giant screen looked like a landscape of some distant planet. The chef's huge pink thumbs peeped over the rim of the plate.

"Maybe we can take a rain check on dinner," said Jane, smiling nicely at Bob.

"I'm heading back up to our plant in Anacortes tonight, but I'll be back down here next week," Bob said.

"Oh, really?" said Jane, who wanted to get her project up

and running immediately and liked the idea of impressing Gunther with what a fast worker she was. "I'm going to be up that way this week myself. Any good restaurants up there?"

Bob produced a business card with the name of his fish-processing company. "Call me as soon as you get to town," he said. "I'll show you around the plant, too. Maybe you can give us a little more ink. We just put in another slime line, and we've got a new filleting machine that'll knock your socks off."

"I just can't see enough fish-processing plants," Jane said brightly in a Carla voice, thinking of the wet concrete floors, the chilly, fishy-scented air, the stainless-steel equipment spotted with blood and fish scales, the unflattering gum boots, coveralls and hair nets issued to visitors.

"Tell her about the pollock roe separator!" Don put in loudly.

A thin man standing nearby shushed them. "They're announcing the Seattle winners," he said in a peevish voice. Don glared at him and scowled into his drink.

"I think you'll agree," said the woman in beaded chiffon from the podium and also, in a nightmarishly huge version, from the giant screen visible over her own shoulder, "that Seattle has the most totally unique dish of all."

Jane wondered if there were such a thing as "most totally unique" and also doubted whether anyone could top the peculiar and pretentious dishes that had just been honored.

"Get a close-up of this," the woman said enthusiastically. "A world premiere that will send shock waves through the culinary community! I'm thrilled to introduce to the world blue salmon with chanterelle mushrooms, couscous and a mango-and-chili chutney. And ladies and gentlemen, we don't mean blue in the sense of rare. Although I'm sure you'll agree it's rare in the sense of totally unique."

An audible "ah" went around the room as the plate was displayed. The salmon was blue all right, sky blue, the color of the light blue crayon in a box of Crayolas.

The man with the peevish voice gasped. "It's gorgeous! Like a classic pair of faded jeans," he said. "I can see it on a bed of blue polenta. I'm calling my editor in New York tomorrow and telling her we've *got* to get this on the cover."

Jane turned around and read his name badge. He was a stringer for a glossy food magazine.

Up on the podium, Norm Carver was gesturing to the plate as his photographer crouched in front of it and squinted. Evidently blue salmon was going to make the cover of *Seafood Now,* too.

The mistress of ceremonies put an arm around the chef, who was looking tired of holding the plate. "Tell us your secret, Carlos," she said. "How did you get it that beautiful blue all the way through? I've been told it tastes just like regular salmon."

"I was just lucky," said the chef. "I bought the fish whole, and when I opened it up, it was blue. I thought it would make a fabulous presentation, so I devised a recipe that would work really well visually, as well as offer an interesting palate profile and incorporate some of our northwest specialties and a few new-world, Pacific-rim type touches."

"Amanda in New York, what do you think?" gushed the woman in beaded chiffon.

The screen popped back to Amanda's face. It was scowling, and little tears seemed to be springing up in her eyes. Her pretty English skin looked red and blotchy. Her distress was particularly unnerving, considering her screen face was about the size of a Ping-Pong table.

"We'll release a statement about this soon," she said in a tense, trembly voice. "But I think it's important to stress that farmed salmon is a safe, natural food, rich in nutrients. We'll be giving the blue salmon careful scrutiny in the lab to establish a nutritional profile."

Great PR woman, thought Jane. She's got a winner and she's in damage control mode. Somehow, bringing up lab work didn't sound particularly appetizing.

"They must have put something in the feed," said Jane. "Like carotenoids but blue."

Bob nodded his agreement. He didn't seem to be gloating or anything.

"Blue salmon," said Don. "That's ridiculous! How do they do that? Jesus, what a stupid thing! Who wants to eat blue salmon?" He began to laugh heartily. "It's really stupid."

"Yes," she said, smiling at him. "Maybe it's some kind of a joke. I think it's pretty funny. Whoever pulled it off is pretty damn smart." Come on, Don, she added silently. Confess. There's twenty-thousand bucks in it for me.

CHAPTER TWENTY-TWO

"Why didn't you tell me they were turning salmon blue?" Jane was calling from the house phones off the lobby with a report for Gunther.

"How did you find out? Did Putnam tell you that?" Kessler sounded almost excited.

"The whole world found out, Gunther," she said. "And I think it's going to be a big hit. I'd say you'll be able to get a premium price for blue salmon any day. The winning recipe at this little salmon bake was blue salmon all fussed up with some other things, and the foodies adored it."

"My clients will be horrified," said Gunther. "Every time a batch of these damn things shows up, they've managed to destroy them as quietly as possible. All the research shows people hate to eat blue things."

"Roquefort cheese is very chic," said Jane. "And squid ink is sort of navy blue, isn't it? No one minds that. It seems to me blue potatoes were fashionable a few years back. And there are blue tortilla chips—"

Gunther cut her off. "The clients will be horrified," he repeated. "It's more important than ever that the perpetrators be stopped. What about the Putnams?"

"I'm having dinner with Bob in Anacortes this week."

"Where's that?"

"North of here. He wants to show me his fish plant. He must be in love."

"I'll take you up there," said Gunther. "We can wire you for sound."

"Be careful. Anacortes is a pretty small town. Bob has already spotted you in the lobby."

"I'll handle it discreetly," Gunther said with his characteristic pompousness. He cleared his throat to indicate a change of topic. "While you were looking at blue salmon, I was watching the local news. That strange fellow you denounced to the police at the opera yesterday, he's been arrested. In connection with the plot against the Norwegians. Apparently he's confessed everything."

"Everything?" said Jane.

"He's admitted that he and the girl were trying to kidnap Knutsen. I just phoned my contact at the Norwegian Fisheries Ministry. Their chief antiterrorist operative is coming over here to interview this Jeffers. He'd like to talk to you, too. Do you mind? I told him I could arrange it."

"All right," said Jane, thinking that Gunther was trying to take credit for arranging something the Norwegians could have arranged themselves, simply by phoning her up. "Did Jeffers confess to murdering Marcia or anything, by any chance?"

"No. But he is already out on bail, he's got himself a lawyer and the television says he's having a press conference at nine tomorrow morning."

Jane had thought she wouldn't have a chance to ask Curtis Jeffers any questions. But there certainly wasn't anything odd about a reporter for a fish magazine covering a case involving a fisheries minister. She was there the next morning, front and center, when Curtis came in, looking thrilled at all the attention he was getting.

With him was his lawyer, an avuncular but driven older man with wispy white hair and a crumpled suit. Jane knew about James Marshall Embree, a fixture around Seattle. He was a headline-grabbing defense lawyer, stuck in a town with a depressing dearth of celebrity crimes.

There just weren't very many cases in which limo driver witnesses, au pairs and shirttail relatives could retail their stories to supermarket tabloids and *Hard Copy*. Embree had to make do with the occasional University of Washington football star picked up for shoplifting or a local TV news anchor busted for drunk driving. Curtis Jeffers, by virtue of his eccentricity, was about as spectacular as it was going to get around here, and the old guy was clearly milking the case for all it was worth.

Jane eavesdropped on two reporters in front of her. A woman with big tousled hair said, "How can this little wienie afford Embree? Is he taking it on pro bono?"

Her companion, a young Asian man, laughed. "Word is the guy inherited a bundle from some old aunt as long as he takes care of her cats up in some old pile on Capitol Hill."

Jane remembered the smell of cat that came from the Jeffers house. Apparently Curtis's love of animals had paid off.

Embree approached the microphone and said, "I think you'll find that Curtis is an idealistic young man, an unusual, gentle man who sees nature not as others see it, but as an incredible manifestation of God's creation, a man who sees the animals who share our planet as brothers and sisters."

Jane noted Embree was wearing a belt made from one of Curtis's brothers and sisters, either an alligator or crocodile, and she doubted he'd ever ordered a soyburger in his life. But the old boy had a messianic light in his blue eyes as he discussed Curtis's spiritual qualities. His face now took on a sorrowful cast, and he said softly, breathing into the microphone, "He was also a young man who fell in love with a young woman, a strong-minded woman, and came heavily under her influence." Embree put his arm around Curtis's shoulder and squeezed. The party line seemed to be the guy was well-meaning, and anyway, Marcia made him do it. Marcia, of course, wasn't around to contradict this.

"What's he been charged with?" yelled out a reporter, who identified himself as with the *Seattle Times*.

Embree answered, "False imprisonment," in a derisive tone. "A ridiculous charge! The alleged victim flew out of Sea Tac Airport the night he was supposedly detained. The whole thing is ridiculous."

"What about the tape with the ransom demand?" said Jane, shocked at her ability to yell out questions just like the people on CNN, but too embarrassed to preface her question with "Jane da Silva, *Seafood Now* magazine."

"I don't see the significance of any piece of evidence the prosecution wants to wave around, when no crime has been committed," Embree snapped, and turned to point to a TV newsperson who was combing his hair and checking himself out in a little mirror.

"The police say they have a ransom type tape," the TV reporter said, stashing comb and mirror in his pocket while the camerawoman who accompanied him got a shot of his thoughtful face. "Do you deny that the voice on the tape is that of Curtis Jeffers?"

Embree laughed. "Curtis says a lot of things. As I say, he's an unusual young man. In fact, Curtis is going to make a statement himself later, aren't you, Curtis?" Curtis nodded happily.

"Did Curtis go to Trygve Knutsen's hotel room?" yelled Jane.

"The details of the evening in question," Embree said calmly, "will come out in due course."

Jane piped up again, "What about the kidnap victim's slipper? How did Curtis get a hold of it?" The other reporters looked at her with curiosity. A couple of them whispered to each other.

Embree waved his hand as if she were bringing up a trivial point. "My client has already told the police that he drove his companion, Marcia St. Francis, to the Meade Hotel. There's no dispute about that. He was in Mr. Knutsen's room. Marcia St. Francis had the key to that room. An item of clothing—a slipper—was removed from that room. We're not saying it wasn't. But none of this is really at issue. The state must prove a crime was committed."

Just what the hell had Curtis been doing at the hotel? Killing Marcia? Maybe there was some kind of accident with the gun, Jane thought. Curtis was crazy enough to do anything.

"Your client's lover, Marcia St. Francis, was found dead in the next room later that night," she said, indignant at Embree's cavalier manner. "What does he know about that?" There were some gasps around the room.

Embree held up his hand. "My client has not been charged with murder. The issue here is a matter of some alleged inconvenience to a representative of an unrepentant whaling nation."

He narrowed his eyes. "As for the Norwegian government's knowledge of the tragic event to which you refer, I cannot comment on an ongoing criminal investigation."

The implication seemed to be that the Norwegian government had murdered Marcia for trying and failing to fasten a drunken lecher to a radiator. Jane wanted to ask Embree if he thought the Norwegian government maintained a prowhaling hit squad that they sent around the world to rub out ditzy kids like Marcia and Curtis. The disturbing part was, she thought, that a lot of people would like to buy that. There was an alarming tendency for people to want to believe in complex conspiracy theories rather than in simple, ugly answers.

Embree turned away from her and took another question. A woman wanted to know if Curtis Jeffers was a part of any large, underground animal rights movement.

"No, no," Embree said with a throaty chuckle. "Curtis got involved in this movement because of his own personal convictions." He looked grave again. "And of course, he fell in love with a woman whose judgment . . ."

Suddenly Detective Olson appeared at Jane's side. "Mrs. da Silva," he said. "I didn't know you were a member of the press. The first time we met you were singing in the Fountain Room at the Meade Hotel. Next, you're working for Marcia St. Francis's family as some kind of investigator. Now, you're part of the press corps."

He skipped a beat, and Jane just shrugged.

"I guess you're also an operagoer. I got your message last night. It was helpful to have Mr. Jeffers located. I'd already arranged to have him picked up on some old warrants so we could talk. But I gotta say, I'm more than a little curious about you. Could we have a cup of coffee after this is over?"

"Of course," said Jane.

Embree now introduced Curtis, who flapped some papers and began his statement in his flat, monotonous voice. "Many aeons ago, when the first cell divided," he began, "the first precious strands in the web of life . . ."

In front of Jane, the reporter with the tousled hair muttered, "Jesus Christ."

Around about the time Curtis described the first creatures emerging from the sea on stubby fins, a voice from the back of the room called out, "Will copies of this be available?" Jane imagined the room would be completely cleared long before Curtis worked his way up the evolutionary scale to mammals. The more off-the-wall Curtis sounded, the happier Embree looked. He smiled down at the press as if to say "What did I tell you? This guy's just a simple-minded loon. Forget about sending him to the slammer. He's not scary enough."

After Curtis finally wound down with a complaint about the lack of availability of a vegan menu at the county jail ("unborn chicken embryos and the mothers' milk of captive animals may be part of a so-called vegetarian diet to the authorities, but to right-thinking people, they are stolen products"), Jane went across the street with Detective Olson. First the pair of them had to fend off a handful of reporters who wanted to talk to him about the case and to her about the slipper she'd brought up.

Olson managed to deflect them all and took Jane's elbow,

escorting her through the gauntlet. "She's getting an exclusive interview?" a woman pouted. "Who is she, anyway?"

Once they were installed in a corner table at the nearest Starbuck's, Olson seemed to want to know the same thing.

"There isn't much to it, really," Jane said. "I went over there to Norway and talked to Knutsen, and he accidentally gave me the ransom tape. But I also remembered that slipper." She leaned across the table. "When you interviewed me, I got a glimpse of Knutsen and noticed that he only had one slipper on."

Olson nodded as if to say he'd noticed that, too.

"In Norway, he said he'd never found the other one. But Knutsen also told me Marcia wouldn't go up to his room. She wanted him to get in her car and go with her." Jane said she thought that after Marcia had ineffectually locked up Knutsen, she had changed and gone back to the hotel to leave that tape. The slipper, Jane felt, was no doubt the "piece of personal property" referred to in the tape. They had meant to take something from his room to prove they held Knutsen—and were no doubt thrilled at its symbolic content.

"But now," said Jane, "Curtis says he was there, too. He has to say that, because he has the slipper. What does he say happened to Marcia?"

"Jeffers made a complete statement," said Olson. "We've released the basic facts. Jeffers says they were in the room when they heard Knutsen coming back. It all fits. The desk clerk remembered Knutsen coming back to the hotel and saying he'd left his key in his room, and they gave him another one. Curtis says when they suddenly heard him coming back into the room, she was over by the connecting door, opened it and went into the next room. He was by the main door, so he popped into the closet, clutching the slipper.

"Then, while Knutsen was in the shower, Jeffers says he sneaked out the door leading to the hall and waited for Marcia at the car. She never showed, so he finally went home." Olson shrugged as if to say "You figure it out."

"Knutsen did take a shower," Jane said. "His hair was wet.

And that's why I guess you couldn't check him for powder burns or anything."

Olson just smiled. "It's a pretty weird case, to be honest. And you've come up with the tape and the slipper. Got anything else you think might come in handy?"

Jane was absolutely delighted. This was the way policemen in books acted, grateful for help from the talented amateur. "Not on me," she said.

He narrowed his eyes and gave her a this-is-serious look. "But I also want to ask you to keep a low profile. There's been a lot of media attention because of this animal rights thing. Everyone loves whales, right? And the fact that Jeffers has retained John Marshall Embree makes it a high-profile case. I'd hate to see you get hooked into some media hype thing, because we might need you as a witness at some point." He leaned across the table and gave her a sincere look. "If there's a chance you'll be a witness in any case involving Curtis Jeffers, his attorney will try to get some mileage from the fact that you were at the press conference, grilling Curtis about stuff in the evidence locker."

"I'm sorry," she said. "I don't want to jeopardize any case you're working on. If you find out who killed Marcia, I want you to get a conviction."

"That's very gratifying," he said.

She hoped he'd ask her about any theories she'd developed about the case and, in return, share his. Instead he asked for the check and said, "Anything else comes up, let *me* know. Me, not the press. Okay?"

"Okay," she said.

She wondered if she should have told him about the blue salmon. Curtis Jeffers might well have had something to do with all that. It might have been his way of protesting salmon farming. But she decided that first she'd see how far she could get with Gunther's theory that the Putnams were responsible.

And above all, how close she could get to Gunther's offer of twenty thousand dollars.

CHAPTER TWENTY-THREE

Jane found herself somewhat annoyed that Gunther had organized her mission to Anacortes with Swiss precision. Of course, this was his gig and she was being well paid, but she also realized she liked doing things her own way, making them up as she went along.

Before they set out, he briefed her in her living room over coffee. Immaculately tailored, legs crossed, relaxed but all business, he snapped open a briefcase and presented her with a neatly typed sheet of paper, describing the stories she would say brought her to Anacortes. A trip to a state-of-the-art seafood plant, owned by the American subsidiary of a large Japanese company. A story on the history of Anacortes, which at the turn of the century had been a big center for fish canning, salt cod, halibut processing and fish rendering. Hardly something she'd want to read in the dentist's office, she thought.

Gunther's backgrounder helpfully added the fact that Anacortes was a misspelling of a Hispanic lady's name, but that the locals had called her Annie Curtis instead of Anna Cortez.

They would drive up in Gunther's rental car. Jane would stay at an old period hotel, which he assured her had been completely refurbished. "It is really very nice," said Gunther. "So often these restored old hotels are done up so pretentiously. They must have spent a fortune, and they've done a pretty good job. It is like a small European hotel."

"You sound like a travel agent, not a detective," said Jane.

Gunther smiled. "My parents ran a very nice hotel in Lucerne," he said. "I know a lot about the hotel business."

"Including how to get in and out of hotel rooms," said Jane. "Where will you be staying?"

He looked pained but brave. "There is a rather grim motel just a block away."

"I see," said Jane.

In the hall, the phone rang. She excused herself and answered it. It was Jack Lawson.

"Listen, Jack," she began, "I'm in the middle of something right now."

"This won't take long," he said in a tense voice, "I just want you to know that you're a fabulous person. Maybe you're too good for me. . . ."

This was it. The big kiss-off. "You're too good for me" was the telling phrase.

"Jack," she began, "I understand—"

"The thing is, I met someone else."

"I understand perfectly, Jack. I hope you'll be very happy."

"You'd like her a lot," said Jack. "She's a therapist down here in L.A."

"I'm happy for you, Jack," said Jane, wishing he'd just get off the phone.

"She says it's important that I don't have any unfinished business in my life," he said.

"I'm sure she's right," said Jane. "So let's consider it finished. It was great, and you're fabulous, too."

"You sound a little hostile," he said. "What I hear you saying is—"

"What you hear me saying is good-bye," Jane replied. "Listen, I really am in a hurry."

"Laura's a very up-front person," he said. "As a matter of

fact, she'd like to talk to you. She wants to make sure no one gets hurt."

"If I want to talk to Laura, I'll come down there and pay her ninety bucks an hour," Jane said impatiently. "Really, I'm sorry, but I've got to go."

"You are special," he said.

Gunther, now buttoned up in a raincoat and carrying his briefcase, came into the hall and looked pointedly at his watch. Jane made a circular gesture with her hand, to indicate she was trying to get the caller to wrap it up.

"Laura's right here," said Jack.

"I hope you are both very happy," Jane said, trying not to imagine Jack and Laura calling from bed in the nude. "I'm glad you told me about Laura. It was great. Good-bye and good luck. And Jack, I don't think we need to talk again, okay?"

She put down the phone. "Damn," she said. Why hadn't she had the presence of mind to dump him sooner? She hadn't followed her instincts. It was partly because she'd still been fond of Jack and looked forward to his visits.

"Is everything all right?" said Gunther, looking concerned.

"Yes, of course," she said, picking up her overnight bag and thinking what a hash she had made of the whole affair. She wondered if Laura were younger and prettier, then consoled herself with the thought that she sounded like a meddling ditz, wanting to get on the phone and counsel Jane about her loss. Good luck to both of them.

It was raining, and the windshield wipers made a noisy, clacking sound. Gunther was silent. She was sure he had heard enough to figure out she'd just been dumped. It was humiliating, but she wasn't about to cry on his shoulder or tell him her side of it. Instead she mustered what dignity she could and acted all brisk and businesslike.

"I think I should tour Putnam's plant first and then we'll do dinner," she said. "I'll see if we can't build a little rapport before I bring up blue salmon."

Gunther nodded. "Try to get him to take you to dinner at the hotel. I understand the food is very good."

Jane thought this sounded like a cheap move—as if she would be implying that the two of them could pop up to her room right after dessert.

"All right," she said. "Once I have his attention, and run blue salmon by him, what approach do you suggest I take?"

"I'm interested in finding out more about his relationship with his brother."

"From what I can tell," said Jane, "Don is kind of nuts, and Bob keeps an eye on him. Sort of a protective older brother thing. Covers for him. Lets him tag along."

Gunther frowned. "Donald is the one obsessed with fish farming. Robert may share this obsession and simply be more crafty. His desire to get involved with the farmed sector is rather suspicious."

Gunther explained that the sabotage itself was fairly simple, requiring tampering with bags of feed supplement, adding a chemical. "This has been done at the farm. The manufacturers have satisfied us that it has nothing to do with them, and we have discovered tampered products in storage areas at various farms around the world. The problem is, the fish appear normal as they are swimming around. It isn't until they are gutted that you know the flesh is blue, and by then the perpetrator is long gone. In any case, these are remote places, with very little security. The farmers look out for seals or birds or human poachers, but no one has paid much attention to storage areas where the supplies are kept."

"How sophisticated do you have to be to come up with whatever makes the fish blue in the first place?" said Jane. "I can't imagine Don as the mad scientist in the lab coming up with synthetic compounds."

Gunther clicked the tip of his tongue in a European, "no, you've got it wrong" gesture. "Drug dealers often have a working knowledge of chemistry. As for the method involved, there's still some question about the formula."

"Well, if you think Don has been doing this, why am I schmoozing up Bob?"

"Because Bob is attracted to you. This gives us an opening. It is my belief that a saboteur like this one secretly wants to tell the world how clever he has been. And if he thought this would make him seem dashing and clever to a woman, that is who he might tell."

"Am I going to be wired for sound today?"

"No, we'll do that when we think the time is right. These things take time."

Jane had a mad vision in which she got the whole story— Bob chuckling into his drink and gloating about how he and his loony brother had run around the world turning salmon blue—and she wasn't wired up to tape it. She started to say something, then had an unpleasant vision of Gunther fumbling under her clothes with adhesive tape. She'd do it his way. Besides, she found the whole scenario incredibly unlikely. It was better not to think about the twenty thousand dollars and be grateful for the generous per diem he was paying her.

Anacortes was a quick drive up the interstate and a short run on Highway 20 across a bridge to Fidalgo Island. The town was bounded on three sides by the waters of Puget Sound and had a newish downtown with a Kentucky Fried Chicken and Safeway and various strip malls, all of which looked as if it could be anywhere in the country.

Farther down the main drag, Commercial Street, was the old part of town, including a lot of nicely restored Victorian houses and plain, sturdy commercial buildings in weathered brick. The ferry to the San Juan Islands left from here, and there seemed to be a lot of businesses catering to tourists: galleries, bookstores, gift shops and T-shirt boutiques.

The hotel was just as Gunther had described it. In her last cases she had spent a lot of time in depressing motels with cottage-cheese ceilings and cigarette burns on the plastic furniture. Jane got a perverse satisfaction from the fact that Gunther was hunkered down in one of those places, while she was staying in a classy auberge with soft, sponge-painted walls and lots of pretty old woodwork.

She had called Bob Putnam the day before, and he'd suggested she call him after she checked in. He was in his office and sounded pleased to hear from her.

"This place is a zoo right now," he said. "We've got a delegation of important Japanese buyers coming through, and my plant manager is all tied up. Dinner is great, but maybe we can reschedule the plant tour."

"No problem," said Jane, thrilled that she'd avoided a chilly visit, during which she would be expected to admire the heading and gutting equipment and the pollock roe separator. "I've got plenty to do this afternoon." She had her cover stories ready and Gunther's memo in her hand, but Putnam didn't seem interested.

"I wouldn't mind trying the restaurant at my hotel," she said, "I understand it's pretty good."

"It sure is," he said. "I'll be over around six."

After she hung up, she called Gunther at the motel across the street and told him she was set for dinner. "I might wander around the town a little," she said. "Look like I'm researching my story."

"Do what you want," he said. "I cannot risk making an appearance, the town is too small. I shall be here in room seventeen all afternoon."

She felt suddenly sorry for him. "Do you have something decent to read?" she said.

"Thank you. Yes. I have a book. And I will also use the time to do some reports on my computer," he said in his usual stiff way, not acknowledging that she'd shown him a little sympathy.

She took a walk up and down Commercial Street in the light rain, finding the profusion of gift shops and all that careful restoration strangely depressing. There had obviously been a massive civic push here, and the result was a pretty classy upgrade of an old downtown that could have died. Up and down the street, buildings had been dressed up with historical murals, and weedy planters revealed it must look very pretty in summer, full of petunias and pansies. But now, off season in the middle of the week, it was cold and deserted, with no one to appreciate the effort.

She retreated to her hotel room, pretty and pastel but with a gloomy light from the gray muffled sky coming from the windows, took a nice hot bath in the deep tub, tried to read for a while and then decided to mope and wallow a little about Jack Lawson.

She tried to remind herself that what had seemed awfully attractive in the rural setting where they'd met hadn't transferred too well to urban life. Let's face it, she thought, Jack looked a lot better on a horse than he did in town. The injection of psychobabble into his drawling, sexy voice hadn't been an improvement, either. She supposed it was all for the best and told herself that Jack probably wasn't her last lover. Somehow this thought didn't seem particularly comforting, either. Maybe it was time to find the last one and hang on to him.

Bob Putnam called her from the lobby promptly at six. They met in the dining room, an attractive aquamarine space with a high ceiling and a view of a small, walled garden. Jane sat across the table from him and studied Putnam's bland but amiable face.

She decided to launch right into it. "What's the industry saying about the blue salmon incident?" she asked.

He smiled. "These marketing geniuses don't seem to know which way to play it. I got a fax from Amanda Braithwaite saying that it isn't toxic, they're trying to find out more, but she also said that it's a prototype product and still unavailable commercially." He shrugged. "You never know what's going to be hot. Remember when monkfish was a trash fish? Now it costs an arm and a leg."

"I wonder who figured out how to get the fish blue," said Jane. "Don't you think that was kind of clever?"

He shrugged. "Maybe it's a mutation. Listen, there's something I've got to tell you. This Gunther character. After our little confrontation that night in Bergen, I made a few calls, checked into him. He's not what he seems."

"What?"

"That company in Zurich says they never heard of him."

"Really?" said Jane. Should she tell him she'd called Zurich and they seemed to know who he was? Maybe Putnam had been a little more thorough. The woman she'd talked to had certainly acted as if there was a Gunther Kessler on the payroll. Either the man she knew as Gunther had simply expropriated the identity of the real Gunther Kessler or the company policy was to neither confirm nor deny the identity of its employees. Another possibility was that Putnam was mistaken somehow. Or that he was lying. But why?

Keeping the last possibility in mind, she decided to play it perfectly innocently. "Then who is he?" she said. "He seemed to be accepted by all those salmon people."

"Beats me," said Putnam. "Maybe he's the mad genius behind the mysterious blue salmon."

He broke off as a waiter arrived with their drinks, then leaned forward in a confidential manner. "You said he was checking into the death of that little demo girl? Did he tell you that?"

"No, it was just a rumor I heard," said Jane.

Putnam looked thoughtful. "Interesting. Did you ever find out how he got into your hotel room?"

"No," she said. "To tell you the truth, it was all so unpleasant I just wanted to forget about it."

"Those electronic hotel key things are supposed to be pretty secure," said Putnam. "If he can get through them, he could easily get into that hotel room where the girl got shot. Was he in Seattle for that seafood show?"

"I'm not sure," said Jane, who knew that he was. He'd seen her singing in the Fountain Room.

He shook his head. "It's pretty weird. I was kind of shocked when he turned up at the Four Seasons the other day. Are you sure he isn't stalking you?"

"I don't think so," she said, although once she had thought

just that. She smiled at Putnam. "If you hadn't told me he was in Seattle, I wouldn't have known he was in town."

"Well, just be careful," he said. "That's all I have to say."

"I will," she said. Maybe Putnam had a point. She realized she'd decided Gunther was all right because he'd misted up at "O soave fanciulla." Maybe her judgment was a little shaky.

She ordered salmon, thinking it would give her another chance to reintroduce the topic of the blue version, but Putnam took control of the conversation.

"So tell me about yourself," he said. "To be honest, you sure don't remind me of those Women's Seafood Network types."

"Like Carla Elroy?" said Jane. She smiled and said bitchily, "The women in this industry seem to wear tons of that fish jewelry, don't they."

He laughed. "The guys, too. My brother's got that fish-hook tie tack."

"How is your brother?" said Jane. "He's sure got some interesting theories about aquaculture."

Putnam laughed again. "Don't pay any attention to Don. He's always been kind of eccentric, ever since he was a kid."

Jane nodded. "What does he do for you in the business?"

"Oh, a little of this, a little of that," Putnam said vaguely. "The thing about relatives is they're always loyal. It doesn't hurt to have someone around you can trust and who always wants the best for you."

"That's very touching," said Jane. "A lot of people can't get along with their relatives at all. In fact, there are plenty of disloyal relatives and jealous siblings and horrible blowups in family businesses."

Putnam put down his fork. "We're different, Jane. There's just the two of us. Our parents died when we were young, and we were kind of shifted around from place to place together. We've been through a lot. It wasn't always easy for Don. He had learning disabilities, trouble in school. I did what I could."

Jane nodded attentively, encouraging him to continue with her silence and her eyes—wide open and receptive.

"Anyway," Putnam went on, resuming eating. "I figure I'll always look out for him. He'd do anything for me."

"He's lucky to have a brother like you," said Jane.

"To be honest, I think he's the reason I was able to clean up my own act and get through rehab." He took on a slightly smug look of someone who knew that redemption, especially where substance abuse was concerned, was chic. Boasting about one's rehabilitation could mean "I am interesting but no longer dangerous."

Jane inadvertently glanced at his wineglass. He caught the gesture and laughed. "No, booze wasn't the problem. But back in the eighties, like a lot of people, I got into coke. There was a lot of it going around the industry. No one knew how bad it was for you."

"I'm glad you emerged okay," she said. For good measure, she threw in a little talk show host stroke. "It's really great that you were able to admit you had a problem and had the courage to change." He acknowledged the compliment with a humble little nod.

"Did Don have a problem, too?" she asked. Don on coke was an awesome thought.

"No, thank God! But like I say, if it hadn't been for him, I might never have cleaned up my act. He needed me. I've always known I have to be there for him."

He didn't say anything about his brother having served time on cocaine trafficking charges. Jane didn't know quite what to make of Bob Putnam, but she reminded herself that she didn't really have to come up with any conclusions. That was Gunther's job, always supposing Gunther *was* Gunther.

Putnam's suggestion that he was some kind of impostor brought up an alarming question. Would she get paid for the work she was doing now?

Once again Bob Putnam shifted the conversation back to her. He asked her where she came from and what she'd done and how she'd gotten into the fish business. She gave him the basic biographical details, fudging a little on the fish issue. His manner was that of someone on a first date, politely getting to know the other person, looking for things in common, without flirtatiousness but with a twinkly-eyed sense of interest that seemed to say it might develop into something more later.

After dinner he said, "I have an idea! Let's swing by the plant now. Those Japanese guys should be gone, and I've got a third shift running tonight. I can show you around. I think you'll be interested in some of our specialized cutting equipment. We can do amazing things, portion control—wise."

"Sounds great," she said, trying to sound convincing. "And don't forget to show me that pollock roe separator," she added enthusiastically.

They drove a few blocks down toward K Street, then turned toward the water. The plant was an old brick building with a chain-link fence around it, a loading dock with a jumble of big plastic boxes that Jane had learned were called fish totes, and a forklift parked at one side.

"Used to be a cannery when this place was really jumping a few generations back," Putnam said. "We've got a bigger plant up in Kodiak, but I think you'll agree we've used the space wisely. We push some really nice high-value product out of here."

He pulled into a slot marked "B. Putnam," next to one marked "D. Putnam," and took out a bunch of keys to let her into a little hall with linoleum floors. "Come into the office," he said. "I'll just check the fax and the voice mail, and then we can suit up."

Jane smiled and thought, Oh, hell, another set of gum boots that don't fit, another lab coat with arms down to my knees and another hair net.

He gestured her to a guest chair while he sat behind the desk, punched some buttons and, smiling at her, listened to his messages. The fax machine had produced an overseas order.

"Ready?" he asked, putting down the phone.

"Sure," she said.

He rummaged in a cupboard and turned to her and said, "Gosh, I can't find the damn coveralls we keep for visitors. I guess those Japanese buyers used them all up." He gave her a conspiratorial wink. "Shall we be very daring and walk through without all that stuff? You won't tell my quality control manager, will you? Just don't touch any product."

Jane, who had no intention of touching anything in a fish plant if she could help it, said, "I won't tell anyone if you won't. But won't we be setting a bad example for the third shift?"

"Oh, there was a message on the voice mail. The manager sent them home early. Seems we ran out of fish."

She followed him down a dark, narrow corridor until they came to a door that led to a big concrete room with wet floors and walls, filled with gleaming stainless-steel equipment. It was freezing cold.

Putnam turned to her in the half light and smiled, then drew back his arm and hit her across the face with his knuckles. She fell onto the cold, wet concrete. Beyond the ringing in her ears, she heard his voice and its echo. "You lying bitch!" he said.

CHAPTER TWENTY-FOUR

She had to get up. All she could think was that she had to get up as soon as she could. She had to get up so she could get away. She had to get up because the floor was wet and cold and hard. She had to get up so he wouldn't be standing over her, humiliating her as he was now.

She pulled herself backward over the concrete so that when she did get up she'd be out of range of his knuckles. It was ridiculous—he could step toward her, he could hit her again, he could do anything he wanted, but she wanted to stand up away from him.

He let her struggle to her feet, then stepped toward her, into her space. She took a step back. "Don't!" she heard herself say. She sounded scared.

"What the fuck are you doing?" he shouted. "What are you after?"

"I'm visiting your plant," she said, trying not to panic.

He rushed at her, twisted her arm behind her back and leaned into her face. "What are you and that Kraut up to?" he demanded. She closed her eyes, unable to bear his face so close to hers. "You told me at dinner you didn't even see him in Seattle. Now I find out you arrived in town together."

"Ow, you're hurting me," she said.

"That's right. And I'm going to go on hurting you until you tell me why you're spying on me. Why did you lie to me? I don't like people playing games with me." He gave her arm a yank, and she cried out in pain.

"Let go," she gasped, "and I'll tell you." She knew that he was perfectly capable of torturing her until she told him something plausible. What really scared her was the feeling she had that he wanted to hurt her anyway, that he was enjoying it. He'd smiled right before he'd backhanded her.

Putnam was still holding on to her arm. "I'm working for him," she said. "He's a detective. He hired me to ask you a few questions, that's all."

"So you set up that little scene in Norway just so I'd come in there and be the cavalry?" he said.

"No, no, it wasn't like that at all," she gasped, shifting her position a little so that her arm wouldn't hurt so much. "He only hired me a day or so ago. This is the first thing I've done for him."

With his free hand, Putnam grabbed her hair and yanked her face closer to his. Her whole scalp hurt. It felt as if he were pulling it off her skull. She cried out. "What does he want to know?" he hissed.

Jane didn't think for a single moment of not telling him. She wasn't getting paid enough to stonewall under these circumstances. "He thinks you might know something about this salmon sabotage," she said, her face contorted with pain as he gave her arm another tug. "I told him I was sure you didn't, but he wanted me to check it out anyway."

Putnam let go of her hair, and the first, faint feeling of hope came over her. Maybe if she talked more, he'd let go of her arm, too.

"For some reason he thought you and your brother knew who was turning salmon blue. He's investigating the whole thing for the salmon farmers," she said quickly.

He let go of her arm. Jane stepped away, rubbing her arm, then stood up straight, trying through sheer willpower to summon back her dignity. "I'd like to go now," she said. "We can forget this ever happened." Not damn likely, she thought. She would never forget about it, and one way or an-

other she would find some way of humiliating Bob Putnam
the way he'd humiliated her.

"You better be telling the truth," he said.

She stepped back a pace and looked over his shoulder at
the door. His body was beginning to bristle again. Please, she
thought. Please, God, don't let him knock me down again.

His face was twisting back into anger. "Something here
doesn't add up. If you're lying again, so help me God,
I'll—"

"I'm afraid to lie to you," Jane replied truthfully. "Please,
I just want to go." Maybe if she seemed weak, he would let
her go. What else could she do? There wasn't any way she
could be stronger. She could only be weaker and hope it
worked. "It's so cold here," she said in a frightened voice.
Back in Seattle she knew a huge Samoan she could hire to
knock him down, smash his face in, kick him, hurt him.

Putnam smiled unpleasantly. "Your Kraut friend wants
you to fuck me to find out if I've been turning salmon blue,
right?"

She started to feel nauseated, then heard a telephone ring
in the distance. Putnam turned in the direction of the sound
for just a second, as if deciding whether or not to answer it.
While he did, Jane ran.

There was a pair of flat metal doors without knobs at the
other end of the cavernous plant area, the kind of industrial
swinging doors you saw in hospitals or big restaurants. She
didn't know what lay beyond them, but she decided she had
no other choice but to run in that direction. She ran what
seemed like the length of a football field, careening around
the stainless-steel equipment in the half-light, going as fast as
she could without slipping on the wet concrete.

She could hear footsteps behind her, but they weren't running. They were walking, slowly and steadily. Why wasn't
he chasing her? The phone had stopped ringing. Putnam's
footsteps sounded maddeningly calm, as though he knew she
could not escape, while her heart was crashing against her
ribs and her body was covered with prickles of fear.

She flung herself against the doors, making a huge metallic thump. They were locked. She could see an inch or so of light where they met and, halfway down, the black bar of the lock. Now she understood why Putnam was taking his time. His feet echoed steadily, coming closer.

Suddenly Jane heard a tune she had sung hundreds of times coming from behind the steel doors. It was "Some Enchanted Evening" in a slushy string arrangement. There must be a nightwatchman listening to the radio. She pounded on the metal surface, making a loud, hollow, shuddery sound. "Open the door!" she yelled.

Putnam's footsteps came faster now. He had begun to run. Another set of much slower footsteps was approaching from the other side of the doors. She pounded again and again, hammering the door with her closed fists and screaming, "Please! Help me!"

Finally, just as Putnam reached her and laid a viselike hand on her shoulder, the thin column of light that came from between the doors went black, and she heard the click of the lock.

The doors were being pushed toward her from the other side, so she had to step back against Bob Putnam. The feeling of his body behind her filled her with a rage that wiped away the physical sensations of fear.

As soon as the gap was wide enough, Jane tumbled through the open doors into the arms of an astonished-looking man.

"Thank you," she heard herself say to him breathlessly as she stepped into a carpeted hall. A strangely accented male voice began to accompany the lush string orchestration of "Some Enchanted Evening." She took a look at her savior. He was about forty, wearing a yellow broadcloth shirt with a loosened striped tie and gray slacks.

"Hey, Dennis," Putnam said easily. "Thanks. We got locked in there, and the lady panicked, I guess. Good thing you were here. Working late?"

Dennis gave Jane a quick, puzzled glance and turned his

attention to Putnam. "I've got those buyers from Osaka in the conference room. We're having drinks and we've got the karaoke machine cranked up. We were just about to head out for dinner. It's going great. I figure we can move a couple of containers to start and then go on from there."

Dennis's deferential manner made it clear that complaining about her abuse at the hands of Bob Putnam might be a mistake. "I'm Jane da Silva," she heard herself say in an astonishingly normal voice. "*Seafood Now* magazine. Sorry I lost it there. I guess I do get claustrophobic. Any chance you could give me a lift back to somewhere near my hotel? That is, if you're heading that way? I *am* kind of shook up."

Dennis looked to his boss for approval of this plan. Jane gave Putnam a steely, defiant stare, intended as a threat. If he tried to prevent her leaving, she'd make a huge fuss in front of Dennis and the fish buyers from Osaka. "Let's just call it a day," she said to Putnam.

He shrugged. "Okay. I've got some stuff I can do in the office," he said to Dennis. "I'd appreciate it if you'd run her back." He glanced at Jane. "I'll be in touch," he said ambiguously, then walked casually down the hall away from them, his hands in his pockets. Jane willed herself not to break down and collapse. She had to wait until she was safely away from here.

Dennis led her through an open doorway into a smoke-filled room with a big conference table, a collection of executive-style swiveling chairs and a teak sideboard with doors open to reveal a well-stocked bar.

Four Japanese men in blue suits were laughing and applauding a fifth, who was bowing, microphone in hand, in front of a karaoke machine with screen and speakers, apparently having concluded his version of the Rodgers & Hammerstein classic.

Dennis introduced her to the men, who lined up and presented her with business cards, while she apologized that she didn't have hers with her. "We're giving the lady a ride to town," he explained. Jane wondered if her face showed signs of having been struck. Bruises would take some time to develop, she supposed. No one seemed to be scrutinizing her face, so she decided she must look normal.

"But first she must sing for us," said one of the men with a big smile. Jane had a feeling that the happy hour had been going on for some time.

"No, no," she said, trying to look modest and shy. All she wanted to do was get the hell out of here.

"Yes! Come on!" the man said playfully while the others laughed, sipped whiskey and chatted among themselves in Japanese.

"They can be pretty insistent," Dennis said apologetically. "They're really big on this karaoke stuff."

"I know," said Jane. "They invented it." This had to be one of the most bizarre evenings of her life. One minute she was struggling with a maniac, the next she was asked to entertain some out-of-town businessmen over drinks.

Dennis gave her a pleading look.

"Okay, okay," she said, trying to sound like a good sport. In a perverse way, she actually didn't mind that much. She felt grateful to her unwitting rescuers, and the idea of singing made her feel that she was safely back in her own normal world again.

They loved her "As Time Goes By" and appreciated the fact that she didn't even need to read the crawling white letters. After a round of enthusiastic applause, they finished their drinks, crushed their smokes and followed her and Dennis out through the rain to his car.

They all piled into some kind of van and drove back up K Street. The windshield wipers were cranked up to full speed. Jane wondered what Bob Putnam was doing right then. It didn't matter. She was safe. "Just let me off in front of my hotel," she said, practically falling out of the vehicle in her haste to get away.

She went into the lobby for just a second, but as soon as she figured Dennis and his customers had left, she went back out and walked up the block to Gunther Kessler's motel. She knew that as soon as she saw pedantic, irritating old Gunther, she'd feel much better. She wanted him to take her back to Seattle that night.

She couldn't help imagining Bob Putnam stalking her for that one block in the dark. The street was completely deserted, and she was very cold. She walked briskly, ignoring the rain that came down hard, her feet lit by the pale yellow of the occasional streetlight reflecting in a smear from the puddles of the old, uneven sidewalk. The brighter lights of his motel served as a beacon. Room 17 was on the bottom floor, around the corner from the office, and there was light coming from behind the curtains. Jane rapped hard on the door.

There was no answer. Had he gone out to get a bite to eat? His rental car was there. A wind came up and rattled the door. Jane tried the knob. It turned. She stepped into the room.

Gunther lay sprawled across the bed, a thin, mustard-colored bedspread twisted underneath him, a blood-spattered pillow next to him, his arms flung to either side, a massive splotch of red covering his chest. From the wide-eyed stare and the gaping mouth, the horrifying, abandoned look of a face without a soul, she knew right away that he was dead.

CHAPTER TWENTY-FIVE

She went into the room, picking her way over an upturned lamp that sent a crazy oval of light into one corner of the ceiling, leaving everything else in semidark, past Gunther's highly polished black shoes, arranged neatly next to the bed, side by side. The door slammed shut behind her, which almost made her scream. By force of will she turned it into a sharp intake of breath and told herself that the wind had done it. She had to stay calm.

She looked around the tiny room, peered into the bathroom. There was no one here. She picked up the telephone receiver and, shaking, held it to her ear, all the while trying not to look at Gunther's face, focusing instead on his feet—long, rather elegant feet in smooth, black, silk ribbed socks. She stabbed at the 0 button, but the line was completely dead.

She would have to go to the motel office, somewhere on the other side of the building. She let the receiver fall from her hand with a clunk that sounded very loud in the still room and backed away from the phone, working her way around those shoes and then quickly back to the doorway.

As soon as she opened the door, she felt herself pushed back into the room by large hands. A meaty arm wrapped itself around her throat, and a sharp metal object jabbed her in the ribs.

"Shut up, okay?" said a voice. She found herself face-to-face with Bob Putnam's brother, Don. At the level of her chest, he held a small black gun.

"It's okay," he said in a voice edged with panic. "Just be quiet. Be quiet or I'll shoot you. I gotta find out what to do."

She stared at the gun, willing it not to go off. "I was going to get some help," she said innocently, as if Gunther had merely fainted.

"Too late. He's dead," said Don. "His chest is all blown away. I didn't mean to. He tried some weird martial arts thing on me. I didn't have a choice. It's just a little chicken-shit gun. It doesn't even make noise. Just a little pop. It's a ladies' gun." His voice was shaking, and when Jane looked down at the gun, ridiculously small in his big paw, she saw his hand was shaking, too.

"Don't shoot me," she said. "Please don't shoot me."

"Bob will know what to do," said Don, his confidence returning slowly. "He might be mad at me, but he'll know what to do."

"You can explain everything real easily," she said, desperate to calm him down so he wouldn't panic and fire. "It sounds like it was all in self-defense. Bob knows that Gunther knew that martial arts stuff. He tried it on Bob, too, back in Norway."

"It's the gun. He'll be mad I kept the gun," said Don, biting his lower lip. "He told me to get rid of it in Seattle. I had an accident with it."

She forced herself to look at the gun. It was small and black, with a rubber grip. And he'd called it a ladies' gun. She had a good idea just what that accident might have been.

"We won't tell," Jane assured him. "Maybe if you give it to me, then he won't know. I can throw it away."

Suddenly he stiffened. "You think I'm stupid, I guess," he said. "Well, I'm not. No way."

"Of course I don't think that, Don," she said, hoping that if she used his name, it would all seem more personal and make it less easy for him to shoot her. "You've just had a few bad breaks. You didn't mean to kill Gunther, I know that. You didn't mean to hurt that girl, either. Like you said, it was an accident."

He looked frightened all of a sudden. "How did you know?" he said in a whisper.

"Bob told me. Bob told me what you did," she said.

"No, he couldn't have," said Don, looking confused.

"It wasn't your fault," Jane said.

Don's voice caught. "She pointed the gun at me," he said. "I tried to take it away from her, that's all. The fucking thing went off."

There was a timid knock at the door. Maybe someone had heard something. Maybe the manager was coming to investigate. As soon as the door opened, she'd hit the ground in case Don panicked and fired.

Don smiled. "There he is," he said. "Open the door, okay?"

But Bob Putnam opened the door himself, just wide enough to insinuate himself inside the room. He closed the door gently.

"Jesus Christ," he muttered, taking in Gunther. Then he looked over at Jane. "Oh, great," he said. "She's here."

Don shrugged. "She was here when I came back from calling you."

"Keep that gun on her," Bob said. "If she moves or tries to make any noise, you know what to do." He moved back to the door and slid the brass bolt into the door frame. "We gotta figure out what the fuck we're going to do."

He put his hands on his hips and looked over at the two of them. "Why don't you sit down in those chairs over there," he said. "This might take a while."

Jane and Don moved obediently across the room to two vinyl-covered chairs arranged in front of the drawn curtains. As she sat down, Jane realized how much she'd been shaking. Bob perched coolly on the bed, sharing it with Gunther's corpse. "So where'd you get the gun?" he said to Don.

Don wet his lip with the tip of his tongue. "A guy in a bar," he said. "He sold it to me for fifty bucks."

"No guns," Bob said plaintively. "I told you, no guns. It's a parole violation, you could go back to the slammer." He stared down at the revolver. "It's not the same one, is it?"

"No. I ditched that like you told me."

Bob looked over at Jane. "Okay, how's this sound? You checked in with this guy. You had some kind of a lovers' quarrel. You shot him, then turned the gun on yourself."

"It won't work," she said quickly.

"Okay, honey," he said to her. "Tell me why it won't work."

"Timing. I was seen alive and well by a handful of Japanese fish buyers around the time he died. I was happy. I sang."

She turned to Don. "The police will see right through it. Right now, Don, you can claim self-defense. If you kill me, too, there's no way you can do that. It's too risky. You'd go back to jail. Or even face the death penalty."

Bob rubbed the skin between his eyes wearily. "Okay, maybe this is better. You and Gunther here had some kind of sicko thing going. He knocks you around a lot. You have dinner with me, cry on my shoulder. He finds out. Knocks you around some more." He looked very pleased with himself and ran a thumb along his knuckles. "You'll have a nice mess of bruises on your face to go with the story. You shoot him. You panic and call me. I show up here, and being the good citizen I am, I take the gun away from you. Then I pick up the phone and call the cops."

"That would be good," said Don. "But the phone doesn't work. The guy made like to use it and I kinda pulled it out."

Bob sighed loudly. "Okay, she called me on the pay phone and I call the cops on the pay phone." Then he smiled at Jane. "Hey, that's even better. If there's a record of Don calling me, I'll say it was you."

"Where did I get the gun?" said Jane.

Bob shrugged. "You bought it from a guy in a bar. Same

as Don. For fifty bucks. Gunther was getting jealous. Beating you up, You were scared."

"The gun could be traced somehow," said Jane. She looked over at Don. He gave her a pleading look, but he kept the gun pointed at her. She gave him an "I won't snitch" smile. He smiled back.

Bob watched the little exchange. "What the hell's going on?" he said.

"We need to know what really happened, Don, if we can come up with a story that will work," Jane said. "You're the one who'll suffer if we don't."

"Shut up!" said Bob.

But Don leaned forward eagerly toward Jane. "I was following him, like Bob said to." So that was how Bob had learned she had arrived in town with Gunther.

Don turned to his brother. "I knew he'd spotted me, so I went across the street to phone you, and when I came back, he was standing in front of the car in his stocking feet, writing down the license number. I followed him back into the room and told him to lay off."

"Yeah?" Jane said softly.

"Go ahead. Get him to talk," Bob said in a fierce whisper to Jane. "Then we'll have to kill you for sure."

"I already explained why that won't work," she said. "Don might have to go back to jail."

Don wanted to go on with his story. "I just gave him a little push, and he whipped me around in some weird hold. I took the gun out. I just wanted to scare him. Somehow the thing went off, same as before. I guess the action's kind of light."

"Just give me the gun," said Bob. "We'll say she killed him."

Jane turned to Don. "If you give him the gun, he'll give it to the police. They'll find out about that other time. They'll find out, because that gun belonged to the dead girl's sister. It's legally registered. They can trace it. You might end up on death row."

Don licked his lips. "Maybe you're right," he said.

Bob jumped in. "Shit! It's the same one. I'll get rid of it for you, Don, like you should have when I told you to."

"Don't give it to him," said Jane. "He can make you go to jail again. You went to jail before, for dealing. He didn't save you then, did he?"

Don hung his head a little. The gun wasn't pointed at anyone in particular just then. "I was doing the deals for him. I got caught. It wasn't his fault. He paid for the attorney."

"You were doing the deals so he had enough money to stuff coke up his nose, weren't you?" said Jane.

"Give me the gun, Don," Bob said. "Don't be stupid."

"He's not stupid," said Jane. "But you think he is." She turned back to Don, whose large foolish eyes were now glazed over with tears.

"I'm in big trouble," he said in a childish voice.

"Don't give him the gun, Don," she repeated.

Bob jumped up and slapped her hard across the face. "Shut up!" he said. Her face stung, but she knew she had Bob scared.

"Hey, Bob, don't," said Don. "She's trying to help me."

"*I* help you!" said Bob, sounding enraged. "I'm the one who always takes care of you, got that?"

"Then why did you tell me he'd killed that girl in Seattle?" said Jane.

"Yeah," Don said. "How come you told her that? You said no one but us should ever know."

"For Christ's sake, she's lying. Don't be stupid," said Bob.

"He called you stupid again, Don," said Jane. She clicked her tongue. "How did you get into that room at the Meade Hotel? Was that Bob's idea, too? Like following Gunther?"

"He wanted me to scare that Carla bitch," said Don. "He gave me the key to her room he got from Norm. I went in there, gave her a push. Then I realized it was the wrong one. They looked sort of the same. Hair, eyes. I never noticed much what she looked like. Plain little broad with light hair. He told me she'd be there, so scare her so she wouldn't write shit about us. I gave her one little push and out comes this gun. I grab it and she tries to grab it back."

"An accident," Jane said soothingly. "Happens all the time. You could get out of that easy, I bet."

"That's not what Bob said," Don said dubiously.

"Just give me the goddamn gun," said Bob. "Jesus Christ. Just do what I fucking say."

"Keep the gun," said Jane. "If he has it, he can send you away again."

"Don," said Bob, "I just wanted to help you. Protect you. Keep you out of jail. You know I've always taken care of you."

Jane kept talking to Don. "If Bob had gone and pushed Carla around himself, you wouldn't be in trouble, would you?" she said. "He's been making you do all the dangerous stuff, the stuff that can get you in trouble. Like selling coke."

Don nodded, his lips clenched and his eyes full of tears.

"I know the truth can hurt," she said gently. "I bet he's been doing that since you were kids. He pretends to care about you, but he doesn't. He'll send you back to jail again. Or the noose. In this state, they hang you, Don."

"Give me the gun," said Bob, "Right now."

"If you give it to him, Don, we're both dead," said Jane.

"Don't listen to her!" cried Bob. "You can make her shut up. Just shoot her. We'll ditch the gun afterward. No one will ever know."

"Don," Jane said, "he wants you to kill me so he can get rid of you. He wants your prints on the gun, powder burns on your hands. He'll call the cops and hand you over. He's wanted you out of the loop for a long time. He thinks you're unstable. He thinks you're stupid. He probably won't even visit you in prison. He'll just be laughing about how he managed to get you sent away."

"Stop it!" Bob screamed. "Shut the fuck up!"

"Bob wouldn't do that," said Don. "He says I'm a big help. He's always said that."

Jane shook her head sadly. "That's not what he tells other

people. When we were having dinner tonight, he told me you were stupid, but that you were loyal and always did what he said. He said when you were a kid you always had problems in school because you were stupid, but that you were stupid enough to do whatever he wanted."

"No," said Bob. "No, she's lying. Give me the gun, Don, please. We'll take care of this bitch. I'll make sure you make out okay on this deal."

Jane didn't take her eyes off Don's face. "I don't think so," she said. "He told me you always did what he says. He thinks you're going to do it again. But you have the gun, Don. The gun he didn't want you to have. You kept it so he can't make you do anything, ever again. Not as long as you have that gun."

"Give it to me right now," Bob said in the firm voice of a parent delivering an ultimatum. He seized his brother's hand and tried to wrestle the revolver away from him.

"It's mine!" Don said with a sob.

There was a dull, slapping sound, like a heavy book falling onto the floor. She didn't realize it was a shot until she saw Bob reel away, clutching his chest. He collapsed, falling backward on the bed on top of Gunther's body.

CHAPTER TWENTY-SIX

Don turned and looked at her. Tears were streaming down his face. "Oh, my God," he said. He still held the gun. He went over to Bob's body, bent down and kissed his brother's forehead. "Bob, I didn't mean it. I'm sorry. Jesus, no," he sobbed.

"Maybe he'll be okay," said Jane. She didn't think so. A trickle of bright blood and spittle oozed out of the corner of Bob's mouth. "We can call the medics. Let's go find a phone."

"I don't know what to do," Don whimpered. "What shall I do?"

"We'll get him some help," said Jane, trying to sound confident. She got up from her chair.

"It's not my fault," he said. He backed away from Bob's body and turned to face her.

"No, it's not," she said. "You didn't really want to hurt him."

"You made me do it," he said, sounding surprised. "You told me to." He looked down at the gun, then over at his brother's corpse. The room was completely still.

"If Bob could talk, he'd ask me to shoot you," he said.

"No, he'd want you to get help," she began.

"Shut up!" he said, bringing the gun up to her chest. "I listened to you before, and Bob is dead!"

Jane said, "Please, Don, no," in a terrified whisper.

He didn't move, and there was indecision on his face. "If I kill you and go away, no one will be able to prove anything. I'll get rid of the gun. I have to kill you. Bob would tell me to. Right?"

He seemed to want her to help him come up with a plan that was in his best interest, even if it meant her dying. She couldn't come up with an argument that would stop him from killing her, even to save her life. It would have been better to have let them hand her over to the police, as Bob had planned.

"Besides, it was your fault," Don said.

He steadied the gun and took aim. She closed her eyes, but the shot did not come. She opened them again, and only then did she hear the rhythmic beeping that penetrated the silence.

"What the fuck's that?" Don demanded.

She looked over at the table across the room and saw Gunther's laptop computer, lid open, a row of green lights glowing. Maybe Gunther didn't have an adapter for American sockets and relied on the built-in battery, which was now about to fade out.

"Gunther's tape recorder," said Jane. "It's voice activated. He always taped everything. That beeping means the tape needs to be turned over."

Don looked horrified. "You mean everything here is on tape? We gotta stop it."

"I'll show you how it works," said Jane.

He didn't seem to find anything odd about her apparently helping him to destroy evidence of her own murder. She went over and flipped down the computer's cover, forming a compact mass.

He came up behind her. "It looks like a computer," he said, sounding confused.

She held it up and turned it around. "There's a tricky little catch back here," she said. "Maybe you can figure it out."

Don put the gun on the table. "Okay," he said politely, reaching out to take the laptop.

She whirled around and pushed the hard corner of the computer into the middle of his face. He let out a howl and fell to his knees. His hands covered his face, and blood welled between his clenched fingers. "You broke my nose," he said in a muffled voice. "It hurts so bad."

She grabbed the gun and pointed it at him. She wanted to pull the trigger and end it once and for all, but instead she backed toward the door.

"My nose hurts," he said, yowling in protest. "That was so mean."

Jane unbolted the door and threw it open. There was no one outside. A light rain fell softly. She ran out the door, into the parking lot toward the red neon smudge of letters reading "Office."

She made it to the smoky little room, where a startled older woman sat nodding in front of *The Montel Williams Show*. Jane blurted out her story, and the woman called the police and bolted the office door until they arrived. The police listened to her, took the gun and evacuated the motel. Jane and the clerk and a traveling salesman clutching a big sample case, and a couple who wore robes and nothing else and begged to be allowed to get their clothes and go home to their respective spouses, were herded away behind a yellow plastic tape.

Police cars parked at crazy angles surrounded the area, and their radios crackled. A series of officers asked Jane over and over again how many people were in the room and if Don was armed. An attempt was made to call the room, even though Jane told them the phone had been yanked out of the wall. An officer put a bullhorn to his lips but was restrained by another, who said a negotiating team was on its way; finally, the door to the room opened slowly and Don, his face covered in blood, walked out into the rain and blinked at the wall of lights in front of him, holding up his hands.

CHAPTER TWENTY-SEVEN

About a week later, after all the activity had died down somewhat and Jane was beginning to feel more normal, Carla called. She was anxious for Jane to turn in her salmon story to Norm Carver. Jane said she would, although everything seemed unimportant and pointless just now. She drove over to the office at Fishermen's Terminal and handed over the copy and the disk, and Norm handed her a sheaf of faxes. If they hadn't had "Blue Salmon" in the headline, she wouldn't have paid any attention.

The first one was from Amanda Braithwaite's company. It said there was no need to panic, blue salmon was just a genetic anomaly and wasn't being prepared for sale.

The second fax came directly from the International Salmon Exporters Association. It was a press release that said that blue salmon was a tremendous hit and a triumph of aquaculture. The salmon was being featured in a dozen gourmet magazines. It added that production was extremely limited, and demand was overwhelming. Apparently enough had been found, worldwide, for a state dinner at the White House.

The third fax also came from the International Salmon Exporters Association. It announced tersely that Amanda Braithwaite had resigned the generic salmon account because of "creative differences" and acknowledged her important roll in "uniting salmon farmers around the world."

Poor old Amanda had apparently shot herself in the foot, thought Jane. A hit fell in her lap and all she could think was how to kiss off the whole thing.

"Anything interesting?" said Norm, paddling through his messy desk.

"Kind of," Jane said. "But I'm through with the fish business. Why don't you pay me off right now? I've had some expenses, you know. And make the check out to Carla. She's been writing all this stuff. It's pretty good, too, though I doubt you've been reading any of it."

"Really?" said Norm. "Maybe I should let her come back."

"It better be at twice the pay," Jane said. "She's got a good offer for a good state job." Norm looked as if he were thinking it over as she left the office.

A week later another Swiss sat in Jane's living room. He had come, he said, to prepare a final report on the death of his company's operative. He was French speaking, young, blond, with soft hazel eyes. She found it easier to tell him her story in French. It gave some distance to the proceedings.

When he had noted down everything with a fountain pen and put the papers in his briefcase with a decisive click, he said, "We were able to retrieve the last entry from his computer. He made a positive report about you. You will be receiving a check from Zurich in the next two weeks for your work on this case. We will pay you in American dollars, unless you prefer Swiss francs."

Jane nodded, touched at Gunther's punctiliousness. "Another agent will be assigned to Gunther's case," the young man went on. "Perhaps he will want to ask you some things about it."

"Gunther said he would pay me twenty thousand dollars if I got someone to confess to tampering with farmed salmon," she said. "Does that offer still stand?"

He raised an eyebrow. "Yes, that too is in his report. The amount was approved by the client."

"Did you know Mr. Kessler?" she asked him.

He looked uncomfortable. "Not very well. He was a very hard worker."

"His parents owned a hotel in Lucerne," she said.

He nodded. "Yes. They are retired now. I have already spoken to them."

"He loved Puccini," said Jane. "That's all I'll ever know about him." She began to cry, and he handed her a crisp white handkerchief.

"None of this would have happened," she said, sniffling, "if it weren't for guns. We have these guns here, and things that never would have turned out deadly do, because of guns. That's what happened to that girl, too. Gunther did everything right, but he didn't have a gun."

The blond man with the hazel eyes cleared his throat. "I am a Swiss. I have a gun in my closet," he said. "Mr. Kessler did, too. It's the law. But this doesn't happen to us."

After that she spent a few days getting her report together for the board. She would attach the letter the Hunters had written her, thanking her for finding out who had killed their daughter and helping them learn about her last months. Jane had the feeling the board would go for this case, release some of Uncle Harold's fortune and keep her out of the Fountain Room or its ilk for quite a while; but she didn't have a sense of triumph. The memory of Gunther Kessler dying in that miserable motel room overwhelmed everything else.

Jane had a few months before Curtis Jeffers and Don Putnam came to trial. She was to be a witness in both cases. She thought she'd have enough time to give Gunther's case one last try, even though it would mean one more gasp out of her Visa card.

The agent in charge of the case was very helpful. He arranged for her to stay in a large old house in Wimbledon, outside London, and lined up everything with the same precision Gunther would have brought to the task.

When Amanda Braithwaite arrived for dinner, huffing and puffing from her walk from the tube station, everything was ready. Jane started by plying her guest with an incredibly stiff gin and tonic.

"Wasn't it nice of my friends to lend me their house," she said, as Amanda browsed around, examining knickknacks with an appraiser's eye.

The two women sat on facing puffy sofas in a living room that overlooked a nice little English garden. Now that it was early spring, the forsythia were blooming.

"Jolly decent of you to have me round," said Amanda, sounding uncharacteristically humble. "After I lost the account, the rats all deserted the sinking ship. Haven't heard a damn thing from any of those fish people. Of course, the worst of it was I lost my job at the agency as well. Sniveling little gits that run the place have no understanding of the terrible problems I faced. I've a mind to emigrate. Go somewhere where they understand marketing."

"You'd be a mad success in America," said Jane. "I think Britain may be too confining for you."

"This country's going back to the dogs," Amanda said. "I can see myself in a more freewheeling atmosphere." She knocked back some more gin. "Somewhere where they reward spirit and gumption."

Jane leaned forward. "How about another drink. Dinner won't be ready for another half hour." Dinner was a collection of prepared entrées from Marks and Spencers that Jane would give a quick blast in the microwave whenever she felt like it.

"I wouldn't say no," said Amanda. "God knows I deserve one. Had a terrible interview today. Wrong sort of firm entirely. An insultingly low salary. I just marched right out."

"I'll tell you how someone could make a lot of money in the fish business today," said Jane, freshening up Amanda's drink with a massive belt of gin.

"How?" said Amanda.

"Well, it seems that blue salmon is a big hit," Jane said. "Too bad there's not much of it around."

"Don't mention the stuff," said Amanda, shuddering.

Jane leaned forward confidentially. "The word is, the salmon producers are all scrambling to come up with the formula. They want to get the stuff on the market as soon as possible. A matter of years, of course, because of the grow-out period, but they're very eager."

Amanda's eyes narrowed.

Jane leaned back on the sofa cushions. "I'm trying to find out who masterminded that little operation. I could serve as a front woman, and we could clean up."

"We?" Amanda said suspiciously.

"You know," said Jane, "the first time I saw you was at the seafood meeting in Seattle. You wore a lovely blue dress to the salmon reception. Remember?"

"Yes," said Amanda.

Jane gave her a girlish look. "I think that was a clever PR move. You knew that it was the threat of blue salmon that brought all those guys together. Wearing that dress was a nice psychological nudge."

"Well, it did cross my mind that the chaps might need a subliminal reminder of their problems," said Amanda. "Little did I know they'd turn out to be such bastards. No understanding of communication with the consumer."

"Let me be frank," said Jane. "I've already made inquiries. The salmon producers want to figure out how it was done, no questions asked. They're willing to pay."

"How much?" said Amanda.

"The sky's the limit. I figure we go for a royalty on each fish," Jane said.

"Each kilo of fish," Amanda said eagerly. Then she said coyly, "But why are you telling me all this?"

Jane smiled. "I'm hoping very much my hunch is right. Because I'd love to do business with a sharp businesswoman like you. Let me run it past you. You had access to all those farms. You were a food technician, and presumably had some training in chemistry. And you wanted all those salmon farmers to perceive an external threat so you could nab their business. After all, you got your start during an egg scare. You decided to kick-start things with a salmon scare."

Amanda smiled. "I'm not saying I did and I'm not saying I didn't," she said.

"I think you were a very clever girl," said Jane, wagging a finger at her. "It seems a shame that others will profit by your genius."

Amanda's bulky body drooped in defeat. "That's the damnedest part," she said. "It seems jolly unfair."

Jane clapped her hands together. "I was right," she said. "You did dose up those fish with something. Brilliant."

"It was pretty easy, actually," said Amanda. "Just used regular old food coloring in high doses. Perfectly safe." She leaned forward. "If you say I did this, I'll deny it. I'm only telling you because I believe you really understand. It was for the good of the client."

She leaned back. "I think we should patent the process. Then gear up with a big marketing program. Recipe development is key." She looked over at Jane. "Before we go further, we should draw up some kind of partnership agreement."

"Excellent," said Jane.

"I'd like to run the whole thing from the States. Better business climate," Amanda said. "I love New York. The energy!" She set down her drink. "Where's the loo?" she demanded.

Jane pointed up the stairs. As soon as Amanda had left the room, she went and tapped gently on a narrow door in the hall.

It opened a crack. A man, sitting at a table with earphones on, smiled at her and pointed to a slowly revolving tape recorder. "We have it," he said.

All through dinner, while Amanda spewed forth her grandiose plans, Jane mentally spent her twenty thousand dollars. She'd be able to get away to somewhere quiet. A crofter's cottage in the Shetlands appealed to her immensely. Right now she was exhausted, but after a while, she knew, she'd be up for another case.

Welcome to the Island of Morada—getting there is easy,
leaving . . . is murder.

Embark on the ultimate, on-line, fantasy vacation with
MODUS OPERANDI.

Join fellow mystery lovers in the murderously fun MODUS OPERANDI, a
unique on-line, multi-player, multi-service, interactive, mystery game
launched by The Mysterious Press, Time Warner Electronic Publishing and
Simutronics Corporation.   •

Featuring never-ending foul play by your favorite Mysterious Press authors
and editors, MODUS OPERANDI is set on the fictional Caribbean island of
Morada. Forget packing, passports and planes, entry to Morada is
easy—all you need is a vivid imagination.

Simutronics GameMasters are available in MODUS OPERANDI around the
clock, adding new mysteries and puzzles, offering helpful hints, and taking you virtually by the hand through the killer gaming environment as
you come in contact with players from on-line services the world over.
Mysterious Press writers and editors will also be there to participate in
real-time on-line special events or just to throw a few back with you at
the pub.

MODUS OPERANDI is available on-line now.

Join the mystery and mayhem on:
- America Online® at keyword MODUS
- Genie® at keyword MODUS
- PRODIGY® at jumpword MODUS

Or call toll-free for sign-up information:
- America Online® 1 (800) 768-5577
- Genie® 1 (800) 638-9636, use offer code DAF524
- PRODIGY® 1 (800) PRODIGY, use offer code MODO

Or take a tour on the Internet at
http://www. pathfinder.com/twep/games/modop.

MODUS OPERANDI—It's to die for.

632-c